GIFT OF GODS

GIFT OF GODS

Cover design by Elizabeth Mackey

Editing by Shannon Page

ISBN-13: 979-8-9856303-5-0

First Edition: January 2024

GIFT OF GODS

MAGE LORE BOOK 2

E. MENOZZI

For Mom and Kaitlin

1

THE cold wind blowing down from the mountains nipped at my face and hands as soon as I stepped out of the forest and onto the plains. The grasses that had covered the land surrounding the Nahl clan holding no longer bobbed their heads to me in greeting. It was too late in the season for that. They'd all gone dormant. Now their frosty stems crunched under Arge's hooves as I rode across the field, heading home.

I couldn't bring myself to hurry, even though I knew, with just a few days left until the Midwinter Festival, I was cutting it close. Still, another few moments of silence under the clear night sky wouldn't matter. Not enough to make me push Arge to move any faster.

I was still processing my incomplete training with the Inahi. It had been almost a full moon cycle since I'd seen or spoken with another human. In that time, the Inahi had taught me how to identify the potential mages and connect them to their magic, at least well enough that they wouldn't lose their dormant abilities after reaching their maturity.

As I approached the compound, I dropped the hood of my cloak to give the guards plenty of time to identify me. They bowed as I passed through the gate, signaling that they still recognized me. I must not have changed that much in the few months I'd been away.

On such a cold evening, so close to nightfall, there weren't many people out. Still, heads turned and whispers followed as I continued past the market to the stables. I didn't bother waving as I led Arge the long way around, preferring to avoid unnecessary conversations.

When I arrived at the stables, I found Dern leaning against the door frame, watching my approach. "When the guards sent a bird to alert us of your arrival, I didn't believe it. Shouldn't you be on your way to the city?"

"Good to see you, too, brother." My voice croaked from lack of use. I grimaced, then cleared my throat before dismounting and leading Arge inside.

Dern called to the stable hand, waving the closest one over to help me, as he pulled the door shut against the winter winds. "Don't get me wrong. It is good to see your smiling face. But haven't you been in some sort of novice mage seclusion? I would have thought you'd be in a hurry to get back to your betrothed, what with that Midwinter wedding you have planned. Unless you've come to drop more family secrets on us…"

I couldn't help scowling. Both at the reminder that I should have gone straight to Ezri, and at the memory of what my father and the late Jahl had done.

"You didn't," Dern said, setting a hand on my shoulder. "Come with more secrets? Please tell me you didn't. We've only just managed to sort out the mess you left behind last time you passed through here."

I reluctantly handed Arge's reins to the stable hand. I would have preferred to take care of my horse and get her settled, but it appeared my brother would not give me any peace until I responded. Watching the youngster lead Arge away, I wondered what sort of magic she held in her slight frame.

A wave of panic hit me, and I reached for the pouch I'd tucked into the inner pocket of my cloak. She turned the corner, and I caught another glimpse of her profile. Then I forced myself to take a calming breath. This girl couldn't be more than a year or two past her naming. She was in no danger of losing her magic. There would be time to test her after Midwinter.

I turned my attention to my brother. "I didn't come to share secrets." *Yet*, I added silently.

Dern exhaled loudly. "Thank the gods."

"Indeed." I paced toward the stable door, whispering Solnat's blessing as I reached out to brush my fingertips against the wall. *Home in my heart, hearth at the core. Blessings to all who shelter within these walls.*

That I still considered this home after everything that had happened, after everything I'd learned, was something I would consider later. Or not. In the meantime, it wouldn't hurt to make sure that our clan was ready.

"Has the group celebrating their maturity left?" I asked, stepping outside.

"You would know that if you'd gone to the city instead of coming here." Dern hugged his arms around himself to keep warm as he hurried after me toward the lodge.

"You didn't answer my question." I took the shortcut through the pasture, once again avoiding the market.

"They're supposed to depart in the morning." Dern blew warmth into his hands, then rubbed them together. "And now that I've answered your question, perhaps you will answer mine? Why are you *here*, Ayla-ruh?"

Dern's use of the Ruhl family's suffix instead of the one used for members of our clan's leadership family made me pause. I shot him a glance over my shoulder. "Stop it. I'm not married yet. And I'm still your sister."

"And you're certainly not acting like someone who is getting married in a few days." He shook his head as he pushed past me, leading the way through the great hall to open the door to Father's study.

"I suppose you'd prefer if I were gushing and bossing everyone around like Cala?" I scowled at his back.

"Gods, no. Please don't." Dern stepped aside as he entered the study, revealing the figure hunched over the desk.

Goff looked up from the stack of papers he'd been reading. The soft glow of lamplight hit his face, illuminating shadows and creases that made him appear much older than I remembered. "Ayla?"

My eldest brother didn't even stand to greet me. No matter how high I rose in the hierarchy of the united clans, I could always count on Goff to see me as his little sister. His consistency was a relief after Dern's uncomfortable attempt at deference and repeated reminders that this holding was no longer my home.

"You didn't come to burden us with more family drama, did you?" Goff set his pen down and leaned back in his chair.

"No." I sank into one of the empty chairs facing him.

"Well, if you came to see Father, you just missed him." Goff massaged the hand that had been gripping the pen.

Dern leaned against the side of Father's desk. "I'm beginning to suspect she came to check up on us."

"No." I glared at Dern. I couldn't tell them what I knew, or where I'd really been. But I was worried. For the good of our clan, I needed to make sure I didn't miss a single potential mage. "I came to make sure everyone reaching maturity is going to the Shal clan festival."

Goff ran his hand through his hair. "It's just a party, Ayla. I don't see what all the fuss is about, even if it is to celebrate you marrying the Ruhl."

"It's more than that." I wanted to tell them why, but I couldn't without revealing secrets that might destroy this new fragile peace between the clans. "It's a new beginning."

"If you say so." Goff shrugged. "As long as you're here, perhaps you could accompany the caravan to the city so that Mage-nah doesn't have to leave. He's getting too old for Midwinter camping. Without him, you can bypass the roads and maybe make it in one day."

"I said I'd take them." Dern stalked over to the hearth, staring at the flames before adding another small log to the fire.

"And I said I need you here." Goff grimaced. "I'll need all the help I can get just to get through the naming ceremony without mucking things up."

"What about Mother and Father?" I asked. "Why can't they help you?"

"Mother and Father left for the city this morning to prepare for your wedding," Goff replied.

Dern squinted at me. "You are still getting married, aren't you?"

Just as I was about to say, "Yes, of course I am," a knock on the door frame stole our attention. Instead of confirming my intent to marry Ezri, I found myself facing the last person I wanted to see.

Rys stood in the doorway, eyes locked on mine, fingers gripping a tube sealed with the wax imprint of the Ruhl. "I have an urgent delivery for the Nahl."

My brothers greeted him like nothing had changed. Dern clasped Rys's hand and slapped the back of his shoulder as he ushered him into the room. Goff grinned and welcomed him back from the city.

They acted like Rys was still a Nahl clan guard. Someone they trusted with their life. Not someone who had been spying for the Ruhl for years.

"Hand it here." Goff half-stood so he could stretch his hand across the desk.

Rys glanced at Goff long enough to place the tube in my brother's open palm. Then his eyes found mine.

I glanced away, fixing my eyes on the fire in the hearth. An awkward silence followed the crack of the seal and the unfurling of paper.

"It's been a long day." I stood, deciding to make my escape while Rys was forced to wait for Goff's response. "I'm going to bed."

Goff lifted his gaze from the message he'd been reading and looked at Dern. "We haven't put anyone in her room yet, have we?"

I set my hands on my hips. "You can't just give away my room. I still live here."

Dern shrugged. "Do you though?"

"He has a point, Ayla." Goff sifted through the loose papers covering the desktop. For a tense moment, I stood there, glaring at him, until he plucked a scrap of parchment out of the mess and waved it at me. "Ah-ha! Here it is. You're in luck. Father hasn't signed it yet."

"Signed what?" I snatched the paper from him and skimmed

the few lines my cousin had written. "He is going to give my room to Wesl? Really?"

Someone behind me snickered. I wasn't sure if it was Rys or Dern, but it didn't matter. I needed to escape the heat from the blazing hearth, as well as my exasperating brothers and the piercing eyes of the guard I used to love.

"Be reasonable, Ayla. You aren't using it, and he's already almost a year past his naming. It isn't fair to leave your room empty when there are others in the family who can use it. Father already gave Cala's room to Megh. Wesl is the next eldest of Uncle Feln's children. He honestly should have signed off on it half a moon ago, but I suppose there's been so many other things to deal with..." He gestured toward the desk with a sweep of his hand.

I took a breath and let the tension drain from my shoulders. "Fine. Wesl can have my room, but not until after I leave for the festival. I'm staying in it tonight."

Dern shook his head. "The others won't be ready to leave early enough to make the entire journey in one day. Really, Goff, I can take the caravan and return before our clan's festival. That way, Ayla can return with Rys at first light."

"Why would Rys be returning to the city?" When I'd last seen him, he'd been packing to leave the Shal clan's barracks. I'd assumed he'd returned to the Nahl clan guard, never bothering to tell them about the childhood oath he'd sworn to Ezri. The one that turned him into a lying spy.

Both of my brothers looked at me with wide eyes, but it was Goff who responded. "Rys transferred to the Shal clan guard."

I glanced at Rys, my eyes searching his tunic shoulder. Instead of the Nahl clan sunburst, there was a rose embroidered on his uniform tunic. "Why?"

"Father made a deal with the Ruhl," Goff responded, returning his attention to the paper in his hand. "One of our guards in exchange for three units of Shal clan guards to help protect us in case the Merluks return. Rys volunteered to be the one to go."

Dern had his eyes fixed on me, and I knew he was watching how I reacted to the news. I tried to keep any hint of emotion from my face.

"One guard for three units? What sort of deal is that?" I asked.

"A symbolic one among allies," Goff replied, sounding distracted. "I believe that's how Father explained it."

Dern smirked. He crossed the room and slung an arm around Rys's shoulder. "I thought you might be pleased at the news, Ayla. I mean, it's *Rys*. We've all been friends since before you could walk. Won't it be nice to have a familiar face in the city?"

I sighed. I'd always suspected that Dern knew about my relationship with Rys. Cala had told me Dern tried to warn Rys off declaring for me. I hadn't forgotten, and a part of me was still mad about it. That part was tempted to smack that smug, teasing grin off my brother's face.

The greater temptation was the urge to explain why Rys was not a friendly face. But the solution of sending Rys to the city must have been Zan and Ezri's way of extracting Rys without ruining his relationships in our clan. As long as he was no longer in a position to spy on our clan, maybe it was better that my brothers didn't know. He could still be a friendly face to them.

The only problem was, I didn't want Rys in the city. Regardless of my brothers' fondness for him, I wasn't sure I could ever forgive him for the way he'd betrayed me.

"I'm going to my room to get some sleep," I said. "I'll go see Mage-nah in the morning and let him know I'll lead the group going to the city."

Dern stepped aside to let me leave, and I squeezed past, careful not to look at Rys.

I made it halfway down the hall before the soft scuff of boots scraping against stone caught up to me.

"Ayla, wait." Rys fell into step beside me.

I squeezed my eyes shut and kept walking. I knew these hallways like the back of my hand. I didn't need to see to find my way safely back to my room. "I have nothing to say to you."

The footsteps beside me stopped.

I opened my eyes. A quick glance confirmed Rys was no longer at my side. I'd expected to feel relieved, but instead, anger burned in my chest.

I spun to face him. "Why did you follow me? What are my brothers going to think of you chasing after me down a dark hallway after everyone's gone to bed?"

The corner of his mouth lifted. "The Ayla I knew never cared about that sort of thing."

I stalked closer to him. "The Ayla you knew wasn't betrothed to the Ruhl."

His eyebrows quirked upward. "That's not true. The Ayla I knew was always destined to marry the Ruhl."

I sighed. "I'm tired, Rys. What do you want?"

"Why are you here?" He gestured back toward my father's office. "Why didn't you go back to the city? To your betrothed?"

"I live here." The words came out in an exasperated rush and were much louder than I'd intended.

"You haven't lived here since the morning I kissed you

goodbye in your room." He took a step closer to me. "Why are you really here, Ayla?"

I lifted my eyes to meet his, but the only thing I could think, looking at him like that, was *spy*. I stepped back and wrapped my arms around my waist. "Nice try."

"What do you mean?"

"I mean, I'm sure your captain would love to know what I'm doing here, but I'll be the one to tell him when I see him. He doesn't need to hear it from you." I let my arms drop to my sides and turned to leave.

"I'm not asking for him." Something in his voice made me pause. "I know that may be hard for you to believe, but I'm not."

"Then why are you asking? Why did you come after me now?" I asked, my shoulders dropping with exhaustion.

"Because I wanted to talk to you. I..." His voice trailed off. When he spoke again, it was barely above a whisper. "I wanted to know."

"Know what?" I glanced back at him.

"What happened? You found them, didn't you? The Inahi?" He rubbed the stubble shading his cheeks. "That's where you've been for the past moon cycle, isn't it?"

"I don't know anything about the Inahi," I lied. "I was in seclusion for my training at the Magery. I told you."

"You're lying." His eyebrows lifted, daring me to challenge his statement.

"I suppose you would know all about that. Wouldn't you?" I glared at him.

When his eyes fixed on mine, the look I remembered so well had returned. That look of curiosity and hunger. The one he got whenever we talked about finding the Inahi. "What are they like? What did they teach you?"

As much as I wanted to share this with the boy he'd been, I owed the man he'd become nothing. I shook my head before pivoting and continuing down the hall to my room.

"Goodnight, Rys," I called over my shoulder.

2

I WOKE at first light out of habit, only slightly disoriented when I didn't feel the presence of the Inahi surrounding me. When I stretched out my awareness, I could just sense them, out beyond the compound. If I needed to, I could call to them with my mind from where I lay, but it would be easier to reach them if I rode out to the plains. Not that I needed to.

I had everything I needed to activate the potential mages. Which was good, because once I set foot inside the stone walls of the city, I would be cut off from them. Before my eyes opened, my hand reached under my pillow to grasp the leather sack I'd tucked there before falling asleep. It was now the most valuable thing in my possession.

After checking that the curtain covering the door to my room was pulled shut, I sat up and loosened the strings holding the leather sack shut so I could dump the contents out onto my cot. It was the first time I'd been alone with the stash of clear crystals given to me by the Inahi, and my fingers itched to touch them. They varied in size and shape, but all were perfectly clear. Until you used them to channel.

I lifted the smallest of them, cradling it in my palm. As Labharon, I had the ability to channel every color, and I'd spent my time with the Inahi learning how to do exactly that. Most of the potential mages I needed to test would only be able to connect with one or two colors. The most powerful would be able to tap into more with time and training. That training had been the true purpose of the Magery, back before Ruhala led our clans to this protected land. So long ago that even the clan elders had long forgotten what it was like to wield magic.

It was up to me to waken that dormant ability in every person who had yet to reach their maturity. To do that, I needed these crystals and some way to make it appear it was Ezri and not me who had been called by the Inahi to act as Labharon. For now, magic was still a secret. My secret.

I'd yet to channel on my own, outside the forest and away from the watchful eye of Inahi Prime. From the secure familiarity of my old bedroom in the Nahl clan lodge, the Gods' Seat seemed like a dream I'd had rather than a place I'd lived for almost a full moon cycle. The crystal in my palm was proof that I hadn't imagined it. And I wanted to test my powers. To reassure myself that my magic hadn't disappeared the moment I stepped out of the forest.

My eyes scanned the room for something I could practice on. They settled on the tunic I'd taken off and draped over the back of the single chair before climbing into bed. I needed to get dressed, anyway. I might as well use a little magic to call it to me.

The last thing I learned before leaving the Inahi was how to wield white magic, which required me to channel all the colors at the same time. When it worked, I could move objects using only my mind. The Inahi said that with time and practice, I may even learn to transport myself to another location, but I was nowhere near strong enough to do that yet.

They also explained that eventually I wouldn't need the crystal to focus my power. I'd be able to sense each wavelength in the natural world and bend them to my will as needed. But channeling all the colors at the same time was hard enough with the crystal. I wasn't ready to try it without.

Holding my palm open so that the crystal was positioned between me and my tunic, I focused on its clear facets before closing my eyelids. To start, I plucked at each color with my mind, strengthening the sense of my magic by trying to memorize the feel of each. Starting with red, I worked my way through them all until I felt ready. Then, gathering up the sensations in my mind, I opened my eyes and reached out my other hand, directing the power through my fingertips to draw the tunic to me.

It fluttered once, as though blown by a breeze, but otherwise didn't respond. I refocused and tried again, sending the fabric billowing up and zipping across the room. Reaching up, I snatched the tunic out of the air before it flew past and giggled with the thrill of success.

The white haze that had gathered inside the crystal in my palm faded as I released my hold on the magic. A swell of pride and awe filled my chest. I could still hardly believe that I could do this impossible thing. And I wasn't the only one.

Everyone in all the clans who had yet to reach their maturity had the potential to wield magic now that Vehlm-jah's dealings with the Koto had broken our pact with the gods. The group of Nahl clan youth who had stood with me on my naming would all be celebrating their maturity this Midwinter, just like me. For the next few days, they still had the potential to use the magic that had been returned to our clans. It was my responsibility to make sure they didn't miss their opportunity.

Not wanting to waste a moment more, I stuffed the crystals back into the pouch, counting them to make sure they were all there. Then I dressed quickly and hurried to find Mage-nah before it was time for me to leave. But when I pulled back the curtain covering the entry to my room, I found myself staring at Goff.

"Oh. Good. I found you." Goff's eyes scanned the empty room behind me. "Can I come in?"

I stared at him. "I was on my way to Mage-nah's tent."

"Kilm's taking care of that." He pushed past me. "We need to talk."

I let the curtain fall closed and turned to find Goff pacing. "What happened?"

"That message. The one Rys brought for Father from the Council?" He waited for me to nod before continuing. "It's a new treaty meant to settle things after Vehlm-jah's death."

"All right." I frowned. "And?"

Goff shoved a hand in his hair. "Did you know about this? Is that why you're here?"

"Know about what?" My intuition pinged a warning that trickled down my spine.

He stopped pacing and faced me. "This treaty forbids the Ruhl from marrying into the leadership family of any of the clans."

I gaped at him. "What?"

"And it's signed, Ayla. By Ezri-ruh." He paused, watching my reaction, before adding, "And Filna-sha. Even Vorn-jah signed it. And there's a note from Uncle Feln saying they've all agreed. They just need Father to sign and bring it with him when he comes to the city for the Midwinter Festival."

"But Father's gone already. Why wouldn't they just wait for him to sign it when he gets there?" I asked while all I could think was, *Why would Ezri sign that?*

Goff rubbed his palm across the stubble on his cheek. "I needed to sign it as well. As Nahl clan heir. All the heirs signed. I guess after what happened with Vehlm-jah they want to be sure..."

"But Ezri has no heir." The words tumbled from my lips as though such an insignificant detail mattered when, if what Goff had said was true, my betrothal was off. I sat down on my cot in a daze.

A voice in the back of my mind reminded me that Father hadn't signed it yet. Maybe Ezri had sent the treaty here on purpose, knowing it would miss my father and delay the signing. If I'd gone straight back to the city like he'd been expecting, he would have been able to explain.

Goff's words finally filtered past my thoughts. "...if the Ruhl dies without an heir, the title dies with him."

"What?" I blinked up at Goff.

He pulled the roll of unsealed parchment from a pocket in his tunic and handed it to me. "It's all in here. You can read it yourself. I was going to send it back with you, anyway."

"You didn't send it with Rys?" I asked.

Goff shrugged. "I thought he was going with you."

I didn't want to travel with Rys all the way to the city, but I also didn't want Goff to send him ahead with a treaty that was only missing Father's signature. Ezri had tried to end our betrothal when he thought I was still in love with Rys. But I'd chosen Ezri. If he'd changed his mind while I was with the Inahi, then I wanted to hear it from him, not from my brother or from the dry diplomatic words written in a Council treaty.

I lunged for my cloak and hurried to the door. "I need to go."

"Ayla," Goff called as I pushed the curtain aside.

I half turned toward him. "What?"

He took a step toward me, not bothering to hide the pity on his face. "I just wanted to say... You'll always have a home here, all right? I won't give away your room yet."

"You're not the Nahl, yet." I scowled at him, not wanting to let on how much I appreciated his words.

"And you'll always be my little sister." He wrapped his arms around me, squeezing me in a brief hug before letting me go. "May Lorjad's Wind be at your back."

"Thank you." I swallowed the urge to cry. "Midwinter blessings to you."

I wrapped my cloak around my shoulders as I hurried down the hall, letting my hand drift over the fabric to reassure myself that the little pouch of crystals was still securely tucked inside. Once I stepped outside the lodge, I jogged the short distance to the stables.

Kilm and Mage-nah were waiting outside when I arrived. The other six from my year were scattered around, readying horses and saying goodbye to family. Several spotted me as I approached. More and more heads turned my way, then quickly looked away, pretending not to stare.

Their curiosity reminded me that the last time I'd seen this group I'd once considered friends, I'd been dancing with the Ruhl under two full moons. They'd been there when he declared for me. When I'd accepted and then run away. They'd watched us enter Cala's wedding hand-in-hand, then watched me depart with him for the city. And now they'd been asked to attend my wedding festival.

It must have seemed more like an order than an invitation. Only a few looked genuinely excited to be leaving. The rest eyed me like some spoiled Nahla who wouldn't think twice about ordering them about.

When I reached Kilm, I wrapped my arms around him. "They all hate me, don't they?" I whispered.

"I wouldn't say they *hate* you..." Kilm teased before stepping back and picking up a bag I hadn't noticed laying near his feet.

"Are you coming with?" I asked.

Kilm grinned. "Did you think I was going to miss your wedding?"

My fingers squeezed the roll of parchment I still clutched in my hand. I dipped my head, attempting to hide the worry I knew Kilm would be able to read on my face, and stuffed the offending document into a pocket inside my cloak. Then I turned to greet Mage-nah.

"How was your seclusion?" he asked after returning my greeting.

I thought of the Inahi and yearned to tell him everything. "Enlightening."

Mage-nah nodded. "I was pleased to hear that your marriage will not keep you from studying at the Magery."

"The Ruhl is very supportive of my desire to train as a mage." It was too bad I couldn't tell Mage-nah how much and why. I would have loved to see the look on his face if he knew I had not only found the Inahi, but they'd chosen me to be their Labharon.

"Good. Good." Mage-nah stepped aside as a stable hand arrived with Arge, saddled and ready to go. "It appears it is time for you to depart. Solnat's blessings to you and your betrothed, my dear."

"Thank you, Mage-nah." I dipped my head as he turned to go.

He paused a few steps away and turned. "Do give my best to Sera, when you see her."

I gaped at him, shocked that he'd acknowledged in front of so many others the aunt my father had banished from our clan before I was born. "I will, Mage-nah."

He nodded once, then continued along on his way back to his tent.

"Sera?" Kilm asked.

"I'll tell you once we're on the road." I hoped our aunt would be back in the city by the time we returned. She'd been badly injured when I left her in Delna-jah's care, and I still didn't know why Vehlm-jah had ordered Tavo to capture her and bring her to the caverns.

I glanced around, checking to see how many others were ready to ride, and noticed one very conspicuous absence from our party. "Where's Rys?"

"Here." His deep voice spoke from behind me, and a shiver ran down my spine.

I grimaced, then turned to face him. "Don't sneak up on me like that."

"Seems like you're the one who has let your training get rusty." He smirked.

I shook my head. "Just stay at the back of the group and make sure no one wanders off."

"Yes, Nahla." Rys dipped his head before leading his horse away.

"What's up with you two?" Kilm whispered.

"Nothing." I boosted myself onto Arge's back, then called out a greeting to the group.

"Thank you for accepting our invitation to celebrate your

maturity at the Shal clan's Midwinter Festival. The Ruhl and I promise to make it a celebration you will never forget." I paused to scan the mix of emotions written on their faces and for a moment wished I was skilled enough at sensing blue to shape eager excitement in place of the skepticism and annoyance I noticed. "With this small group of skilled riders and a dash of Lorjad's Luck I believe we can reach Shal city before nightfall. So let us be on our way."

Without waiting for a response, or checking to make sure anyone was following, I rode Arge around the market and toward the gate in the wall surrounding the compound. I trusted that Kilm and Rys would make sure everyone fell in behind me, and I didn't look back until I'd ridden past the guards. Only then did I do a quick count to make sure all six of the Nahl clan's potential first true mages were still with us.

Kilm rode up beside me as soon as we were clear of the gates. "Nice speech. Did you learn how to do that in the city?"

I ignored his teasing. "Tell me what I need to know about this group. What have I missed in the few moons I've been away?"

"And the many moons before that when you only had time for folklore and a particularly surly guard who seems intent on pursuing you despite your imminent marriage?" Kilm stared expectantly.

"He's not pursuing me." I shut my mouth on the words that wanted to come out, explaining how the guard I once loved turned out to be a lying spy.

"Could have fooled me." Kilm shrugged. "But if you don't want to talk about it, that's fine."

I sighed. "Just tell me about the others, please?"

"Abi and Paj are paired, but not yet married. You may have missed Abi's declaration at the Gathering. They're a sweet couple, though. Both training as leather workers.

"Ivn has been helping teach the youngsters in the crèche, but I think that's only so he can spend more time with Dern, even though our brother hasn't seemed to notice because he's still pining over Tavo.

"Oly started apprenticing with Mage-nah after you left. I've worked with her a few times, because she seems to have a natural affinity for potions and elixirs. Her bedside manner could use some work. Scared Wyn half to death because... Well, let's just say she said something that made Mother's assistant believe she was much worse off than she actually was when she came in asking for a basic tonic. Probably shouldn't share all the details if I ever want Mage-nah to certify me."

"You could come train at the Magery, you know," I said, interrupting. "You might want to after you meet Sera."

"Is she one of the masters or something?" he asked.

"She's a mage, but she doesn't teach at the Magery." I paused, not sure how best to break the news to him. "It was her notebook you found. She created it while studying at the Magery and lost it on one of her visits home."

"Home? She's from our clan?"

I nodded. "She's our aunt."

Kilm turned his head to stare at me. "What?"

"Father's sister, but he kicked her out. Banished her." I shook my head. "There's so much more to tell you. Like, Uncle Harn? Father's brother who died? He had a baby with Ezri's aunt."

Kilm's eyes widened. "No wonder Father never wants us to go to Shal city. That's where all the good stories are. We just get boring folklore about gods stealing scepters from each other."

"Forsla's Flame wasn't a scepter."

"Fine. Sorry." Kilm waved a hand at me. "Whatever stories I have about this group pale in comparison to what you just told me. I feel like you should be the one doing the talking."

"But Lon and Bez—"

"Are the only two besides me who are actually excited about going to Shal city, and that's because Bez has family there and Lon is fascinated by the sea and wants to become a trader. Don't ask me how I know that. Just consider yourself warned and don't bring it up unless you want to know more about ships and sailing than you ever thought possible."

Kilm shuddered, then turned to me with an eager smile. "Now. Tell me all about Uncle Harn's secret baby. Did you meet this mystery cousin? Tell me everything."

I hesitated before deciding to split the difference between the story Jace had told me and the truth I'd learned from the Inahi. "Everyone thinks the baby died."

"Oh. Well, that's disappointing." Kilm slumped in the saddle and pouted for a moment. Then he bolted up straight. His head turned so he could look at me. "Unless...they're all wrong and it didn't die!"

"What didn't die?" Bez asked, riding up alongside us.

"Nothing," I said at the same time that Kilm said, "My mystery cousin!"

"What mystery cousin?" Bez asked.

"It's just family gossip. There's no mystery cousin," I said, flashing a look at my brother that I hoped would make it clear he needed to keep his mouth shut. "How are you? Kilm says you have family in the city? Are they coming to the Midwinter Festival?"

Bez's face scrunched at my obvious change of subject, but she went along with it. "My father grew up in the Shal clan. He met my mother when he was a novice at the Magery. He was out gathering herbs and ran into her in the Heartgrove. At the end of the summer, when he found out her family was returning to the compound for the Gathering, he packed up his things and went with her."

"And they've been together ever since?" Kilm asked, clearly touched by the romantic gesture.

"More or less." Bez grinned and shrugged. "There was a rough patch when he wasn't the only one to declare for her, but they all worked it out in the end."

Her response triggered a memory of Bez running around in a pack of similarly aged children, most who had their naming the year after us. She'd always been so surrounded that it had been intimidating for me to approach her. Because of that, we'd never been close. If I'd known that her father had studied at the Magery, even briefly, I probably would have braved her flock of siblings just to hear her father's stories.

"Have you met your father's family before?" I asked.

Bez frowned. "Yes. But I don't remember. They didn't approve of his leaving his studies and chasing after my mother. He says he brought me to them when I was a baby, and they wanted him to leave my mother and stay in the city. He refused and never went back."

"And you want to see them now?" Kilm asked, his voice rising on a note of surprise.

Bez laughed. "I thought it would be nice to meet them. If they're awful, I don't need to stay. But maybe they've changed their minds about the Nahl clan now that..." Her voice drifted off as her eyes found mine.

"I can't say I've made much of a positive impression on the Shal or her clan," I said.

"But the Ruhl chose you. That must mean something," Bez replied.

I thought of the treaty tucked into the pocket of my cloak. "I wouldn't be surprised if the Shal is still trying to find a way to change his mind."

"Is that why you wanted us to come to the wedding?" Bez asked.

An image of me, surrounded by the six other Nahl clan potential mages, facing off against the Shal surfaced in my mind and made me smile. "Partly... But Ezri and I also have a surprise for everyone reaching their maturity this Midwinter."

"That's what the invitation said." Bez raised her eyebrows. "And I suppose you aren't going to give us any hints before we get there?"

"It wouldn't be a surprise then, would it?" I grinned at her.

Bez and Kilm both groaned.

A glimmer of water on the horizon caught my eye. "Come on. I'll race you to the river crossing."

3

W E stopped at midday to rest, not far from where I'd first taught Ezri about Lorjad's Laws for Travelers. The memory felt like something that had happened a lifetime ago. There wasn't much time to get lost in remembering, though. Not with Bez and the others laughing and joking all around me.

Kilm retrieved a wrapped bundle from his pack and handed it to me before taking Arge's reins. "Go join the others," he said when I dismounted. "I'll get Arge settled and join you in a moment."

"Are you sure?" I asked, casting a tentative look over my shoulder to where three of the six potential mages from our clan were gathering on a flat rock in the sunshine while Rys and the others led the horses down to the river.

"Go on." Kilm pried my hand off Arge's reins. He gave me a light shove toward the group before taking my horse and leaving me with no choice but to do as he'd suggested.

"...first thing I'm doing is marching straight to the barracks and..." Lon's voice drifted off when Ivn and Abi turned their heads to watch me approach.

"Has Rys convinced you to join the Shal clan guard?" I asked, trying to break the tension.

Lon swallowed. "Um. No. I was just..." He looked to the others as though he needed help.

Abi, who'd been one of Cala's best friends before Cala married and left for the mountains, took a seat on the rock and gestured for me to join her. "We were discussing our plans for after the festival."

I tucked my legs under me before unwrapping the bundle Kilm had given me. "You won't be returning to the plains?" I asked Lon.

"No, Nahla. At least, not right away." Lon's cheeks flushed. "I plan to be a trader. If the Shal will take me."

I cocked my head to one side, only then remembering what Kilm had warned me about not getting Lon started about ships. It was the part about the Shal I found more interesting, anyway. So, I steered him in that direction. "What do you mean? Why must you get permission from the Shal?"

"Well. It's the Shal clan who controls the trading with Agrion and beyond, right?" He rubbed his palms on his thighs and didn't wait for me to respond before continuing. "Anyone who wants to join the traders has to appeal to the Shal, through the commander of her fleet. I'm hoping the commander will be stationed at the barracks this time of year. They don't make as many trips across in the winter due to the harsh weather. At least, that's what Jem says. My older sister, that is. She joined a few years back and writes home when she can. Said she put in a good word for me with the commander. All I need to do is go straight to the barracks and—"

"Not this again." Oly plopped down on the rock next to

Lon and gave him a shove.

"Who let him get started?" Paj tucked himself in next to Abi.

Kilm reached past my shoulder and plucked the travel cake from the wrapping. He split it down the middle and handed me half. "Told you," he whispered to me.

"Do you think we'll have a chance to visit the Magery while we're in the city?" Oly asked, focusing her attention on me. "Now that you're a novice and all, I was hoping you could give us a tour."

I'd just been about to agree when Bez elbowed her. "She's not going to have time for that. She's getting married, fool."

I closed my mouth as I scrambled for a new response. "I'm sure it can be arranged. Even if I'm not available to take you. I can introduce you to Mage-sha. I'm sure she would be willing to show you around." I remembered what Kilm had said about how Oly had started apprenticing with Mage-nah after I left. "Are you thinking of staying in the city to study at the Magery?"

Oly snorted. "Who? Me? No."

"Why not?" I asked.

Oly raised her eyebrows, then shot a glance at Abi. Next to me, I caught Abi giving her a tiny shake of her head. The others all became suddenly very absorbed in their food. I looked to Kilm, realizing I must have said something wrong without realizing.

Whatever it was, Kilm saved me by changing the subject. "You all can tour the Magery if you want, but I'm not leaving without exploring the city."

Ivn perked up at that. He turned to Rys with wide eyes. "Is it true that you can see Agrion from the top of the tower?"

Rys glanced at me before responding. As though he was

waiting for my permission.

I took a bite of my travel cake and waited to see what he would say.

"On a clear day," he said, returning his attention to Ivn. "Sometimes."

"I'm just excited to finally dip my toes in the sea," Abi said.

"It's a bit cold for that," I said. "But you'll get a glimpse of it soon enough. Once we pass through the Heartgrove and cross the Lower Stone, we'll emerge on the plateau. That's where it first comes into view, but the view is much better from the tower balcony."

I thought nothing of my response to her until I realized everyone was staring at me. Kilm raised his eyebrows, but I had no idea what I'd said wrong.

After a brief, uncomfortable silence, Paj spoke. "Don't know about you all, but I haven't yet found an offering stone for the Midwinter blessing." He stood and offered his hand to Abi to help her up. "Want to have a look down by the river before it's time to go?"

I opened my mouth to remind them not to dawdle, but Kilm caught my eye and gave his head a slight shake.

Bez looked up at them, shielding her eyes from the sunlight. "A rock, huh? That would have been easier. My mother insisted I carve my offering. Lost track of how many times I stabbed myself in the process."

Ivn snorted. "Glad I'm not in your family."

"I'll go with you." Oly stood, and when no one else did, the three of them started down to the river.

"I already stitched mine up," Lon said, digging in his pack. When he pulled his hand out, he held a scrap of cream fabric with the rune representing Lorjad's Stick embroidered into the center.

I hadn't put any thought into my offering. My eyes followed Paj, Abi, and Oly's progress along the bank of the river. I would have gone along if I hadn't got the impression they were leaving specifically to get away from me. It hurt to realize that I no longer seemed to fit among my own clan. Maybe I never had. But that thought didn't make the realization any easier.

I let the others' conversation wash over me as I finished my half of the travel cake. Then, without a fuss, I stood, brushed off my leggings, and edged away from the group, toward the spot where Kilm had left Arge near the river's edge. When I reached Arge, I ran a hand down her neck and along her back.

After Midwinter, the others from my clan would return to their families, gathered at the Nahl clan compound. They'd return with magic, though they didn't know that yet. And I'd be alone again, surrounded by a clan that didn't want me. At least I had my studies at the Magery to look forward to. Perhaps I'd make friends there, surrounded by people as consumed as I was by folklore and our connection to our gods.

Besides, I'd have Ezri. Assuming the treaty hidden in my cloak pocket wouldn't really keep us from marrying. We had to find a way to make it work. We needed to be together to keep the clans united. Without me, he wouldn't be able to maintain the illusion that he was the Ruhl.

I rested my cheek against Arge's neck. Petting her, my mind drifted, and I lost all sense of the others in our group. The sound of rushing water lulled me into a now-familiar trance-like state.

She was here. The voice of the Inahi Prime spoke in my mind. The words came with an image of Mia hunched over a small fire in a clearing not far from where I stood.

Where is she now? I asked, allowing the question to form in my mind.

I'd asked the Inahi to help me find Mia, who had run away after killing Vehlm-jah. She'd taken swift action to banish the Koto from our lands, at least temporarily. They would be able to return once the veil fell, but by then we would know how to use our magic. We wouldn't be at their mercy.

Mia's quick thinking and skill with her knife had bought us time, and I refused to see her punished for it. Besides, I wanted to believe we'd become friends. I had so few of them, and I valued them so much. I would never let one of them down. Not if I could help it.

We can no longer see her. The response squashed the hope that had bubbled up to fill my chest.

Where did she go from here? I asked, letting them sense my frustration.

From here to the Flamehunt, the Prime's voice answered. Another image, this one of Mia trudging through a forest, then slowly fading away. *After that, we cannot see.*

I turned toward the mountains, rising like sharp, snow-capped teeth at the edge of the horizon behind me. The thin strip of green at their base thickened into a dense forest near the spot where the Stone River tumbled down the rock face and started its journey across the plains.

"Ayla?" A familiar voice spoke, pulling me from my connection to the Inahi.

I blinked, turning toward the sound, and sighed. "Rys."

"Are you all right?" he asked. "You looked..."

I glanced around at the others as his voice trailed off, reassuring myself that they were all still there. We hadn't lost anyone. "I'm fine."

But Mia was out there, and the Inahi had given me a clue

where I could find her. The only problem was, I couldn't go chasing after her. I needed to get this group safely behind the Shal city walls before nightfall, and I needed to speak with Ezri.

"How long until everyone is ready to ride?" I asked.

"That's what I was coming to tell you." Rys gestured to the others, already moving toward their mounts. "We're ready when you are."

I moved to walk past him, giving a tug on Arge's reins. Rys closed his hand around my arm, pulling me to a stop beside him. "Oly's parents were killed in a Merluk raid just before the Gathering."

"Oh." I tensed, embarrassed that I should have known. I'd been so single-minded in my pursuit of the Inahi that I'd missed so many of the things going on in our clan. No wonder they all hated me.

"It's all right." Rys reassured me as though he'd read my thoughts. Then he added, "What was left of their onk herd went to her mother's brother, but he wouldn't take in Oly and her younger siblings. Her father's parents took them in, but they are too old to tend a herd. So Oly started apprenticing with Mage-nah to help support her younger siblings."

That would explain why she didn't join Mage-nah until after I left, and why Kilm thought her bedside manner needed work. She was probably still grieving. My eyes scanned the group until I spotted Oly. She didn't notice me watching as she talked with Ivn and Bez. "Have you talked with her about it?"

Rys and I had both survived a Merluk attack, but he'd lost his father to them in the summer before his naming. I'd had an entire company of Shal clan guards to defend me.

"A little," he said. "She doesn't like it when people make a fuss."

"Thank you." I turned my head to meet his gaze. "For telling me."

He nodded once. "Have you picked your rune? For the offering? You didn't say."

"It didn't seem like I could say anything right, so I just..." I shrugged.

Rys took a deep breath. "You forget sometimes. That you're a Nahla. But they can't forget, just like I couldn't."

"What does being a Nahla have to do with anything?" I glared at him.

"The Nahl's family lives in the compound, only leaving for diplomatic visits to the other clans. But this is where our families go. After the Scattering." Rys gestured to the land surrounding us. "I'd guess their families have all grazed their herds out on the plateau a time or two. It's not good land, but it will do in a pinch. Especially if you're traveling back toward the Flamehunt."

I sighed. "They've all seen the sea. I'm the only one who hadn't."

The corner of his mouth lifted. "It's cute how excited you are to share it with them, though."

I shoved at his arm. "Don't."

He laughed and took hold of Arge's reins. "Come on. Saddle up. Gotta get out on the plateau before nightfall or you'll miss the view."

I rolled my eyes. "You're just jealous that you weren't there to tease the sheltered little Nahla on her first trip across the plains."

He stared up at me as I settled into the saddle. "I am."

Something fluttered in my stomach in response to his words, but I swallowed it down. He released the bridle as I nudged Arge into a walk, eager to rejoin the others and be on our way back to the city. To Ezri.

4

EZRI and Jace were waiting for us at the stables when we arrived. I spotted them before they noticed it was me leading the pack of Nahl clan potential mages. Ezri's face lit up the moment he recognized me. My heartbeat sped in response.

Jace said something to him, and his smile faltered for a moment. But then it was back, and he was rushing forward to greet me. Zan, who had been standing guard nearby, moved with him.

I didn't pay much attention to anything after that. Everything that wasn't Ezri—running a hand down Arge's neck before reaching up to help me down from the saddle, wrapping me in his arms and nuzzling his face against my neck, holding me tight against his chest—fell away.

"I missed you," he whispered.

"I missed you, too," I said.

He held me close a moment longer before releasing me. "Is everything all right?"

I wasn't sure if he was asking about me or the Inahi or any of the hundred other things we couldn't talk about until we were alone. But I was back, and despite the words on the papers in my cloak pocket, it didn't feel like anything had changed between us, so I nodded.

"Good." He curled his fingers around mine. "Let me greet the others from your clan, and then we can go somewhere quiet, and you can tell me everything."

It took longer than I liked to introduce Ezri and Jace to everyone and get the horses settled in the stable. All the while, Rys and Zan lingered at the edges of our chatty cluster, seamlessly working as a team to make sure no one got too close to Ezri or Jace, except me. Kilm, who had gone uncharacteristically shy, stayed at my side while Ezri focused his attention on charming the potential mages I'd brought with me.

Just as the last threads of my patience began to unravel, Ezri started leading the guests back out of the stables and up the hill toward Ruhl house. When he told them that was where they'd be staying for the duration of their visit, I wasn't surprised. I didn't imagine the Shal wanted an entire group of Nahl clan youths in her house when she didn't even want *me* there.

"Considering how quickly you can flee back to the forest, Nahla?" Jace asked as he fell into step beside me.

Kilm, on the other side of me, snorted.

Jace's eyes flicked past me to my brother. "You didn't mention having a twin."

I glanced over and caught a hint of color on Kilm's cheeks before turning a knowing scowl on Jace. "He's only sixteen."

Jace raised his eyebrows, feigning innocence. "I thought we only invited the ones celebrating their maturity."

I continued to glare at Jace with narrowed eyes I hoped

conveyed my unspoken warning that he stay away from my baby brother. "Kilm is here for my wedding. He's going to be my witness."

Kilm gasped and clutched my arm. "Really? You want me to be your witness? In front of everyone?"

"Of course." I twisted out of his grasp so I could wrap my arm around his shoulders. "There's no one else I'd rather have by my side."

Jace cleared his throat, drawing my attention, and frowned. He knew about the treaty, then. I shouldn't have been surprised. Jace made it his business to know everything. Though I was curious who told him. The Shal wanted Ezri to be her heir, not Jace, so I didn't imagine she'd been the one to share Council secrets. It wouldn't have been my uncle, or Tavo, both of whom hated the Shal clan. That left Ezri and the Council's secretary, Pim.

I stared ahead at Ezri's back as he laughed at something Paj was saying. A blast of winter wind blowing across the sea hit us as we reached the crest of the hill, stealing our breath for a moment. I tugged the edge of my cloak across my chest.

"Is everything ready for the festival?" I asked once I'd recovered.

"The Jahl clan should arrive tomorrow, and the festivities I've planned will begin with dinner in the evening." His eyes sparkled in what remained of the waning moons' light. "It will be a Midwinter unlike any our clan has celebrated since Hyant was Shal."

"Hyant?" I cringed at the reminder that I still hadn't bothered learning the clan lineages.

"He was the fifth Shal. Last of Ruhala's direct line," Kilm said, staring up at the Council tower at the center of the courtyard. "After that, leadership passed to a cousin."

"Impressive." Jace grinned at my baby brother like he was a delicious treat.

Ezri called to us from outside Ruhl house, distracting me before I could smack that look off the face of the Shal clan heir.

"Sixteen," I hissed at Jace as soon as Kilm turned toward Ezri.

"Did I ever tell you that I'm also celebrating my maturity this Midwinter?" Jace's grin slipped into a smirk.

I'd never asked, just somehow assumed he was older, closer to Ezri's age than mine. But if he was only seventeen, like me, then that made him a potential mage like the others. It also made him only a year older than Kilm.

"I never did get a chance to thank you for giving me the opportunity to plan the perfect party to celebrate the Shal clan heir's coming of age." Jace's eyes sparked with satisfaction. "Sleep well. I'll see you in the morning."

I groaned as I realized I should have been more suspicious when he'd readily agreed to plan the Midwinter Festival for me. I'd unknowingly given Jace a chance to somehow make this about him. Especially if my wedding to Ezri got called off because of the treaty in my pocket.

Jace leaned around me to wish Kilm a good night, and my brother waved as Jace retreated across the courtyard to Shal house.

"No," I said. "Don't even think about it."

"What?" Kilm asked. "He seems nice."

"You have no idea." I rolled my eyes. "He'll eat you for breakfast."

Kilm's wicked, teasing grin returned. "That doesn't sound so bad."

"Ugh." I shook my head and started walking toward Ezri.

"Just be careful and don't say I didn't warn you."

"I'm only here for a few days," he said, hurrying to keep up with me. "It's not like I'm going to get attached."

"Attached to what?" Ezri asked, as we approached. "The city?"

"Your cousin." I marched past Ezri and started down the hall toward his suite of rooms.

Behind me, Ezri directed Kilm to the room he'd be sharing with Ivn and Lon. Whatever else he said, I didn't wait long enough to hear. Jace's comments had flustered me, and I was impatient to finally be alone with Ezri and to hear what he had to say.

He appeared in the doorway a moment later and hesitated before coming into the room. "We left your rooms for you. You can stay there if you prefer."

"Do you want me to?" I asked.

"No." He took a step inside the room, hesitated again, this time glancing back toward the door he'd left open. "It's just..."

"Are you waiting for someone?" I unhooked the clasp at my throat, slid my cloak off my shoulders, and draped it over the back of a chair.

Ezri hurried back out into the hall, looked both ways as though checking to see if anyone was around, then came back into the room and shut the door behind him. "I thought Zan was going to join us to hear your debrief."

"Is that what we're doing?" I stalked toward him. "A debrief?"

Ezri's hands clenched and flexed at his sides. "I wasn't sure."

I closed the distance between us, stopping just in front of him. "Did you change your mind?"

"No." He paused. "But there's something you should know."

"The treaty?" I asked.

His eyes widened. "Did the Inahi tell you?"

I laughed. "No. I was there when Rys brought the papers for my father to sign. Only Father wasn't there. Goff read them instead."

Ezri ran a hand through his hair. "I'm sorry. I wanted to be the one to tell you."

"To tell me this doesn't mean what I think it means?"

He frowned, then took my hand and led me to one of the cushioned couches in his sitting room. "Once your father signs, our betrothal will be off."

"Why?" I sat beside him.

Ezri cradled both my hands in his. "It was the only way to keep the clans united after what happened in the caverns. My mother dug her heels in, refusing to cooperate with clans who she now had proof were working together, aligning themselves to challenge her."

I sighed. "They weren't planning an attack."

"Vehlm-jah and your father were only trying to balance the power between the clans." Ezri squeezed my hands and gave me a reassuring smile. "I know. I think my mother probably knows that as well, but she wasn't about to let this opportunity pass her by."

"Of course she wasn't." I clenched my jaw.

Ezri lifted a hand to cup my chin. "Maybe it's for the best. I still don't know how much damage the poison—"

I cut him off. "Have your feelings changed? For me?"

"No." He answered without hesitation but let his hand fall from my face. "But Zan and I have gone round and round, trying to find a way for us to be together. Everything leads to a dead end."

I'd been thinking about it on the ride to the city, and I

knew what he meant. "Even if we tell everyone the truth—that I'm the Labharon, not you—the Council will make me the Ruhl, and your mother will make you the Shal clan heir. We'll have the same problem as we do now."

"And if I try to decline in favor of Jace, she'll only refuse to cooperate on the Council until I agree." Ezri flopped backward against the cushions.

I leaned back next to him, curling myself against his side. "We could try to find Belyn and Harn's baby. Whoever it is, they're the true Ruhl."

Ezri shifted so he could wrap his arm around me. "Even if we could find them—which seems impossible—I'm not sure the Council would accept that. Everyone thinks the heir to that title is the one who can speak with the Inahi. Once they find out that's not true, the Council will be at each others' throats, arguing and pointing fingers."

"Which will make it easy for the Agrisse mages to invade and conquer us."

"If Valthonia doesn't beat them to it." Ezri sighed.

I lifted my head so I could see his face. "I don't want them to tell me who I can and cannot marry."

Ezri brushed his fingers down the side of my face. "Me either."

"There has to be a solution." I set my hand flat against his chest. "If you still want us to be together."

"Do you?" he asked, curling his fingers under my chin and drawing my face closer to his.

I stared into his eyes for a moment, allowing myself to relax into the closeness of him. The warmth of his body next to mine. The gentle caress of his fingers on my back. And the emotions swirling in my chest at the sight of him, so close after so long apart. "I do."

His eyes flicked to my lips as he leaned closer. I kept my gaze locked on his until his lips brushed against mine. Then they fluttered closed, and I lost myself in his kiss. All the doubts and fears flew from my mind. His words had reassured me, but it was his mouth on mine that told me all I wanted to know.

By the time we finally broke apart, I was certain. "We can't let them keep us apart."

Ezri tucked me close against his chest, then rested his cheek on the top of my head. "So we go along with the treaty, for now, and pretend to end our betrothal while we try to find the true Ruhl?"

I lay there for a moment, considering his suggestion, unsure where we would even start if we wanted to try. The Inahi didn't seem inclined to tell us. But there was someone we knew who had been close with both Belyn and Harn.

I lifted my head to look at Ezri. "Have you heard anything from Sera?"

"Oh!" He sat up with a start, shifting me aside so he could stand. "I almost forgot."

I watched him cross the room and disappear into his office. When he returned, he carried a wrapped package.

"You got me a present?" I asked as he handed it to me.

"Maybe." He grinned as he resumed his place next to me. "But that's not from me."

I glanced down at the red seal marked with an inverted V. "The Jahl sent me something?"

"Perhaps it's from your sister?" he suggested, reminding me that Cala was now the Jahlini. "With news about your aunt?"

I frowned as I peeled open the wrapping to reveal a slim journal bound in leather. There was a note tucked inside the cover. I read through it once, quickly, then passed it to Ezri. "It's not from Cala. It's from my aunt."

"It says she's returning with the group from the Jahl clan." He paused to glance up, but I had already turned my attention to the first page of the journal. He finished the rest of the note, then leaned closer to read over my shoulder.

I paused before turning the page and looked up to meet his gaze. "It's about Belyn and Harn."

"Do you think there's something in there about the baby?" he asked. A glimmer of hope lit up his eyes.

"That must be the secret she mentioned in the note. It has to be." I closed the journal, hugging it to my chest. "I don't think Sera knows, though. About me."

"Not unless Delna-jah told her." Ezri frowned.

"Do you think she would?" I hadn't asked Delna not to tell anyone else what she'd guessed. I'd just assumed she would keep my secret. "If she told Vorn…"

Ezri shook his head. "No. If she did, then Tavo would know as well. And he's had more than enough opportunities to tell the Council as we've been negotiating this treaty. But he hasn't. So, no, I don't think Delna said anything. At least not to her children."

"You said they'll be here tomorrow?" I stared down at the journal in my hands. "That doesn't give me much time to read this."

Ezri set his hand over mine on the cover. He grinned at me. "Do you want to stay up and read it to each other?"

"You'd do that?" I asked.

"There is nothing—" He caught himself and paused. His eyes darted to my mouth. "Well, almost nothing I'd rather do."

I leaned forward and kissed him. "We can do both."

"It is a love story." His lips captured mine again.

"A tragic love story, though," I added when we paused for a breath. "They both died."

"But they may have left us a cousin." Ezri tucked a strand of my hair behind my ear, then he stood.

"Where are you going?" I watched as he crossed the room.

"We need tea," he said, walking toward the door. "I'll send for some and be right back."

I listened to the murmur of voices in the hall as I reread the note my aunt had sent with the journal. My eyes lingered on the first sentence in her final paragraph.

I only ask that you keep this information to yourself, for now.

Would she mind if I shared it with Ezri? After everything that happened with Rys, I didn't want there to be secrets between me and the person I loved. She would understand. I hoped.

Ezri returned with a pensive look on his face. "Zan's in the hall."

"Oh." I wasn't surprised, and it didn't seem like Ezri was, either.

Zan took his responsibility seriously, and he only trusted one other person to protect Ezri: Mia. Who had run to avoid the punishment she'd face for killing Vehlm-jah. Punishment that Zan, as captain of the Shal clan guards, would have been tasked with serving. And I doubted that Filna-sha, despite the fact that she was probably secretly thrilled to be rid of the old Jahl, would let Mia off lightly.

"The Inahi don't know where Mia is," I said, realizing I still hadn't told Ezri about my stay in the forest. "They said she fled to the Flamehunt, but now they can no longer see her."

"The Flamehunt?" Ezri's brow creased with worry. "But that's at the foot of the mountains. Why would she go back and risk being so close to the caverns?"

I shrugged. "It's winter. Few in the Jahl clan will travel that way this time of year. And they'll be looking for her here, won't they? In the city."

I chose not to mention that the Flamehunt, being Forsla's domain, was widely feared among the Nahl and Jahl clans. There was an old story that claimed the Merluks as Forsla's children. Because of that, many believed that the Flamehunt was crawling with them. It was a guard's right of passage to journey to Forsla's temple at the core of the Flamehunt and ask for her blessing. Other than that, no one dared venture deeper than the outer edges of the forest where it was said the veil would protect us from Merluk attacks.

After what we'd experienced on my first journey to the city, I wasn't convinced the Merluks kept to the Flamehunt, exclusively. We were camped closer to the Wandering Woods when they attacked. But that time, the Koto may have been coordinating and controlling their actions. We still didn't understand all that the Koto could do, or what connection they had to the Merluks. Mia was the only person outside the Jahl clan who had experience with the Koto and knew what they were capable of. Another reason we needed to find her and bring her home.

"I should tell Zan," Ezri said. "So he can send someone after her."

"It will need to be Zan, I think. She won't trust anyone else."

"He's waiting for the tea. When he joins us, we'll tell him." Ezri sat in one of the chairs opposite me. "Can you do it? Did they teach you? Can you wield magic?"

My eyes slid past him to my cloak draped over the back of his chair. Thinking it would be more fun to show him, I considered attempting to call the cloak to my hand with magic. But, I doubted my ability to command white without the prism, and it wouldn't do to try and fail in front of him. Not when he was relying on me and the powers the Inahi had given me to save our clans.

"I'll show you what I learned." I stood and reached over him so I could extract the little pouch from the inner pocket. But first, I found the treaty Rys had brought to the compound and handed it to Ezri. "Here. You can give my father this to sign tomorrow."

"Are you sure?" he asked, looking up at me.

I clutched the leather pouch in my hand and dug my teeth into my lower lip as I considered my response. "We'll have to pretend we've broken things off between us. Do you think they'll let me stay at Ruhl house?"

"The rest of your family and clan are here, so I don't see why not. At least until after the festival." Ezri's eyes narrowed. "But then…"

"I'll have come of age. Father can't make me return with him. Especially not if I'm studying at the Magery." I settled myself in Ezri's lap.

"I don't want to break things off with you. Even if we're only pretending." He cupped my cheek in his palm.

A knock on the door interrupted us just as my lips brushed against his.

"Zan," Ezri muttered. "Has the worst timing."

I laughed and moved to the couch as Ezri called for Zan to enter.

"Nahla." Zan dipped his head to me and then to Ezri. "My Ruhl."

"Enough of the formalities. It's just us." Ezri nudged Zan further inside and shut the door before taking the tea tray from Zan. "Go sit down. Ayla was just about to show us what she learned from the Inahi."

5

AN didn't sit. He turned hungry eyes on me and asked, "Did they tell you where she is?"

"Where she was," I said, trying to keep my voice calm and gentle. "But they aren't sure where she is now."

During my short time with Ezri, I'd learned that Mia was more than just another guard to Zan. They had both been taken in as children and raised by a woman they called Mamma Fae, which made them practically family. I knew if it had been Kilm who had gone missing, I would have been equally desperate to find him.

"Where?" A muscle in his jaw tensed as he braced for my response.

"They said she fled to the Flamehunt. After that, they don't know."

"If the Jahl guards captured her..." His hand went to the knife sheathed at his waist.

The Inahi had not been able to sense the caverns. But that had been before Mia killed Vehlm-jah, when the Koto had been welcome there. Now that they were gone, that may have changed. But I didn't know for sure, so I couldn't reassure Zan. All I could say was, "Few from our clans venture into that forest. I doubt anyone would find her there."

Zan's mouth pressed into a line. He glanced at Ezri. "I need to go after her."

"I know," Ezri said. He set the tea tray down on a table. "Go. I'll be fine."

"I don't like the timing." Zan shook his head. "With the events Jace-sha has planned, you'll be surrounded by strangers from the Jahl and Nahl clans. I don't trust them not to try something. I should be here to keep you safe."

"Perhaps there's something Ayla can do? With magic?" Ezri cast hopeful eyes in my direction.

I considered the properties of the colors. "In theory? Maybe. But, not without more practice. It's definitely beyond what I can do right now."

Zan gave me a skeptical look. "What can you do right now?"

I loosened the strap securing the pouch in my hand, then plucked out one of the crystals at random. Cradling it in my palm, I reached past red for the sensation of orange. With my eyes closed, I pictured myself clothed in the tunic and leggings I was wearing. I imagined those same clothes were made of stone rather than cloth. Then I projected that image onto my body as I wrapped that sense of orange around me.

When I opened my eyes, Ezri was staring at me. His open-mouthed awe nearly caused me to drop the illusion I'd cast. Then, with one swift step toward me, Zan had the tip of his knife pressed against my breastbone, and I lost my grasp on the magic.

"Useless," Zan muttered, stepping back and sheathing his

knife. "As I expected."

"But it looked so real." Ezri edged closer to me, stretching out a hand to touch my sleeve. "How did you do that?"

"It was an illusion." I opened my palm to show him the crystal. "You know the beginning of the story about the origin of clans?"

Ezri nodded. "Long ago, when color was magic..."

"Right. I always thought it was something poetic, but it's actually quite literal. Colors *are* magic. If you can tap into that sense," I explained.

"And you can't after you've reached your maturity, can you?" A portion of the excitement drained from his face.

"You can't *start* after your maturity," I clarified, not that the detail changed anything for Ezri or Zan. "That's why we need everyone who is reaching their maturity this Midwinter gathered together. I have to help all of them activate that sense before it's too late."

"So they can create useless illusions?" Zan scoffed.

My fingers closed into a protective fist over the crystal. "That's only orange, and just the very easiest form of what that color is capable of. There's so much more."

"And you think they'll all be able to do this?" Ezri asked.

I dropped the crystal back into the pouch. "According to the Inahi, they should all have an affinity for at least one color. Some will have more. Most will be able to tap into more with time and training. And they all should be able to develop deeper levels of power. At least with the color they are most comfortable with. If they practice."

"And you think this is going to save us from an Agrion invasion?" Zan asked. "A bunch of children casting illusions."

"Zan." Ezri laced his voice with a hint of warning.

"He's not entirely wrong, though," I said. "If the rumors are true, then Agrion is crawling with mages."

"Not to mention their army," Zan added.

Ezri turned to me. "Is there anything we can do to convince the gods to restore the veil?"

"That's the other thing." I tugged at the pouch strings, wrapping them around my fingers. "The gods are missing."

"Missing?" Ezri tilted his head to one side as though convinced he must have misheard me.

"How do gods go missing?" Zan asked, gesturing at the air around him. "If they're gods, can't they just exist everywhere all the time?"

"No," Ezri and I said at the same time.

Ezri grinned at me. "Go ahead."

"If that were true, then we wouldn't need the Inahi to speak with them on our behalf," I said.

"Do you remember the campfire story Mage-ruh used to tell us about how Solnat fell from the sky one Midsummer, bringing with him his children and causing the change in seasons?" Ezri asked.

Zan frowned. "A bit. But that was just a story, wasn't it?"

Ezri shrugged. "Maybe? But if the Inahi are real, then maybe the gods really did walk among us. Solnat at the peak of the mountains, where in the darkness of winter, Estrel could reach down to him from her home in the night sky. And their children, one deep in each of the three forests. Like the story says."

"Well, there is another story," I said. "The mages don't tell it very often. Mage-nah used to let us act it out as part of our Midwinter celebration each year. Cala always got to play Estrel. Not that it matters."

"You wanted to be the god of hope and healing?" Ezri asked with a smirk.

"No." I scowled at him. "I just didn't want to be Jusala."

"You and me both." Ezri chuckled. "Who got to be Lorjad?"

"Dern, of course," I said, grinning at the remembered vision of him dressed in a shimmering gold jacket worn over tight gold trousers, carrying an enormous staff with streamers sprouting from the top, flapping behind him in the winter wind as he bounded around us, trying to make it look like each of his human strides were actually godlike leaps accomplished at a blurringly fast speed.

"But what's the story?" Zan asked, making it clear he had no patience for the sharing of memories. "And why Midwinter?"

"Because it was one Midwinter a long time ago when stars fell from the sky and scattered to the Earth. Estrel was calling Solnat and his children home. In exchange, Estrel granted us the gift of magery, and before they left, the gods introduced us to the Inahi." I grinned, adding, "That used to be my favorite part because it meant I could convince Kilm to be Jusala so I could be the Inahi."

"Stormcat," Ezri teased.

I glanced away from the secret sparkle in his eyes and hoped I wasn't blushing so much that Zan noticed. "After that Midwinter, the gods left to continue their journey, leaving the Inahi behind as their messengers."

"But now they're missing?" Zan asked.

I sighed. "According to the Inahi, the gods are not responding."

"Are they worried about this?" Ezri asked.

I shrugged. "I thought they were concerned about it when they first told me, but then they didn't mention it again. Not until I brought it up."

My first few days among the Inahi had passed in a blur. I

had so much to learn and so little time for them to teach me before the Midwinter deadline. I refused to lose any potential mages, so I threw myself into mastering the colors. It wasn't until one day, when I collapsed, exhausted from another failed attempt at purposefully channeling my still-developing sense of the colors, that I recalled what the Inahi who had greeted me at the edge of the forest said.

The gods are missing.

"When I asked, the Inahi said the gods have never gone this long without checking in. They explained that Estrel and Lorjad are always coming and going, traveling between the realms. But, as far as they can tell, Forsla has not set foot in the Flamehunt, nor Jusala in the Heartgrove, in years. They said Solnat was the last they'd spoke with, and that had been just before Ezri's birth. Since then? Nothing."

"So it's Ezri's fault, then." Zan folded his arms across his chest. "I suppose it was his birth that drove them all away? Or perhaps it was Vorn's fault? They were born in the same year."

"Very funny, Zan. I'm sure the timing is purely coincidental. Why would the gods care about the birth of a child to the Shal or the Jahl?" Ezri shook his head. "If the Inahi aren't concerned, then I'm not either. I'm sure the gods will turn up eventually. And when they do, I want the Inahi to be able to assure them that we are worthy of their renewed protection."

"But how?" I stared at him in surprise. I hadn't realized this was something he planned to do. "Now that we have our magic back, I doubt the clans will want to give it up again. The promised return of magic was what had driven Vehlm-jah to partner with the Koto in the first place. Even though Vorn-jah wasn't involved in that plan, I can't imagine he will agree to give magic back to the gods."

Ezri scowled. "We'll see. When the elders see all this power returning, but only for those who have yet to reach their maturity, I think they may be less excited."

Zan nodded. "It won't take long before they begin to feel threatened. And then, who knows? Besides, if all these stories are true, there are still Valthonian rogues out there, hunting us for our magic. What good are some flashy tricks in the face of an invasion? If you ask me, we're better off without it. Won't take the clan leaders long to come to the same conclusion."

I saw the logic in their perspective, but still, something about it didn't feel right to me. I'd need more time to think about it. Instead of arguing, I asked the question I'd been wondering for some time. "Mia said her family was trying to escape Agrion because of the Koto. But why were the Koto chasing them?"

"We won't know until we get her back," Zan said. He turned to Ezri. "With your permission, my Ruhl?"

Ezri reached out and squeezed Zan's shoulder. "Go with Lorjad's blessings. His wind at your back, and his luck in your search."

"Thank you." Zan dipped his head to Ezri. "I'll assign Rys as your guard while I'm gone."

My shoulders tensed at the name. The last thing I wanted was Rys following along behind Ezri the way Zan did. But Zan had been there when Rys pledged his life and loyalty to Ezri. It made sense that Rys would be the one he'd trust in Mia's absence.

Ezri nodded but said nothing. I wondered if he was thinking about my history with Rys and the decision I'd made before I'd left to train with the Inahi. In that moment, I wanted Zan gone so I could reassure any doubts lingering in Ezri's mind. He hadn't said anything about the fact I'd arrived with Rys, or what that implied. That I'd gone back to my clan first instead of returning immediately to the city. To him.

Of course, it had been pure coincidence that Rys had been sent to the Nahl clan at the same time I was there. And this treaty made everything more complicated. Whatever final exchange of guidance or warnings passed between Ezri and Zan, I missed them. My mind had gone elsewhere, only returning long enough to wave goodbye to Zan and watch him step out into the hall, shutting the door behind him.

I rushed to Ezri's side as the latch clicked.

He turned in time to open his arms as I threw mine around his neck. His eyes sparkled as they gazed down on my face. "What's this all about?" he asked.

I pressed onto my toes to kiss him. Then I pulled away and said, "What if we married in secret?"

He grinned. "Tonight?"

My lips curved upward as they met his again. "Sure."

He hugged me close against his chest. "Much as I'd love to, I think maybe we should wait."

I leaned back to look up at his face, trying to interpret the reason he wanted to delay. "Why?"

"Don't you think we should find our secret cousin first? Just in case—"

I cut him off. "We'll find them. If Sera doesn't know where to look, then I'll ask the Inahi to help. And then... Wait. What's the wording in the treaty, again?"

Ezri pulled away, searching for wherever he'd set the papers I'd given him. "That the Ruhl cannot marry into any of the other leadership families, I think. But I'll need to check to make sure."

I caught his hand and tugged him back to me. "You can

confirm it later. Or make sure that it's amended before my father signs it, if you need to."

He cocked his head to the side. "Why? What are you thinking?"

I closed the distance between us. "I'm thinking that once we find our cousin and make them the Ruhl, we can show that the title has nothing to do with who is chosen by the Inahi to be Labharon. We'll use the missing folklore pages to prove it. Then we can get the Council to officially abolish the title.

"Your mother will agree because it will allow you to go back to being her heir. My father and Vorn-jah will agree because they wanted Vorn to have that title, anyway. And none of them will want someone they've never met boosted to a position of power on the Council. And, in the process, they all will have forgotten what it said in the treaty, so won't realize that there is no longer any law stopping us from being together."

Ezri laughed. "That's positively genius."

"Thanks?" I grimaced as the implication of what I'd said hit me. "Ugh. I suppose being around all this political maneuvering is rubbing off on me. I'm not sure I like that."

Ezri kissed me. "It's all right. You get used to it."

I wasn't sure I wanted to get used to it, but that was part of what it meant to be the partner of a clan leadership heir. It was the sort of compliment that would have thrilled Cala, but it only made a shiver of fear run down my back.

Ezri took my hand and led me back to the couch we'd been sitting on. His gaze fell on the teapot and cups we'd left abandoned on the table. "I don't suppose any of that magic of yours can warm these for us?"

I lifted the cup he'd poured for me off the table and took

a tentative sip, confirming that the liquid had cooled to just above the temperature in the room. "In theory, yes? But I've only advanced past the most basic level with two colors, and neither is red."

"Heating things is a more advanced skill?" Ezri asked, settling back on the couch. He pulled Sera's journal onto his lap but didn't open it.

"Not exactly." I returned my cup to the table and curled up next to him. "The way the Inahi explained it to me, there are three levels of ability associated with each color of magic. The first, most basic, level for all of them allows the mage to use the power on themselves only.

"You advance to the second level when you affect another object or person with your magic. But only one at a time. Then, after much practice, or with an unusual amount of natural affinity, a mage will be able to use their power on multiple objects or people, or both, at the same time."

"So that illusion you cast on yourself? That was only tapping into the most basic level?" He tapped his fingertips on the cover of Sera's journal.

I nodded. "But orange also happens to be the color I have the most affinity for. It was the first one I harnessed when I was training with the Inahi. And it's the only color where I've worked up to casting illusions on multiple items at the same time. I've only done it a few times, though."

Ezri put his arm around my shoulder, tucking me close against his side. "Then that's the one you should demonstrate tomorrow in front of the clan leaders and the Council."

I pulled my lower lip between my teeth as I considered his suggestion. "It's not that impressive. I mean, you heard Zan's reaction."

"And you heard *my* reaction." He brushed a few hairs that

had escaped my braid off my forehead, then tilted my chin up so he could look me in the eyes. "Ignore Zan. He's worried about Mia and about how he's going to defend our city from attacks. By the time you have all these potential mages tested and trained, he'll have a use for your magic. I'm sure of it."

I wasn't quite as sure, but I'd never spent much time considering how to defend a city, or even just our clan, from an army led by mages. If Mia's reaction to the threat of the Koto was any indication, we would need a lot more than a group on the cusp of their maturity, only able to use magic on themselves. We had a long way to go, and we were running out of time.

And the only person we knew who had slipped past the veil and knew anything about Agrion and the Koto was missing. "I'm worried about Mia, too," I said.

"Zan will find her." Ezri squeezed me closer. "The one thing about this genius plan of yours that I don't understand is why we need to marry in secret."

"Oh." I rested my head on his chest and reached for Sera's journal. "I was thinking about Belyn and Harn, and it made me think we shouldn't wait."

"You think someone is going to shove me over a balcony railing?" Ezri asked in a teasing tone.

I heard the worry underneath his words, though. I knew he kept a vial of elixir, made just for him by Mage-sha, stashed in one of his pockets. When I left, he'd thought he might not live long enough to see me return. But that wasn't why I didn't want to wait.

I released my grip on the journal and caught his hand in mine, interlacing our fingers together. "I'm tired of letting everyone else tell me what I can and cannot do. I don't want to wait for their permission."

"Hmm." Ezri's chest thrummed with the vibration of his voice. "While I appreciate the sentiment and agree, maybe we should at least wait until after you come of age?"

"After Midwinter?" I asked, tilting my face up to look at him.

"It's what we've been saying we'd do all along."

"All right." I kissed his jaw, then the corner of his mouth before he captured my lips in a soft kiss that slowly deepened.

"All right," he sighed when we paused to catch our breath.

"Even if things aren't settled," I said. "Let's ask Mage-sha to marry us later that night, after the Midwinter ceremony."

Ezri snorted a laugh. "You're serious about not wasting any time."

"I am." I pouted, expecting him to argue with me.

He tilted his head to one side and smiled at me. "All right. You have a deal. Only, I was thinking, maybe we ask your aunt instead of Mage-sha?"

"Really?" I knew Ezri respected Mage-sha. She'd been the one to do our reading. But it had been my aunt, who he'd nicknamed Mage-ruh, even though that title did not exist, who had been the one to teach him our folklore. She'd been the one who believed he would inherit the title of Ruhl when he came of age. "Are you sure?"

"I think she's the perfect choice. We already know she's good at keeping secrets." He grinned.

I slid my hand from his so I could pick up the journal. Then, once I'd made myself comfortable, curled up against his side, I opened to the first page and started reading.

6

EZRI and I entered the tower with Rys just a few steps behind. I remembered the first time I'd been led into this room, on my way to meet the Shal clan as Ezri's betrothed. The vaulted ceiling and stone columns were just as impressive as I remembered. The light from the slitted windows high in the tower walls beamed down on the stone floor, illuminating a pattern I hadn't noticed before. I'd been so nervous then, and so focused on the looming figure of Ezri's mother framed in the open doors at the far side of the circular room, that I must not have even looked down at the floor.

The slightly curved stones we walked over were laid in a circular formation that centered on one large disk. The effect made it appear like a rock had been dropped in the middle of a flat pond, sending waves of ripples out toward the ring of columns standing sentry around the outer third of the room. Perhaps it was just a trick of the light, but it appeared that some of the rings of surrounding stones were lighter in color than others. One ring, only a few rows out from the center, looked like it was composed entirely of the same white stone that had been used for the columns.

I marveled at it as Ezri and I made our way through the center of the design and across to where Mage-sha was waiting for us. It wasn't until she moved that I spotted her standing near the base of one of the columns. Her white hair and robes were a near match to the stone, causing her to blend in with her surroundings.

Mage-sha raised her palms to me in greeting and dipped her head as we approached. "Welcome home, Ayla-nah."

I wrapped my hands around hers. "Thank you for organizing this meeting, Mage-sha."

She raised her eyes to meet mine. In a low voice she asked, "Have you decided how you will handle it?"

I nodded. "Ezri will do all the talking."

I turned at the sound of voices echoing off the stone walls. As they stepped out of the dim entryway and into the filtered sunlight in the central chamber, I recognized the faces of my parents. They walked at the center of a group with Kilm keeping pace alongside my mother and my uncle Feln matching my father step for step. Behind them trailed the group of potential mages from our clan.

Mother beamed when she caught sight of me. Beside her, Father scowled. His eyes flicked back and forth between me and Ezri. My stomach fluttered in anticipation.

Father had wanted this union between me and Ezri, and he knew about the treaty. Ezri had given him the papers after breakfast, then left him to discuss things with my uncle rather than waiting for him to sign. I wondered if my father would surprise us and insist the Council revise the treaty. It wouldn't be the first time he'd disagreed with Uncle Feln on a Council vote.

I would have to wait to find out, though. As I greeted my family, Filna-sha and Jace entered the tower, accompanied by an enormous group of Shal clan youth who all appeared to be my age. There were so many of them that they found it difficult to keep their distance from the representatives from the Nahl clan.

The stone room echoed with whispers as the two groups clustered into small huddles, eyeing each other across the aisle-like chasm that separated them. Filna-sha and Jace ignored the hushed voices behind them. Filna-sha kept me and Ezri pinned under her sharp scrutiny, holding back her satisfied grin until she stood before us, alongside my parents.

"Ayla-nah, welcome back to the city. I trust your Magery isolation was enlightening." Filna-sha didn't wait for my response before turning toward my father. "Will you be joining us for our Council meeting this afternoon, Teron-nah?"

"I will." My father's eyes narrowed. "I have several questions—"

Whatever he'd been about to say got drowned out by a commotion in the entry. Shouting outside, followed by angry voices near the door and murmurs of unrest from those already in the room, had Rys moving closer to Ezri. He positioned himself between Ezri and the potential threat, preparing to protect the Ruhl from danger.

The chasm between the clans widened to let a grey-haired woman seated in a rolling chair through. Despite the new scars on her face and the dark circles under her eyes, I recognized my aunt, looking unusually fragile under the blankets tucked around her body. Delna-jah strode alongside my aunt's chair, which was pushed by her son, Katz.

I glanced over to catch Kilm's reaction as Ezri leaned closer and whispered, "Why did they bring all their guards?"

It took me a moment to realize that everyone in the Jahl clan party, except Delna-jah and Sera, was wearing black with red chevrons embroidered on their chest. The uniform of the Jahl clan guard. Delna stood out from the others, dressed to honor Estrel in the color of mourning. She wore a long violet tunic with red embroidery at the cuffs and collar, worn over loose-fitting lavender pants.

"What is the meaning of this?" Filna-sha's voice boomed out to the new arrivals.

Beside me, I caught my mother's whispered question to my father. "Is that...Sera?"

Tavo emerged from somewhere near the middle of the Jahl clan group. He patted his younger brother's shoulder as he increased his pace to make his way around his mother to the front of the group. "The Jahl clan has arrived."

"Yes," Filna-sha replied as he approached us. "I see that. But what is *she* doing here?"

Father's body tensed as he locked eyes with the sister he'd banished from our clan. I guessed he was asking himself the same question, even though I wasn't sure if Filna-sha was referring to Delna or Sera. I knew she hated my aunt, so I suspected Sera was the reason for her venomous tone.

Delna replied, breaking the moment of tension. "The Jahl clan accepts responsibility for removing this mage from the Magery against her will. It was done under orders of the former Jahl, may he shine with Estrel. Since he is no longer with us, I have come to accept Jusala's judgment on his behalf."

"Yes. Fine. Take it up with the master mages. Now is not the time, nor is this the place." Filna-sha waved a hand in the air as if trying to sweep Delna and my aunt back out the door they entered. "This meeting is for clan leaders, Council members, and those celebrating their maturity."

Katz's hands tightened around the handles on Sera's chair in response. He took a half-step back, pulling the chair with him, then stopped when his mother set a hand over his.

"I am also here on behalf of my son, the Jahl, and as his representative," Delna answered. "I bring with me those from our clan who have been invited to celebrate their maturity at the Shal clan's Midwinter Festival."

With the mention of the invitation, Jace stepped forward, edging just past his aunt. "We are pleased you could join us, Delna-jah. Welcome."

"Yes. Welcome." Filna-sha adopted a softer tone when she echoed Jace's greeting. "Your guards may wait outside, though. This meeting is not for them. Or the mage."

"These guards are here to celebrate their maturity," Tavo said.

Ezri moved forward. He set a hand on Filna-sha's arm. "They'll stay, Mother. All of them."

Filna-sha's jaw clenched. She stared up at her son with narrowed eyes. Everyone waited, watching to see how she would respond to his open defiance of her authority. But I only tensed for a moment. Then I reminded myself that she believed, like nearly everyone here, that Ezri was the Ruhl. The head of the Council. It was his call, and she wouldn't challenge him. Not now, when she still needed a majority of the Council to agree to the treaty.

"All right," she said, pivoting away and pacing back toward the gathering of Shal clan celebrants. "Let's get on with it, then."

Ezri nodded to Jace, who turned to face the group with his arms spread wide. "Welcome. Everyone. On behalf of the Shal clan, I would like to say how pleased I am that you have accepted our invitation and joined us for this momentous occasion."

Jace paused for a moment as all eyes slid past him to stare at me and Ezri. They didn't know, yet. They still thought they were here to attend a wedding. I curled my fingers around the weight of the pouch in my pocket and tried to keep my swirling emotions from reaching my face.

"And now," Jace's honeyed voice pulled me from my thoughts. "Our Ruhl would like to say a few words. I give you, Ezri-ruh."

Jace dipped his head, and the rest of the gathering followed, bowing to Ezri as he stepped forward. Across the room, Filna-sha barely bobbed her head. When she looked up, she caught me staring. I watched as the realization hit her that I also hadn't bothered bowing to Ezri. Her eyes narrowed, but she said nothing. She wouldn't. She thought she'd won, but she had no idea what was coming.

I fought the smile that pulled at my lips as I waited for Ezri to begin the speech we'd planned.

"United clans, I bring you a gift from the gods, granted through their messengers, the Inahi." He paused to let the surprised murmurs die down. "As it is written in our folklore, long ago, when colors were magic, our people traded their power to the gods for protection. Unfortunately, we broke our promise to the gods. And now, the protective veil surrounding our lands will fall."

I kept my eyes on Filna-sha, noting her reaction. But, if she was surprised by this news, she hid it well. Her clan and mine both began shouting questions and talking among themselves. Meanwhile, the Jahl clan representatives, all dressed in black, stood in silence, waiting for Ezri to continue. They knew what their Jahl had done.

Ezri held up a hand, and the Shal and Nahl clans fell silent. "The gift I bring you is that the gods have not left us defenseless. They have returned our magic to us. Starting with all of you who are about to come of age."

This announcement was followed by a momentary shocked silence, and then gasps of surprise along with more hushed whispers and a flurry of shouted questions.

Kilm edged closer to me and whispered, "You already knew this, didn't you?"

Rys overheard Kilm's question and glanced over to catch my response.

"Not now," I whispered to Kilm, avoiding the piercing look Rys gave me. I could almost hear him putting pieces together in his head. If we weren't careful, he'd figure out exactly what Ezri and I were trying so hard to hide.

Across the room, Filna-sha stood staring at Ezri with a look of disbelief. The only other time I'd seen her so discomposed was when Ezri had been poisoned. She looked at her son like he'd just announced that the gods themselves would be attending the Midwinter Festival.

I supposed that Filna-sha, who seemed to put no faith in the divine and didn't ever believe the Inahi existed, let alone that her son would be able to find and speak with them, probably never considered the possibility that magic also existed. Unlike Vehlm-jah who had been so determined to return magic to the clans that he'd aligned himself with the Koto.

But none of that mattered anymore. We couldn't go back. We could only move forward. And that meant it was almost time for me to take my turn as the focus of everyone's attention.

Ezri had his hand up again and was waiting for everyone to quiet down. When the group had settled enough for him to be heard, he said, "I know you have questions, and I promise to answer them, but first, I think it would help if we had a demonstration.

"Unfortunately, I am unable to tap into the magic that has been returned to us because I have already reached my maturity." Ezri turned to look at me and motioned me forward. "So I have shared what I learned with my betrothed, Ayla of Nahl clan."

"You *did* know," Kilm hissed at me as I joined Ezri in front of the others.

Ezri and I had decided that there was nothing I could do without more training that would convince anyone that having our magic returned to us was better than having the protection of the veil. The Council would see that immediately. So we settled on something that would excite the potential mages enough that they would be eager to come forward for testing.

Clutching a crystal in my palm, I closed my eyes and tapped into the sensation of orange to create another mirage. Only this time, I needed to stretch my abilities. As I merged the sensation with my intention, gasps from the crowd gave me hope that I'd succeeded.

I cracked open my eyelids to peek at my progress. Catching sight of the colorful flowers dangling from the vines that appeared to have grown up out of the floor to line the inside of the tower walls, I released the breath I'd been holding. Then I blinked my eyes the rest of the way open and gaped with the others at the mirage I'd cast. Ezri reached over and curled his fingers around my free hand. He squeezed it, and I glanced over to grin at him.

"You did it," he whispered.

Ezri and I had stayed up most of the night alternating between me practicing and him reading to me from Sera's journal while I rested and prepared for another try. He'd believed in me even when I was ready to give up and insist we try something easier.

"It worked." I grinned at my creation.

Heads were starting to turn in our direction, so Ezri released his grip on my hand. "I would like each clan to choose three candidates who will be the first to be tested. They will need to be prepared to assist us as we work to make sure all of you have your magic activated before Midwinter. After the celebration feast, we will announce our plans for training the rest of the youth in all the clans, as well as continuing training for those attending the Midwinter Festival. Now, I will answer your questions. One at a time."

I found my aunt's eyes in the crowd as hands raised in the air and Ezri began to call on people. She inclined her head when she noticed me looking. Her eyes narrowed in a way that made me think that she had already easily seen through our ruse. The number of people who knew or suspected the truth about my connection to the Inahi was growing. Though I believed we could trust Sera and just hoped Delna had not said anything to the rest of her clan, I worried that with this many people aware of our secret, it wouldn't remain a secret for long.

If someone overheard any of us discussing things, word would get back to Jace. He had ears everywhere. And if Jace could find out, Filna-sha would be able to as well. I glanced at each of them in turn.

They seemed absorbed in Ezri's response to a question about who would have magic. The shock of his announcement would wear off, though. More quickly for the clan leaders, who were probably already beginning to think through what this news meant for clan power dynamics. It wouldn't be long before they turned their scrutiny to Ezri. Once they did, I doubted even his considerable charm would be able to hold off the inevitable. They'd see through him and everything would fall apart if we weren't prepared.

"What else can magic do?" someone from the Shal clan asked. "Or is it all just illusions?"

Ezri's shoulders tensed, but he didn't hesitate or look to me before responding. "More. Much more. It will depend on your affinity, at first. Which makes me think it would be best if we get started with the testing."

Almost everyone with a hand raised lowered their arm, but a few waved theirs in the air, hoping to get in one last question.

Ezri shook his head. "Bring your remaining questions to your clan leader or Council representative. I'll give you all a few moments to decide who will be the first three for testing from each clan. Come forward when you're ready."

As soon as Ezri turned his back to the assembly, Jace intercepted him. I started toward them, but Kilm tugged at my sleeve.

"Ayla, I know I can't be one of the three, but will you teach me anyway?" He stared at me with wide eyes. "Please?"

I nodded once. "I will, but go tag along with Father and the others for now. Tell me what they say."

Kilm smirked. "You want me to spy for you?"

My jaw clenched at that word. "No. Just...listen."

Kilm held up his hands. "All right. Sure. Whatever you want to call it."

I watched as he made his way over to where Father and Uncle Feln stood with Bez and Oly, who appeared to be making an animated case as to why they should be chosen. Abi stopped whispering with Paj when she spotted Kilm moving toward their group. Her eyes slid past him and locked with mine. I couldn't tell from the look on her face if she was mad at me or merely curious.

Having a small group would give our clan an initial advantage. With only six of them, it wouldn't take long at all before they were all able to tap into their magic and start practicing together. The group from the Jahl clan was more than twice as large, and the Shal clan's group was even bigger. With so many to train, whichever three the Shal clan put forward would spend almost all their time leading up to Midwinter just getting everyone else tested. Ezri would probably insist we help them, just to make sure no one was missed.

Our clan would walk away from the Midwinter Festival with stronger magic than any of the others, but there were so few of us, it wouldn't matter. There just weren't enough of us to stand up to the other clans, if it came to that. The only advantage we had was me. Once Father figured that out, he'd lose any hesitation he had about ending my betrothal to Ezri.

Someone tapped me on the shoulder.

I turned to find myself facing Delna and Sera. I bowed my head. "Greetings."

Sera scoffed. "No need for that. Not when you outrank both of us."

I raised my eyes to meet theirs. "But Delna-jah..."

"Is no longer the Jahlini." Delna spoke in a soft voice, barely above a whisper.

"Your sister holds that honor now," Sera added. Her lips pursed as though she'd tasted something sour.

"How is Cala?" I asked.

"Pregnant," Sera answered, frowning.

"She's managing her new responsibilities well." Delna set a

hand on the back of Sera's chair. "Though she's not been very accepting where your aunt is concerned."

Sera glanced away when I looked at her. She winced when she realized she'd turned her head toward Father and Uncle Feln.

I followed her gaze and caught Uncle Feln turning his head to look at us. A brief shadow crossed his face before he looked away to respond to something one of the others had said.

"Delna is going to take me to the Magery," Sera said. "We're only in the way here, and despite what Delna thinks, it will go better for me if I stay out of Filna-sha's way. But I was hoping you'd come see me when you're done."

"If you're not too busy preparing for the wedding," Delna added.

Then it was my turn to wince.

Sera caught my reaction before I could hide it. "What happened?"

"We'll talk later." I shook my head. Behind her, I spotted Filna-sha walking toward Ezri with three Shal clan youths in her wake. "I'll join you as soon as I can get away."

Filna-sha and Jace had begun a spirited conversation, punctuated by expressive gestures that made me think they might be arguing beneath the seemingly calm and polite tones they were using. Tavo was starting toward them with three others from the Jahl clan.

"I think I need to go," I said. "I'm sorry."

"Don't be, dear. We understand," Sera said.

"Lorjad's Luck to you," Delna said, brushing her fingers against the arm of my tunic as I passed her. *Labharon,* she spoke the word directly into my mind as she'd done in the caverns.

I nearly stumbled, but caught myself, glancing back only

to catch the back of Delna as she pushed my aunt's chair around the crowd toward the tower door. Then Kilm was at my side, along with Bez, Oly, and Ivn.

"I see we're not the only ones who chose four instead of three," he said, gesturing toward the others surrounding Ezri.

I hadn't realized it until he pointed it out, even though I knew both Jace and Tavo were the same age as me. "They're too busy to take on the responsibility of testing and teaching the rest of their clan."

"Exactly," Kilm said. "But they're also too important to be among the last to get their powers."

I had to admit he had a point. "This is going to make things interesting."

1

EZRI led the small group toward the balcony doors on the far side of the room. Rys followed, keeping close to Ezri, and in the process, positioning himself between Ezri and me. I might not have noticed if it were Zan. But because it was Rys, I took the way he blocked access to my betrothed personally.

I fell back, joining the small group trailing behind Ezri. Once he'd put some distance between our group and the rest of those gathered in the tower, Ezri stopped. Annoyance flashed across his face when he turned to face us. I turned my head, following his gaze, to see what was bothering him.

"Mother, you are not needed here," he said.

Filna-sha raised her chin. "I am the Shal. This is my tower, and I will stay if I like."

Ezri continued to stare her down. "Your presence will only fluster those we are testing, making this process take longer than necessary."

"If this magic is so finicky that it can't stand up to a bit of scrutiny, what good is it?" Filna-sha waved her nephew forward. "Have Jace go first, then. He isn't intimidated by me."

Ezri's eyes found mine, and I understood his look without a word. Arguing with Filna-sha would only make her suspect we were hiding something from her. And we were. Better to go along with her and do our best to make sure she didn't catch on.

I gave him a tiny nod, and he directed Jace toward me. As I reached into the pouch to extract a crystal, Tavo spoke up.

"My Ruhl, I don't think it's fair for the Shal clan to be tested first," he said. "You've already allowed your betrothed to gain access to her magic and kept all this a secret from the Council. You should have brought this information forward and allowed the clan leaders to decide who would be trained and when."

"He has a point," Filna-sha said.

A muscle in Ezri's jaw flexed, but he managed to bury his frustration and address their concern calmly. "Ayla was with me when I met with the Inahi. It was their decision to activate her magic. Not mine."

It always surprised me how well he handled these situations. It was one of the reasons why I believed it was better that everyone continued to think he was the true Ruhl. I'd ignored too many of Goff's lessons in diplomacy to deal well with the pressures of clan politics. But Ezri had been raised for this. And the best part about his answer was that everything he said was true.

"Fine," Tavo conceded. He turned to me. "If that is the case, then I think it's only fair that you test both Jace and me at the same time. Then all three clans will be on equal footing again."

I looked to Ezri, waiting for his nod of approval before

fishing a second crystal out of the pouch. "Hold out your hands, palm up."

Tavo stepped up alongside Jace. The pair stood shoulder to shoulder in front of me. I dropped a crystal into the center of each of their palms. Then I stepped aside so a beam of sunlight streaming in from the high windows illuminated the clear stones.

"See the colors reflected by the crystal in your hand? Concentrate on them. Try to see each one separately from the others. Focus on each for a few breaths before moving on," I said.

Tavo dropped his eyes to his palm immediately. Jace hesitated a moment. He raised his eyebrows like he didn't understand or expected me to say something more. But there was nothing more to say. He would have to keep trying until something happened.

I motioned for him to get started, just as the temperature dropped suddenly. My eyes went to the balcony doors, but they remained closed. As others began to shiver and whisper, I glanced at the stone in Tavo's hand. A red haze had filled the once-clear crystal and was beginning to fade.

Tavo stared at me with wide eyes.

I grinned back at him. "Red. Nicely done. On your first try, too."

"Should I keep going?" he asked.

I plucked the crystal from his hand. "Not now. That was enough to activate your magic. You can practice more once I've finished testing the others in your clan."

As I finished speaking, Jace gasped.

I turned to find the fingers of Jace's hand had nearly doubled in length. The crystal in the center of his palm swirled with a golden hue. "Yellow. Well done."

"But…" Jace stared, at a loss for words for the first time since I'd met him. "My fingers!"

I set a hand on his shoulder. "Breathe. Release your focus."

"How?" His breath came short and shallow as he continued to stare at his hand.

When I'd first grasped the sensation of yellow, I'd made my nose grow, so I hadn't noticed right away. The fact that I couldn't see what I'd done at first made it slightly less shocking, but I remembered the panicked feeling that I'd changed myself forever and would remain stuck that way. But I'd had the Inahi in my head to help me. Jace would have to make do with my words.

"Close your eyes and think of something else," I said. "The sea. A book you've been reading. Someone you love."

He blinked a few times, unable to tear his gaze from his hand at first. Then he squeezed them shut. After a few breaths, the color faded from the crystal and his fingers shrank back to their usual length.

"Good," I said, taking the crystal from him.

Jace bent and flexed his fingers a few times, staring at his hand in wonder. "Magic did that?"

"*You* did that," I said, giving him what I hoped was a reassuring smile. "With magic. And you'll be able to do more, with practice. But not until after I've tested the others."

"Is this some sort of joke?" Filna paced over to examine Jace's hand. "A trick of some sort?"

"No, Mother." Ezri sighed. "The gods are not playing a trick on us."

"Not the gods." Filna pinned me with her glare. "The Nahla."

"What?" I squeezed my fingers around the crystals in my hand and took a step back.

Filna stalked toward me. "That is exactly the question I have been asking myself this whole time. What, my dear, is the point of all this nonsense?"

"Nonsense..." I froze under the force of her scrutiny, my mind unable to form coherent thoughts. Not that it mattered, because my tongue refused to respond and form words, anyway.

"Mother, please." Ezri rushed forward, putting himself between me and his mother. "Ayla-nah is just doing as I've asked. If you have questions, bring them to me. Leave her alone so she can finish testing the others."

Filna turned to face her son, and a wave of relief washed the tension from my limbs. But she wasn't finished. "Then you tell me. What is the point? What use have we for these... these...party tricks? You should have come directly to the Council for guidance. This is an unacceptable trade. You go back and tell the Inahi that the gods can keep their magic. We want the veil restored and will settle for nothing less."

Ezri's eyes flicked past Filna-sha to meet mine. Then he gently touched her shoulder and began guiding her back toward the rest of the group. "Perhaps we should discuss this further in the Council chambers with the representatives from the other clans."

Tavo hurried after Ezri and his mother, and Rys went with them.

Once they were gone, I turned to the others. "Who wants to go next? Now that all the clans are even again, let's have three more. One from each clan."

Bez pushed past Oly and Ivn to take her place before me alongside an equally eager and intense young woman from the Jahl clan. But the three volunteers from the Shal clan hesitated. They stared after the Shal and whispered with one another, holding up the process.

Bez turned to see what was taking so long. "Just start without them."

"If one of you doesn't join us, we're moving on without you," the Jahl woman said.

Bez flashed her an approving grin as two of the Shal clan representatives shoved forward the third, a short young man with a patchy beard. He stumbled to a stop between Bez and the Jahl clan woman.

I placed a crystal in each of their outstretched hands. "Angle the crystal into the light until it casts a rainbow of colors onto your hand. Concentrate on one at a time. Focus on each for a few breaths before moving on."

Nothing happened at first. I began pacing in front of them, my eyes shifting from crystal to crystal, waiting for a swirl of color to appear in one of them. The power associated with many of the colors required more focused practice before achieving a noticeable effect. Unless one of these three also had an affinity for red or yellow magic, the connection would be more subtle. Likely, the only indication would be a change in the focusing crystal.

I had paused in front of the Jahl clan woman whose crystal seemed to be taking on a rosy haze. I wasn't sure if it meant she was close to connecting with violet, which would show an affinity for healing magic, or if I was only imagining the change in hue. Violet was slippery, so just in case, I reminded her to hold her focus.

Then, out of the corner of my eye, I noticed a sudden movement. I turned as a chair came rushing across the floor toward Bez. Everyone standing scrambled backward, their startled exclamations breaking her concentration. The chair skidded to a stop and toppled over at her feet.

"Woah." Bez stared at me with wide eyes. "What just happened?"

"I think you just channeled white magic." I looked back at her in awe.

That someone from my clan would have a natural affinity for white magic, so strong that she'd drawn a large object to her without even trying, surprised me. I had been expecting everyone's first attempt to result in one of the seven base colors because that was how it had worked for me. I hadn't turned out to be an especially strong mage. It had taken me nearly a full moon cycle before I'd mastered white.

"Nice work," I said. "Give your crystal to Ivn and wait with Oly and Kilm."

Bez nodded. Ivn hurried forward, eager for his chance to try, and I turned to the Shal clan man and the Jahl clan woman. Both had lost their focus due to the commotion surrounding Bez. If they had successfully channeled any of the colors, I'd missed it.

"Let's start again at the top, once Ivn is ready," I said. "All together this time. Waiting for my signal before moving from one color to the next."

Ivn took his place beside the others with a crystal in his palm.

"When you're ready, find the rainbow and focus on it." I waited while they adjusted their hands, tilting them into the light. "Let's start with red. Focus on it. Let your mind relax."

I talked them through each color, waiting until they had a few breaths of focus before checking their hands. None of them showed an affinity for red, orange, or yellow. When we reached green, the Shal clan man shivered, drawing my attention to him. One glance at the green haze forming at the center of his crystal had me moving closer.

"That's it. Hold your focus there," I said, digging another crystal out of the pouch. I let it settle into my palm and held my hand alongside his. "Now direct that sensation toward the crystal in my hand. Imagine you're pulling it like a string, tying them together."

It took him a few tries to establish the connection. Sweat beaded on his brow from the strain of focusing, but he kept at it. The green hue at the center of the stone he held pulsed with power. Then the one in my hand colored to match his.

"Good. Well done." I closed my fingers over my crystal. "You can relax now."

He blinked at me. "But nothing happened."

"Not like the others, no. Green magic allows you to draw on the power from other mages. Eventually, you'll also be able to bolster their power with your own." I realized something with a start. "You may even have done that already."

"Borrowed someone's power?" he asked.

"No." I paused. "Well, yes. I was just allowing you to borrow some of mine, as a test, just now. But I was thinking of Bez, with the chair."

"You think he might have been helping me without realizing it?" Bez asked.

"Possibly." I took the crystal from him. "We can test that theory later, though. Who's next from the Shal clan?"

When neither of the remaining pair rushed to take his place, I paced over to the Jahl clan woman while I waited for the Shal clan trio to sort it out. "What's your name?" I asked.

"Cyn," the woman responded.

"Ivn," I pitched my voice louder to make sure he heard. "You and Cyn can move on to blue."

I stayed near Cyn, watching for any change in her crystal. Blue magic was mind magic. It wouldn't have any outward effect. Just as I was about to turn away so I could check Ivn's crystal, he spoke up.

"Did you...say something?" Ivn asked, staring past me at Cyn.

I glanced down at his hand and noticed the blue swirl at the center of his crystal.

Cyn remained focused on her crystal. I didn't think she realized Ivn was talking to her.

"You're not," Ivn said, responding to something only he could hear.

That got Cyn's attention. Her eyes cut to Ivn, and she frowned.

I looked back and forth between them. "Can you hear her?"

Ivn scowled. "She said she was a failure."

"I did not." The woman glared at him.

I set my hand on her forearm. "Maybe not out loud."

"He better not be inside my head." Her fingers curled into a fist around the crystal in her hand.

"Not on purpose." I glanced over at Ivn. "That's enough. Give the crystal to Oly."

Cyn continued to glare at Ivn.

"Blue magic allows the mage to communicate without speaking," I explained, loud enough for the whole group to hear. "At first, you will only be able to hear the thoughts of others. Even animals, in some cases. With practice, blue allows you to communicate across great distances using only your mind."

Blue magic was how I communicated with the Inahi. It was my strongest affinity and the one I'd used first, without even the aid of a focusing crystal. The Inahi explained that they'd always allowed their chosen Labharons access to blue magic because it was the only way they could communicate with us.

In a softer voice, meant only for the Jahl clan woman, I said, "Let's try violet. I think you may have had it before, but it's a tricky one to grasp."

She let her fingers relax and unfurl. "All right."

I talked her through it, and once she had it, I explained. "Violet, or rose, is healing magic. So if you have an injury, you could try directing your focus toward that."

I let her practice a little longer while I got Oly and the woman from the Shal clan set up. By the time I'd activated everyone, I was swaying on my feet with exhaustion. The lack of sleep, combined with the stress of teaching others how to connect with their magic, had caught up to me. I picked up the chair Bez had drawn to her and set it on its feet so I could lean on it.

"Nahla." The stocky man from the Shal clan with the affinity for green spoke up. "This is all very interesting, but I don't see how we are going to be able to teach the others in our clan."

The other two with him nodded their heads. Someone from the Jahl clan trio agreed. Even the faces of the others from my clan looked grim.

I had to admit, they had a point. Looking over at those who had lingered in the tower, watching us from a respectful distance, a sinking feeling took hold of me. There were too many, and we didn't have enough time for me to walk through every color with every person. We would never finish before Midwinter.

8

THE icy wind blowing from across the sea hit me as soon as I stepped out of the tower. I shivered, realizing that I'd left my cloak back in Ezri's room. The calm morning had lulled me into thinking I could leave it behind for the short walk from Ruhl house to the tower at the center of the courtyard.

The Magery was a ways down the hill, past the stables, and I'd be exposed to the wind for most of that trek. I wrapped my arms around my body, taking a moment to call on my weak red magic to rub some warmth into my biceps. As the sensation traveled inward to warm my core, I hurried across to the front of Ruhl house, hesitating a moment on the front step as I wondered if I should knock before barging in.

This was my home now. All of my belongings were inside. I'd packed everything when I'd left my clan, not expecting to ever return. Nothing had changed. Yet.

I threw open the door and stepped inside. After shoving the heavy oak door closed against the wind, I turned and found Nye waiting to greet me.

She dipped her head. "Welcome back, Nahla."

"It's good to see you again, Nye." I started walking, and she fell into step behind me.

"Can I be of assistance to you?" she asked.

"Not right now." I turned in the opposite direction of the suite I'd been assigned and started down the hall that led to Ezri's rooms. "I just need to fetch my cloak from Ezri's room, and then I'm off to the Magery."

"Will you be having your midday meal there?" she asked, continuing to follow me.

In all the excitement of the morning, I'd forgotten about food. But the moment that she mentioned it, my stomach rumbled. "I think so."

She paused in the hall outside Ezri's room and waited while I went inside. When I returned a moment later with my cloak and Sera's journal, she asked, "Which dress would you like me to prepare for you for the welcome dinner this evening?"

Both moons had waxed and waned several times since I'd last considered the wardrobe my mother had commissioned for me from one of the dressmakers in Shal city. "Whichever you think is best."

"Are you sure?"

I retraced my path back toward the front door. "I trust your opinion, Nye. You've lived here longer than I have. I'm sure whatever you choose will be perfect for the occasion."

"Oh. Well." She hesitated a moment, then hurried after me. "The blue is very nice, Nahla. Possibly the most beautiful of the bunch."

I couldn't remember what any of my dresses looked like, except for the one I'd worn that first night. I liked that one, but I also knew I shouldn't wear it again. Not when it was the only dress I'd worn during my time in the city.

"The blue would be fine," I said, more focused on catching up with my aunt than on thoughts of my wardrobe.

"Then again, blue is perhaps..." Nye's voice trailed off.

It took me a beat to realize what she might be trying to imply. Then I cringed as I realized that even the staff of Ruhl house had a stronger grasp of clan politics than I did sometimes.

I needed to be more careful. My initial response could have implied that I thought myself the Ruhlini already. Or worse. Wearing blue, the traditional color of the Inahi speaker, might draw unwanted scrutiny that could reveal the secret I was trying to keep.

"You're right, of course," I said. "Not the blue, then. Let's save that until the Midwinter Festival, when it will be more appropriate."

Nye's steps faltered behind me before speeding to close the distance between us as I reached for the door handle. "Perhaps something in Nahl clan colors?"

I froze. "No. Not that."

What would Cala wear? The thought flitted through my mind.

The dress I'd worn when Ezri introduced me to his mother had been golden. Though I hadn't considered it at the time, I realized that Solnat had been a safe god to invoke on that evening. He stood for wholesome things like family and hearth. Nothing like the colors associated with the gods who ruled the Midwinter Festival. Forsla's black and Jusala's green might be considered overreaching at best, or vaguely threatening, at worst.

"Is there something in a violet hue?" I asked.

"Oh yes, Nahla. There is a lovely purple dress with white embroidery." Nye's hands waved about her midsection and hips to indicate the placement of the design.

Estrel and Lorjad. Perfect. "That will do nicely, I think."

"I'll have it ready for you when you return." Nye dipped her head again.

"Thank you, Nye. I sincerely appreciate your help."

"It is nothing, Nahla," she replied, though her cheeks warmed pink.

I wrapped my cloak around my shoulders and slid outside, trying to let as little of the cold air inside as possible. Then, pulling the edges closed against the wind, I hurried down the hill with Sera's journal tucked under my arm.

Ezri and I had finished her account of Belyn and Harn's tragic affair with damp cheeks and a spark of hope in our hearts. When the Inahi told us our cousin lived, I didn't think much of it. But after reading Sera's story, I wanted to find my uncle's child more than ever. And not just because they would be the key to my own happiness.

I was so lost in my thoughts that I almost didn't recognize the couple standing on an overlook, not even looking out over the wind-tossed waves, but instead absorbed in what looked like a passionate discussion. One of them glanced my way as I hurried past. With my attention focused on the guard barracks just ahead and hoping it would provide a little relief from the stiff wind, I almost didn't recognize the pair as my little brother and Katz-jah.

A shiver of fear ran through me, rooted mostly in the drama I'd been reading about in Sera's journal. They were so close to the edge and the sheer drop down to the beach. I remembered exactly how far down it was because I'd climbed the stairs leading up to that overlook from the sandy strip below. And they appeared to be arguing.

Kilm's wave set some of my worry to rest. His reaction to my presence told me he felt he had whatever was going on under control. I slowed my pace, thinking maybe I should stop, when another figure sauntered out of the barracks, heading toward the overlook.

Katz folded his arms across his chest when he caught sight of what appeared to be Jace walking over to join them. Kilm said something to Katz before turning to greet Jace. Whatever he said didn't have any effect on Katz. The Jahlo remained stiff, his posture unwelcoming.

I sighed and shook my head. I'd warned Kilm that Jace would be trouble. At least it was a trouble that I didn't think would lead to anything worse than hurt feelings. No promises had been made between Kilm and Katz, at least not that I knew of. I hoped whatever tension had developed wouldn't advance to the stage of jealous rage that resulted in fatal tumbles from high places. But I made a mental note to check in with Kilm later, just to be sure. In the meantime, my interference would only make things more awkward. So, I returned Kilm's wave and picked up my pace.

A moment later, I passed the stables and the white stone walls of the Magery came into view. The rose-colored banner attached to a pole on the highest peak of the roof snapped in the steady wind blowing off the sea, sending it streaming toward the city below. I sucked in a breath at the sight.

It still hadn't quite hit me that I would be officially studying there to become a mage once Midwinter was over. I'd be behind the other novices, but I'd be on the path I'd only dreamed of as I shadowed Mage-nah on the plains.

Learning how to use magic with the Inahi had been fun, but it had come with an enormous burden, knowing that I would have to somehow unlock those abilities in everyone when I returned. It was all on my shoulders. I had to be the expert while still working to understand and master my own abilities.

In the process of becoming a mage, on the other hand, I could just be another novice like all the others. All the additional pressure would be gone. I would have friends. People who loved folklore and runes as much as I did. I thought I had that once, with Rys. Until he'd abandoned our shared dream to become a guard.

Of course, now I knew the secret he'd been keeping all these years. I knew why he'd pledged himself to the guard instead of joining me and studying under Mage-nah. It didn't make me feel any better about his choosing Ezri over me, but it did give me the answers to the questions that had plagued me in those first days after leaving my clan.

As I opened the gate in the low wall surrounding the courtyard outside the Magery, excitement and anticipation added an extra spring to my step. I hurried inside and asked the novice behind the desk where I might find Sera.

The youth bent his head to study the scraps of paper that littered the surface of the desk. He pulled one from the bunch, then scooped the rest into a neat stack that he pushed to one side.

"You're Ayla-nah, yes?" he asked, squinting at me.

I nodded.

"It says she's with Mage-sha up in the laboratory," he said, handing me the piece of paper.

"May I go up?" I asked, pointing to the stairs.

He shrugged and gestured to the paper he'd given me. "According to that, you're a novice. You can go anywhere but the masters' suites, and only into the apprentice dorms if you're assigned there for a duty rotation."

"Thank you…" I paused, hoping he might give me his name.

"Jak," he said.

"Thank you, Jak. It's nice to meet you."

He nodded, then turned his attention to someone who had just entered and was waiting behind me.

I tucked the paper he'd given me into my tunic pocket as I jogged up the stairs to the laboratory. It took me a moment to orient myself when I reached the first floor. Another student spotted me and asked if she could help.

"I'm looking for the laboratory. I've been there once before, but I think I've forgotten the way." I'd had Mia to guide me then. I missed her calm presence. It felt strange being out on my own with no guard. No friend at my side.

"I'm heading that way, too," she said. "Come on. I'll show you the way."

"Thank you." I fell into step beside her as she started up another flight of stairs.

"My name's Val. Are you new?" she asked.

"I'm Ayla." I left off the clan leadership suffix, even though I knew it wouldn't take long for word to get around about who I was and where I was from. "I'm a novice, but I'm starting a bit late."

"Well, I'm on my way up to check my exam scores and see which classes the masters have placed me in for second term. It's supposed to be posted today at midday. Is that why you're here as well? To check your classes?"

I blinked at her, unsure how to respond. Mage-sha hadn't mentioned anything about how this worked. I didn't know if I'd be assigned classes like the other novices, or if she had a different plan for me since I had missed the first term. It would be embarrassing if my name wasn't on the list.

"I was on my way to meet with Mage-sha and Sera," I answered.

"Oh! Master Sera is the best. I didn't get into her class on runes last term, and I'm really hoping that I've been assigned to her this time around." Val skipped ahead a few steps, then stretched up to her full height, craning her neck to see up to the landing. "I think I see the postings!"

She reached back to grasp my hand and pull me along with her into the crowd that was gathering around a cluster of papers pinned to the wall at the top of the stairs.

"Second term classes will be on that end." Val nudged me to the far end of the postings. "And the laboratory is through those doors across the hall. I'm going to check my scores first. I'll catch up with you later?"

She turned away before I could respond. Bodies jostled past me, heading in the opposite direction, as I made my way toward the laboratory doors. The crowd was growing as students flowed in from all directions. Most seemed to be prioritizing exam scores, like Val, which left an opening near the second term class assignments.

I hesitated outside the doors, torn between the questions I had for my aunt and curiosity about my future as a novice mage. It would only take a moment to check. A few quick steps closed the distance between me and the papers pinned to the wall. I found the novice class schedule and scanned down the list of names, searching for my own. I'd almost reached the bottom of the list when someone called my name.

"Ayla-nah, is that you?"

I turned to find Mage-sha standing near the laboratory doors. I stepped away from the posting and walked over to where she was waiting.

"I'm not listed on the schedule," I said, trying to hide the disappointment in my voice.

"Yes. I know." Mage-sha put an arm around my shoulder and ushered me into the laboratory and away from the chaos of voices and bodies filling up the landing. "Let's talk in here. Your aunt and Delna-jah are waiting for you."

I followed Mage-sha around shelves filled with jars and books and various bits of equipment that only vaguely resembled anything Mage-nah kept in his tent back on the plains. Stacks of papers covered most of the tables scattered around the room. The mess made it hard for me to see how anyone could get any work done in this space.

On the far side of the room was a hearth containing a modest fire that had mostly burned down to coals. A kettle hung from a hook over what was left of the flames. Close to the hearth sat my aunt in her chair, with Delna across from her on a rocker.

They turned their heads as we approached. My aunt's eyes brightened at the sight of me, and Delna gave me a slight nod.

Sera's eyes fixed on the journal tucked under my arm. "Have you read it?"

"Last night." I hugged it against my chest. "With Ezri. I hope you don't mind."

She pressed her lips into a thin line. For a heartbeat, I thought she was going to scold me. Then she shook her head. "That's good. I'm glad he knows."

"Do you know where the baby is now?" I asked.

Sera glanced around. "Perhaps we should go somewhere with a bit more privacy?"

"Have you eaten, dear?" Mage-sha asked.

"No." I'd forgotten about my hunger again by the time I reached the Magery, but it hadn't gone away. There were just more important things I wanted to discuss.

"There are rooms downstairs, near the dining hall. I doubt any will be in use at this time of day. Not with the term over and everyone fussing over the postings." Mage-sha looked over her shoulder toward the hall.

Delna and Sera exchanged a look. Then Delna said, "I think it will be easier if we stay on this level."

Mage-sha glanced at Sera's wheeled chair. "Yes. The landing is a bit crowded at the moment. Perhaps you're right."

Her response made me wonder how they'd got her up here in the first place. "It's all right," I said. "I can get something to eat later."

"Nonsense." Mage-sha set a hand on my shoulder. "I'll send a novice down to fetch a plate for you, and we'll move our gathering to the masters' retiring room. It's just through those doors there, so we won't need to fight the crowd on the landing."

It took a while to get everyone resettled in the retiring room. Delna helped Sera, and Mage-sha wandered off to find someone who could bring up some food for me. I stood in front of the hearth for a moment, in search of some way to be helpful. Out of the corner of my eye, I spotted the kettle and reached for it without thinking.

The moment my palm touched the hot metal handle, I cursed, snapping my hand back to cradle it against my chest. After shaking some of the pain from my hand, I shoved Sera's journal under the arm attached to the hand I'd injured. Then, after wrapping the edge of my cloak around my uninjured hand, I lifted the kettle from the hearth and found my way to the retiring room.

Mage-sha joined us a moment later. She took one look at me struggling to set the kettle down with my non-dominant hand, and said, "What happened?"

I showed her the burn. "It's not that bad."

She folded my fingers over my burned palm and patted my hand. "Let me get something to put on that."

As she turned away, a thought occurred to me.

"Wait," I said. "There's something I'd like to try first."

I pulled one of the crystals from the pouch tucked into my pocket. "I've only practiced on small cuts, but it's worth a try."

Shutting my eyes to block out the three women watching me, I focused on the color sensations, working my way through each in turn. The color I needed for healing magic was at the very end. The palest shade of violet, closest to the pink of Mage-sha's tent and the banner that flew from the top of the Magery.

I took my time because it was slippery. It always wanted to slide into blue or fade away completely. It took all my focus to hold on to the sensation and channel it into my palm. Just as the pain eased, someone inhaled sharply. The sound made me lose my grasp on the magic for a beat. Before I tried again, I cracked my eyelids open to peek at my hand.

What had been a bright red welt, already starting to swell and blister, had faded into a light pink stripe across my pale skin. The throbbing pain was almost gone, and I decided that was enough.

"Magic," Sera breathed. "Amazing."

I looked up and met her eyes, realizing as I did that she hadn't been there when I'd tested the first batch of potential mages. She'd only seen the illusion I'd cast.

"Hard to believe it's real," Mage-sha said, taking a seat at the table positioned in the center of the small room.

"You've done well," Delna said, adding the word *Labharon* projected from her mind to mine.

"How do you do that?" I asked before remembering that Sera didn't know. At least, she didn't know about me.

From the look Delna exchanged with my aunt, I guessed that maybe Sera did know something about Delna's strange abilities. More than I did, at least.

Someone knocked on the door, breaking the tense silence. I hurried over to thank the novice who'd brought up a steaming plate of food, then shut the door when they dipped their head. Something about the awed look in their eyes told me that it wouldn't be long before everyone knew that the new novice was also the Nahla betrothed to the Ruhl.

Not betrothed once Father signs that treaty, I reminded myself. Then I countered the thought with another. *Soon we'll be married instead.*

"Sit down and eat." Delna spoke the words as a gentle suggestion, not a command. Her soft voice reminded me of my mother, reminding me to extract myself from our clan's library and take care of myself. "Sera's given you her story, but I've yet to share much of my own."

She waited for me to take a few bites before beginning her tale. "My mother was the last Ruhlini, as you know. And I suspect you also know that the title the clan leaders gave to her family has only a coincidental connection to the true power she held."

I nodded. "The Inahi pick their Labharon. It's not a title that can be inherited the way our clan leadership families inherited our titles from Ruhala's children."

"Exactly." Delna glanced at my aunt. "Sera discovered this while helping Mage-sha restore the ruined page in the Magery's book of folklore. My son took her captive under orders from my late husband, who wished to keep that a secret. But you found out anyway. I suspect the Inahi told you the truth?"

"Yes." I spoke around a mouthful of food that I quickly swallowed so I could say more. "When they chose me to be their Labharon."

Sera's eyes widened. "I thought... It's not Ezri-ruh?"

I shook my head. "No one knows. Well, almost no one. We told Mage-sha. And Zan. It's impossible to keep secrets from him. But that was all. Except Delna-jah. She just knew. How did you know?"

Delna frowned. A sadness filled her eyes before she glanced down at her folded hands on the table. "I believe it is because that honor would have passed to me when my mother died. There were signs. Before. They started after she fell ill."

I recalled the bouts of sickness that Sera had described in her journal. Sera had thought someone was poisoning Delna. "But the medicine Mage-sha gave you..."

Delna glanced at Mage-sha. "I suffer from the same affliction as my mother and my nephew. Mage-sha's elixir helped me with that, as it helps Ezri-ruh. But there was something else. Something I didn't dare tell a soul."

"Her father had found a way to stifle her magic." Sera's eyes narrowed. Her disgusted scowl illustrated the frustration she'd expressed in her journal about Belyn and Delna's father.

Delna reached over and set her hand on the arm of Sera's chair. "He thought he could force the Inahi to choose Belyn instead, by denying them access to me. After the lengths he'd gone to, destroying all references to the Labharon until only the clans' belief in the title of Ruhl remained, he had to make sure that Belyn inherited Mother's role. Not a girl still years from her maturity. Too young to secure him the powerful position on the Council that he desired."

"But it's the Labharon who sits on the Council," I said, confused.

Delna sighed. "He'd taken Mother's seat when she fell ill and planned to continue on as representative for the Shal clan after Belyn married Jeln-sha. It was what he'd asked from the Shal in exchange for agreeing to the betrothal. At first, the Shal refused, which was part of the reason why Father decided to bring Belyn to visit the Nahl and Jahl.

"He thought the threat of an alignment with a rival clan might cause the Shal to change his mind. It was a negotiation tactic, as well as a cover that would allow him to get his hands on the Nahl and Jahl clan books of folklore. He didn't expect Belyn to take her future into her own hands."

"Or that you would catch him destroying the Nahl clan's book," Sera added.

"Or that," Delna agreed, returning her hands to her lap as she leaned back in her chair.

"Why didn't you tell someone?" I asked, mopping the remaining sauce off my plate with the last hunk of bread.

"I tried to run away." Delna's eyes dropped to her clasped hands.

"Ber-ruh was threatening her." Sera folded her arms across her chest.

Delna looked at Sera. "You did what you could."

"I should have done more." Sera scowled.

"Enough." Mage-sha's voice cut through the tension. "Both of you. It's done. We have a new Labharon. Our connection to the Inahi isn't lost. And both of you are still alive to pass along your knowledge."

"Yes, Mage-sha." Sera's face softened. She let her arms drop so that her hands rested in her lap.

My eyes bounced between them, wondering at the dynamic between the three of them. After all these years, Sera still behaved as though she were Mage-sha's apprentice, assigned responsibility for the Ruhlini's children. But Delna was no longer a child. She'd been the Jahlini for years.

"How did you end up marrying Vehlm-jah?" I asked.

Sera's jaw flexed. The tension returned to her shoulders as she looked over at Delna.

"Your aunt isn't the first person the Jahl has ordered captured," Delna said. She paused to take a deep breath. "Vehlm figured out what my father had been doing to me and why. Rather than expose my father's deceit to the Shal, he told his father. Once the Jahl knew my value, he ordered Vehlm to smuggle me out of the city and back to the caverns where the two of us would be married by their clan mage. He used the distraction of Belyn's funeral as his opportunity to capture me."

Sera shifted in her chair. "We didn't know where she'd gone until the Jahl announced the marriage of his heir, and by then, it was too late to do anything about it."

"But you didn't become the Labharon," I said.

Delna folded her hands on the table. "The Inahi couldn't reach me in the caverns."

"Because of the Koto." I remembered the Inahi had warned me about that when I'd traveled there to confront Vehlm-jah.

Delna nodded. "It was as the Jahl had planned. He didn't want me to become the Labharon. He had agreed to help the Koto break our connection to the Inahi. The Koto said that was the only way they could, or would, return magic to the Jahl clan."

"But the Koto didn't give the Jahl clan magic." I hesitated. "Did they?"

"They showed Vehlm how to call on the Merluks and control them," Delna said. "They promised more, but not until they were sure the connection was severed. There was still a chance a new Labharon could rise."

Pieces of the puzzle clicked into place. "Is that why they tried to kill Ezri?" I asked.

Delna sighed. "The Koto could sense that Vorn had not inherited whatever power I possessed."

"But if they knew, then why did Vehlm-jah and my father claim that Vorn-jah should be the Ruhl?"

"Your father didn't know," Delna said. "Vehlm didn't tell anyone, even Vorn. He thought he could do what my father had done. All references to the Labharon in our written legends had been destroyed. Few had studied the legend about Ruhala and the origin of the clans well enough to remember the details. There was only my mother's diary, and the page Father tore out of the Nahl clan's book of folklore, to prove the truth. I had them with me when Vehlm captured me, but who was I going to share them with, hidden away as I was in the caverns?"

Sera scoffed. "He was no different from Ber-ruh, forcing you to marry him before you had even reached your maturity. And all so that he could claim that his child should inherit the title."

"They were all wrong," I said, catching Sera's eye. "Neither was the firstborn."

"No," she said. "They weren't."

"But Belyn's baby died," Mage-sha said. "May they shine beside Estrel."

Sera shifted forward. "Mage-sha. There's something I need to tell you."

9

MAGE-SHA sat in stunned silence as Sera explained how and why she'd hidden Belyn and Harn's baby instead of handing it over to Ber-ruh.

"I'm sorry, Mage-sha," Sera said. "When I overheard Ber-ruh telling the Shal that they would get rid of the baby so they could pretend that Belyn and Jeln's eldest child was the true heir to the Ruhl line, I had to do something."

"You could have told me," Mage-sha said.

"You weren't in the city at the time," Sera replied. "And I'd promised Belyn."

Mage-sha shook her head slowly. Her blue eyes shined with unshed tears. "But I don't understand. You knew that Ezri wasn't the eldest, and yet you argued for him to be named Ruhl. You convinced us to put our faith in him, and you didn't know that the Inahi chose their speaker. The clans could have lost their connection to the Inahi. Why didn't you bring the true Ruhl forward?"

"If I had, would anyone have believed me?" Sera leaned

back in her chair. She turned her head to look at Delna. "Would Vehlm-jah have accepted my word and agreed?"

Delna frowned. "No. He wouldn't have agreed to anything that didn't result in Vorn being named Ruhl."

Sera nodded. "And Filna-sha wouldn't have agreed, either, as much as she hates that the Magery chose her son and only heir instead of Vorn-jah. She would never have placed someone she believed to be far beneath her on the Council. She's much happier thinking she has some degree of control over the power behind that title."

"But we'd already gone almost twenty years without a connection to the Inahi," Mage-sha said. "You were putting the clans at risk, keeping the eldest hidden."

"I wasn't." Sera held up a hand when Mage-sha tried to argue. "I've been keeping a close eye on the true Ruhl for years now. I had a plan. Once he began speaking with the Inahi, I would have brought him forward with my proof of his true parents."

"You know where he is." I leaned forward, eager for her to share her secret and wondering if she realized she'd slipped in mentioning the child's gender after she'd been so careful with her wording in the journal she sent me.

"I do," Sera confirmed. "Not that it matters now."

"But it does." I shifted to the edge of my chair, resting both my forearms on the table between us. "I need to know who he is. Ezri needs to know. And don't you think my father and Uncle Feln would like to know that Harn's child lives?"

"Why?" Sera squinted at me. "It won't change how they feel about me. If anything, it will make them hate me more for keeping the baby hidden. I don't see what anyone gains by ripping open old wounds."

I pulled my lower lip between my teeth. Ezri trusted Sera

and Mage-sha, but neither of us knew anything about Delna-jah. If I revealed our plan in front of her, and she told her sons, they might be inclined to stop us. The politics were complicated, and I didn't know how to work through them quickly, on my own. I decided it would be better not to say anything until I had a chance to talk it over with Ezri.

Delna spoke up, saving me from having to respond. "The clans believe the lies my father spread about how the role of Labharon would be passed to the eldest of each generation in the Ruhl clan line." Her eyes locked with mine. "If Sera brings our nephew forward now, we will need to tell them everything."

I stared at her as what she said registered with me. "You know who he is, don't you?"

Delna pressed her lips into a line. Her face flushed with color as her eyes flicked to Sera.

"You're missing the point." Sera gripped the arms of her chair and leaned toward me, drawing my attention. "Are you ready to tell everyone the truth? Is Ezri-ruh?"

A knock on the door interrupted us.

"Will you see who it is, dear?" Mage-sha asked, reaching over to pat my hand.

I broke the tense stare with my aunt to stand and walk over to the door. When I opened it, I found Ezri beaming at me, with Rys standing just behind him.

"Found you," he said.

"Just in time," I replied, before turning to tell the others that Ezri had joined us.

When Rys attempted to follow Ezri into the room, I held out my arm to stop him. "This is a private meeting."

"I swore I wouldn't leave Ezri's side while Zan is gone," Rys replied, trying to push past.

"It's all right, Rys," Ezri said. "No one threatening in here. I'll be fine. You can wait outside."

Rys scanned the room behind me. When his eyes fell on Delna, he opened his mouth to argue the point, but Ezri cut him off.

"No one in here will harm a hair on my head. You can trust them."

"But—" Rys tried again.

"I promise to yell very loudly if I need you." Ezri guided me into the room and shut the door on Rys. Then he turned to the others. "Now. What did I miss?"

"How was the Council meeting?" Delna asked. If her tone didn't make it clear that she knew what they'd been discussing, her next question did. "Is everything prepared for your wedding?"

"About that." Ezri flashed me an apologetic look. "It seems that we won't be having a wedding after all. The Council has ended my betrothal."

All three pairs of eyes fixed on me. Two faces looked at me with curiosity, watching to see what my reaction would be. The other showed only shock.

"What happened?" Mage-sha, who appeared to be the only one who hadn't expected this news, asked.

"The Council doesn't like the idea of the Ruhl marrying into any of the leadership families," Ezri explained.

"But you are not...." Mage-sha let the rest of her statement hang in the air.

"I'm not." Ezri pulled a chair up to the table. "And I believe that you were discussing who is. So. Tell me. What did I miss? Who is the lucky recipient of my title? Hmm?"

"Ezri-ruh." Mage-sha pushed herself to her feet to face him. "Are you sure this is a good idea?"

Ezri looked at me.

"They're concerned that the Council will have a lot of questions," I explained. "Especially when they find out that, despite being the true Ruhl, our cousin is not the Inahi speaker."

Ezri shrugged. "All right. We won't bring them forward. But I would like to know who it is."

I stared at him, unsure if he was saying that only to appease my aunt, or if he really meant to go back on the plan we'd made.

"Who is that guard outside?" Sera asked, her eyes still fixed on the door. "And why did he say that Zan is gone? Where did he go?"

"Zan is following a lead, searching for Mia," Ezri explained. "He left Rys in charge of guarding me while he's gone. Why?"

"Rys. Why does that name sound familiar?" Sera's brow furrowed. "Is that...? The boy from the Nahl clan whose father—"

"Died fighting Merluks to keep us safe? Yes." Ezri nodded. "Now. Are you going to tell us who my cousin is? Or are you going to make me beg?"

"Ezri." Sera's voice carried a note of pleading. "What difference does it make to you? Your cousin is happy with who they are. Knowing the identity of their parents and being handed a title they don't want won't improve their life. You understand that perhaps better than anyone."

"He," I said, drawing both Sera and Ezri's attention. "You said 'he' before. And Delna called our cousin your nephew."

Sera scowled. "I suppose we did."

"So she knows." Ezri grinned, turning the focus of his charm onto Delna. "What if I promise not to tell a soul? Will you let me in on the secret?"

I stared at the back of Ezri's head, unable to believe he'd make such a promise without speaking to me first. What was he doing?

"Come on, Aunt Delna," he said. "I can keep a secret. Please?"

Delna's eyes narrowed. "This is not my secret to tell."

"Enough." Mage-sha's voice silenced us. "Sera's right. We should take some time to think this through. There's too much at risk."

Ezri leaned back in his chair and crossed his arms. "All right. Let's say I die without an heir—"

Mage-sha spoke up to protest, but Ezri continued over her. "No. Listen. The Council has just ended my betrothal. Even with a wedding at Midwinter, there was no guarantee I would survive long enough to produce a child. I haven't recovered fully from the attempt on my life. We both know that your work, Mage-sha, while clearly a miracle of Estrel, will only serve to delay the desired result of my attackers. Now, with no wedding, and no desire on my part to agree to a hasty partnership just to produce an offspring to inherit a meaningless title, what will happen when I die?"

"Vorn and Cala's firstborn will inherit the title of Ruhl," Delna said in a quiet voice.

Ezri nodded. "But our connection to the Inahi, as far as the clans are concerned, will be lost once again, until their eldest reaches their maturity."

"You could easily live long enough to see that happen," Mage-sha said.

"Especially since Cala is pregnant," Sera added.

"I could." Ezri paused. He tapped his toe against the floor, either in impatience or in thought. "But why should we let my grandfather's lies continue? They currently grant me a power I don't deserve, and when I'm gone that power will pass to the eldest of the Jahl's line. A child who would otherwise inherit their father's title of Jahl, and will likely never inherit the ability to speak with the Inahi, at least as long as Ayla lives."

"As long as there is a chance for Vorn to have more than one child, he will never agree to abolish the title of Ruhl," Delna said, her voice barely above a whisper.

"Even if he knows that it means nothing?" Ezri asked.

Delna shook her head. "Inheriting the title will give the Jahl clan two seats on the Council."

"That's half the votes," Sera added, nodding. "Majority, so long as Teron and Goff will continue to go along with him."

"Which they will," Ezri said.

I grimaced. I didn't like it, but he was probably right. I couldn't imagine what would make Father side with the Shal clan against the Jahl.

Delna's eyes locked with Ezri's across the table. "Your only chance of getting rid of the title is to bring forward Belyn's son while you are still alive."

Ezri's face made it clear that he agreed, but he said nothing in response. It hadn't taken Delna very long to guess our plan. He must have guessed that she would when he continued to push the point. Allowing her to get there on her own rather than forcing her hand allowed her to make the choice. She could follow her own heart without her son knowing that she had a hand in taking away his potential advantage.

"You could undo the damage your father did," I said, keeping my voice soft.

Delna looked to Sera.

"If you need time to think it over..." Ezri said, letting his voice trail off.

"Zan." Sera's eyes slipped past Delna to meet Ezri's.

"You want to wait until he returns?" Ezri asked.

"No." I reached over to brush my fingertips against Ezri's. Everything Sera had been saying about keeping an eye on the true Ruhl suddenly made sense. "Our cousin. It's Zan."

———

After going around and around with my aunt, Mage-sha, and Delna, Ezri and I left the Magery without anything decided. But it was getting late, and we needed time to get ready for the welcome dinner Jace had planned. Then hurrying up the hill with Rys, we didn't dare talk about what we'd discovered. We walked in awkward silence, exchanging looks but unable to say what we were thinking.

When we arrived at Ruhl house, we paused in the entrance hall, just before we needed to part in opposite directions: Ezri to his room, and me to mine. Rys continued a few steps down the hall toward Ezri's rooms to give us some space, and I wondered how much he'd overheard in the Council meeting.

Ezri and I stood staring at each other for a few breaths, neither of us making a move toward the other.

"Now what?" I asked, trying to keep my voice low.

Ezri ran a hand through his hair. "You'll be able to stay in your rooms until after the festival."

"We should talk," I said.

He grimaced. "This is going to make it a lot harder to do things like that."

"I know." I tried not to look over at Rys. "We'll find a way."

Ezri nodded. "See you at dinner?"

"From the opposite side of the room." I tried to smile, to show how confident I was that it would all work out, but my heart was slamming against my chest and my palms were damp.

This was it. As soon as we turned away from each other and separated, every step we took would make it that much harder to find our way back to each other. Ezri would be swept up in the currents of the Council, and I would slowly sink back to obscurity. The fourth-born daughter of the Nahl clan leader.

Except that wasn't all. Not anymore. I was the Labharon. Ezri needed me. The clan leaders needed me. And Ezri loved me. We'd get through this.

I reached out, taking his hand in mine, and squeezed.

The gesture lifted some of the darkness from Ezri's face, and he smiled at me. A real Ezri smile. By the time he turned away, his eyes were sparkling again, and my heartbeat slowed to a steady thrum.

Nye was waiting for me outside the door to my rooms. The dress we'd agreed on hung from the wardrobe in my bedroom, but I didn't stop to admire it. I let her lead me to the bathing chamber where my mind spun, working to make sense of everything we'd learned and fit the new pieces into our plan.

By the time I was dressed, I felt more confident. Zan would hate being Ruhl, but he already knew I was Labharon. It wouldn't be hard to convince him to accept the title temporarily. The clans would vote to abolish the title, and we'd restore the missing piece in our folklore. Everyone would know the truth about our connection to the Inahi.

I would have to step forward as the real Labharon, but I could let Ezri represent me on the Council so I wouldn't have to deal with all the politics. I'd be free to study at the Magery, and make sure everyone with the potential learned how to use their magic.

When Nye stepped back to examine her work on my hair, I glanced up to look at myself in the mirror. It had been a long time since I'd stopped to look at the face staring back at me. Violet shadowed the lids of my eyes. My lips had been stained with a deep plum hue. Nye had braided pieces of my hair before sweeping it all off my shoulders and pinning it up into an elaborate configuration that reminded me of Cala on her wedding day.

"Nye?" Even my voice sounded strange to my ears, as I watched my reflection speak.

Nye's eyes met mine in the mirror. "Do you like it, Nahla?"

"Yes. It's only…" I blinked, but the image in the mirror didn't change.

"Nahla?"

"My jewelry chest." I swallowed my hesitation. Everyone would be looking at me. Judging my reaction to the ending of my betrothal. "Perhaps we might add the comb?"

Nye's eyes brightened. "Of course, Nahla."

I would be making a statement wearing the headpiece of the Nahl clan leadership family. It would draw attention to my clan tattoo. Even though I wore the colors of Estrel, it would align me with my family in a way that could be interpreted as defiance. Perhaps Ezri's mother would see it and infer my true message, but that was a risk I was willing to take.

She hadn't won. This wasn't over. I was strong, and I wasn't going anywhere.

10

OTH moons were high in the night sky by the time Ezri crept onto my balcony and knocked on my window. I leapt up from the chair I'd curled into and opened the balcony door to let him inside. His arms wrapped around me the moment the latch clicked closed behind him.

"I think that was the most excruciating dinner of my life," he said, cradling my cheek in his palm so he could kiss me.

His lips were cold from sneaking around outside, but his mouth was warm, and I allowed my worries to slip away as he deepened the kiss. I tugged at his waist, pulling him further into the room until the backs of my legs touched the bed. I pulled him down with me. His hands roamed over the curve of my waist as his lips trailed kisses across my jaw and down the side of my neck.

"That dress," he said, breath hot on my bare skin.

I laughed. "You liked it?"

"Torture." He lifted his head to look me in the eyes. "I was supposed to be pretending as though I didn't care, but I couldn't keep my eyes off you."

Ezri hadn't been the only one staring. Just as I'd expected, everyone's eyes had been on me all evening. Though it wasn't all curiosity behind their gazes. As word spread throughout the crowd, the looks I received fell into two groups. The first, and most obvious, were those searching for any hint of drama. They searched my face for signs of devastation, anger, or elation. Anything that might fuel their gossiping tongues. I hoped I hadn't given them any.

The second group were those, like Ezri, who, once they heard the news, regarded me with an unmistakable heat in their eyes. A Nahla, on the cusp of her maturity, available for courting. They would have swamped me if it hadn't been for Kilm and the small group from my clan who kept close to me all evening, deftly fending off those who approached with lust in their eyes. I suspected their actions were Kilm's doing. Though, whether he'd chosen to rally them to that noble cause for my benefit or because it gave him a reason to steer clear of both Katz and Jace for the entire evening, I wasn't sure.

"I'm glad you liked it," I said, combing my fingers through his silky hair.

Ezri shifted his weight, so we were laying side by side, facing each other. "I talked with Sera."

I sucked in a breath. I hadn't seen my aunt at the dinner. I assumed Jace had deferred to Filna-sha's wishes and left Sera off the list. "When?"

Ezri shrugged one shoulder. "I managed to get a moment alone with her before the dinner. It's all settled. She's agreed."

"To come forward about Zan?" I asked, lifting myself up onto my elbow.

"That." Ezri pinched my chin. "And to marry us after Midwinter."

I covered his mouth with mine. My excited kisses and his exploring hands soon had us both breathless. My heart was racing as we broke apart to catch our breath. "How?"

Ezri grinned. "It seems you aren't the only Nahla who can't resist my charm."

"Ew." I shoved his shoulder. "Really. How did you convince her? She seemed so set on keeping Zan a secret."

Ezri twirled a strand of my hair around his finger. "I may have led with the marriage part. Once she realized we were set on doing this with or without her help, she came around."

"But she knows the marriage is supposed to be a secret?" I asked, quickly adding, "Just until it's all settled."

Ezri's eyes narrowed as he studied my face. "You're sure you don't want to wait?"

I scowled. "Do you know what my father said to me tonight?"

"No." Ezri's brow furrowed with worry.

I smoothed the wrinkles with the tips of my fingers. "He said, 'I know you, Ayla. There's more to this than you're letting on.' Then he insisted that, once this is over and we're back at the compound, I explain exactly what happened with the Inahi."

"What did you tell him?"

I shrugged one shoulder. "That I'm moving into the Magery to join the rest of the novices and begin my studies."

Ezri laughed. "Of course you did."

"Ezri." I cupped his face in my hands, meeting his eyes with my own. "I'm sure."

"All right." He swallowed. "As long as you know—"

"Ezri?" I cut him off.

He had that look on his face again. The one that he got

when he started talking about his illness and the poison he'd been served that had nearly killed him. But we'd been over all that already.

When he fell silent, I said, "I know."

He exhaled. His fingers caressed my cheek. "Well, then we should probably discuss what happens next, since I no longer have any excuse to keep you close to me."

I sat up, positioning myself cross-legged on the bed, facing him. "What does Jace have planned for tomorrow?"

We went over the schedule, and I offered to lead a training session in the tower for anyone who wanted to practice. Ezri guessed it would be most of the group, and promised to keep the clan leaders occupied elsewhere so they wouldn't be breathing down my neck. The less they saw of me, the easier it would be to hide my true abilities. I needed to appear only slightly more advanced than the others so it wouldn't raise any suspicions.

By the time we finished talking, Uthea was close to the horizon, and I was struggling to hide my yawning.

"Get some sleep," Ezri said, pushing himself off the bed.

I reached out to grab his arm. "Aren't you going to stay?"

He bent to kiss the top of my head. "We can't risk it."

I sighed because I knew he was right. "When Zan returns, you'll talk with him?"

Ezri nodded. "Sera wants to be there as well."

I wrapped my arms around his waist and rested my head against his stomach. "See you in the morning?"

"It's only a few more days." He slid down until we were eye level. "Soon we'll be waking up together every morning, Stormcat."

"Promise?"

"Promise." His kiss was warm but much too brief, and then

he was gone.

I wrapped the blankets around me and fell asleep almost immediately. When I woke, Nye had brought me a breakfast tray. She was humming to herself as she laid out my clothes for the day.

"Good morning, Nahla," she said when I finally sat up and stretched.

"Good morning, Nye." I blinked at the sunlight streaming through the windows in the balcony door. When I spotted a single yellow flower resting on the railing, I grinned.

It was going to be a good day. The start of many more to come. I dressed quickly between bites of food, anxious to get started. As much as I tried to hurry, the gathering room on the ground floor of the tower was already crowded by the time I arrived.

Kilm spotted me as soon as I walked in. He nudged Bez and the two of them pushed their way through the others to greet me.

"How are you?" Kilm asked.

"Fine." I scanned the room to avoid the concerned look on his face, noting how quickly the echoing chatter died down, replaced by a hiss of whispers as more and more people noticed me.

I sighed. If I was going to be the center of everyone's attention, I preferred to be teaching them magic. "Let's get started."

"I convinced the other volunteers to get their groups organized," Bez said. She pointed toward the center of the room. "We're going to form a ring here in the center of the room, with those of us who volunteered in the middle. We can monitor the crystals while you provide the instructions. We just need to know how many of those crystals you have, and we'll get the first batch in position with everyone else queued up behind them."

I pulled the pouch from my pocket and glanced inside, even though I already knew the answer. "Ten."

"Great!" Bez pivoted and started back toward the others.

I followed, but only managed a few steps before my toe snagged on a corner of one of the stones in the floor. The bag of crystals tipped over in my palm. I gasped as they tumbled over my fingertips and scattered across the ground, skidding away from me, toward the center of the room. I held my breath until I was sure that none had shattered, and then I realized, in my panic, I'd grabbed for white magic and somehow managed to cushion their fall.

"That could have been tragic," Kilm muttered.

He'd kept his voice low, as though intending the comment only for me, but everyone in the tower had turned to stare in shocked silence at the scene I'd made. So everyone heard.

Ivn and Bez, who were standing closest to me, responded with nervous laughter. Their reaction infected the rest of the group, and soon everyone was laughing with relief. Tavo and Cyn bent to pick up the crystals that fell closest to them. I reached for the pair that landed near me, and Bez rushed forward, scurrying after the ones that had gone flying toward the center of the floor.

She had three in her palm when she reached for the one that had traveled the farthest from where I stood. As her fingers clasped around it, her boot stepped onto the circular stone at the center of the room. A heartbeat later, an invisible blast hit me in the center of my chest, shoving me back.

I landed hard on my bottom and used my forearms and elbows to keep my head from slamming against the stone pillar behind me. My fingers curled protectively around the crystals in my hands, and the force of the impact caused their sharp edges to cut into the flesh of my palms.

Grimacing against the pain, I blinked to clear my vision, but it wasn't my eyes that were the problem. The room was filled with a cloud of smoke that had only just begun to disperse. From my vantage point on the floor, it looked like I wasn't the only one who had been injured.

A group from the Shal clan who I hadn't met were rushing forward from wherever they'd been gathering. They bent to help the others from their clan who had been closer to the blast.

The blast. I scanned from the outer edges of the room in toward the middle where a figure lay sprawled in the center of the floor. *Bez.*

I lurched toward her as I tried to stand. My legs were too weak to hold my weight, and I stumbled to my knees before I got my footing. I must have cried out in the process, because someone turned and spotted me.

There was yelling that I couldn't quite make out over the ringing in my ears, and then someone rushed toward me, followed by another from the Shal clan group. I shook my head and gestured toward the middle of the room. One of them turned to look. They skidded to a stop at the sight.

More yelling and hand waving. Someone pushed past me, then someone else caught me and helped me to my feet before I fell again. I stumbled toward the body at the center of the room, but a strong arm held me back. The first voice I recognized as my ears began to clear belonged to Filna-sha.

"What in the name of all the gods happened here?"

I turned in time to see the shocked faces of the Council and clan leaders as they stopped at the bottom of the stairs to gape at the chaos that had erupted beneath them as they met in the room above.

My father's eyes scanned the room. His shoulders visibly relaxed when he spotted me. His face reminded me that I wasn't the only one of his children who might be hurt.

"Kilm." My voice came out in a croak.

"Right here," he said, adjusting his hold on me so I could see his face. "I got you."

"When did you get..." I squeezed his arm. "...muscles?"

"Good to see you haven't lost your sense of humor." He shook his head as his eyes fixed on my forehead. "But I don't like the look of that gash on your head. Let's get you over to Mage-sha so she can have a look at it."

Kilm started to lead me away until I remembered and dug my heels in.

"Bez," I said, trying to turn back.

"They've got her," he said, keeping his hold on me. "And there's nothing you can do for her until we get you patched up."

"But..." I held up my palm full of crystals.

"I'll make sure we get all of them." Kilm guided me forward a few steps.

"No." I shook my head, trying to clear it, to get the right words out. "Rose. Magic."

Kilm squinted at me. It took him a moment before he realized what I was trying to say. "Healing magic. Of course. Right. I'll find someone who can give it a try."

I tugged on his arm as his eyes scanned the room. "Me. Let me."

"I don't know..." Kilm frowned at my forehead.

"Kilm," Sera called out as she approached us. She moved slowly, alternating careful steps with her good leg and shuffles forward of the one that had been broken as she leaned her weight on a staff. "Get your sister over to Mage-sha."

Kilm turned his head toward her. "She wants to try to use magic to help Bez."

Sera frowned. Her eyes slid past me to the center of the room, and I craned my neck to look behind me.

On the ground, Bez wasn't moving. Ivn was crouched next to her head, his fingers on her neck. A mage in master's robes stood over them. He waved to a pair of youth wearing cream-colored tunics over brown trousers. They rushed toward him when he called, and I realized they were carrying a frame stretched with canvas, big enough to hold a body, between them.

I broke loose from Kilm's grasp and started moving toward the master mage. As I walked, I dropped all but one of the crystals into my pocket. I wasn't sure where the little pouch had gone, but it didn't matter. I could find it later, after I healed Bez.

The pair of youths with the stretcher arrived just ahead of me. They dropped it on the ground alongside Bez and knelt, ready to move her onto the platform.

"Wait," I called, causing the master mage to turn.

"I'm busy," he said, pointing to something behind me. "Go over there and one of the other mages will take care of you."

"No." I held up a crystal, pinching it between my fingers so he could see. "I want to help."

When he shut his mouth, his nostrils flared. "I think we've had quite enough magic for one day."

I ignored him and bent down next to Ivn. "Is she...?"

"Her heart is beating," he said. "And she's breathing."

The master mage loomed over me. "Go and see to your own wounds. Both of you. Let the trained mages repair the damage you've done."

I glared up at him. "I have been trained. By the Inahi. Now

stand back and let me help my friend."

While the master gaped at me, I scanned Bez's body. The upper half of her body covered most of the circular stone at the center of the floor. One arm was bent, so her clenched fist lay next to her head. Her other palm was open at her side. When I reached down to touch her hand, a jolt ran through me, knocking me back on my heels.

The master took several steps back, and the two youths who had been kneeling next to the stretcher scrambled to their feet. Only Ivn didn't move.

I caught my breath, then motioned to Bez's fist. "Can you try?"

Ivn moved his fingers from Bez's neck and brushed them against her hand, tentatively. When nothing happened, he wrapped one hand around her wrist and used the other to gently peel her fingers away from her palm.

The three crystals nestled in her palm were no longer clear. They were solid black and pulsing with an energy I could sense. It wasn't the same as the colors I'd been taught by the Inahi. This was something different.

I waved Ivn's hand away before he could reach for the crystals. "Wait."

Closing my eyes, I reached out with my newly developing sense of magic. There was something strange about the way it felt. Almost like the sensation was radiating up from the stone floor, through Bez, and into the crystals in her hand.

I opened my eyes and glanced around for something I could use to knock the gems out of her hand without touching them. "Kilm, give me your boot."

"My boot?" Kilm stared at me.

"Fine. I'll use mine." I sat back, swiveling my legs around in front of me so I could yank one of my boots off my foot.

Sera shifted her staff and shuffled forward a step. "Let me."

Sera's staff.

I motioned for my aunt to move closer. "Can you use your staff to knock those crystals out of her hand?"

Kilm hurried to Sera's side to help support her as she maneuvered herself into position.

"We're wasting time," the master mage grumbled.

"Did you see what happened when I touched her?" I asked.

"Perhaps it's you who are the problem." The master pointed at Ivn. "Nothing happened when he was touching her."

I glared at him, wanting to argue, but unsure what to say. I was acting on a hunch I couldn't explain.

Ezri rushed over just as Sera swung her staff in the direction of Bez's hand. "What's going on?"

I caught the end of the staff and guided it toward the target. Gently, I nudged the crystals off Bez's hand and onto the floor. Then I used my foot to push them off the center stone. The moment they were free of whatever pull that disc in the floor seemed to have over them, the blackness drained away.

"Now you can take her," I said.

Ezri helped me to my feet as Ivn and the two Shal clan youths worked together to maneuver Bez onto the stretcher.

"Are you all right?" Ezri asked, reaching for the cut on my forehead.

I winced as his fingers brushed against my skin. "I will be. I just need a quiet place to heal."

Sera bent down and scooped up the crystals from the floor as Kilm joined Ivn and the others, helping them lift the stretcher. She studied them for a moment before holding them out for me to take.

"What happened?" she asked.

"Everyone keeps asking me that." I grimaced at the circular

stone set into the center of the floor. "I'm not entirely sure. But if I had to guess, whatever happened has something to do with that."

"The floor?" Ezri asked.

"Maybe. I don't know." I looked at him. "I need to have a closer look, but I'd prefer to do it when there are fewer people watching me."

He took my arm and led me toward the area where Magesha was working alongside the others who'd come up from the Magery to help. There were more people gathered around them than I had expected.

I squeezed Ezri's arm. "I don't need their help. I can heal myself. I just need—"

While I searched for a place where I could sit and focus for a few moments, I missed Filna-sha marching toward us with my father, my uncle Feln, and Tavo hurrying to keep up. By the time I turned back to Ezri, it was too late to escape. She had reached us, and she did not look pleased.

"What is the meaning of this?" She waved her hand in the air as though batting away whatever remained of the smoky haze that had followed the explosion.

"Mother," Ezri said. "Can't you see? Ayla-nah is injured. Perhaps we could let the mages tend to her before we start asking her questions."

"The Ruhl has a point." My father's eyes fixed on my forehead briefly before cataloging the various scrapes and cuts on my arms, hands, and knees. "My daughter's safety is more important right now."

Filna-sha spun on him. "The safety of all the clans is more important than a few minor injuries to one individual. We were clearly wrong to leave these young people unsupervised. They should be trained by the Ruhl, not the random woman the Inahi used for the purpose of demonstrating the potential of magic."

"Now see here." My father stepped toward Filna-sha, using his height to tower over her. "My daughter is a Nahla, not some random woman. Just because—"

"Come on," Ezri whispered in my ear. As my father continued to argue with Filna-sha, Ezri guided me to a position just out of his mother's line of sight.

I winced when he took hold of my elbow to guide me further away.

"Sorry," he said. "Can you manage on your own?"

"I'll be fine. Just... Is there someplace we can go?" I asked.

Ezri stepped between me and the clan leaders, blocking their view of me. "Go up to the Council room. I'll make some excuse and meet you up there as soon as I can."

As I hurried toward the stairs, Rys rushed past me, heading in the opposite direction. He froze when he caught sight of me.

"Gods. Ayla. Are you hurt?" He stepped toward me.

I held up my hands to stop him from coming any closer. "Why aren't you with Ezri?"

"I... He..." Rys looked past me. His eyes fixed on Ezri before returning to meet mine. "Zan is back."

"Zan? Where?" I sucked in a breath, and my heart started racing in anticipation. He was back. Our cousin. I wanted to run back to Ezri and tell him, but I held myself in place. In a low voice, I asked, "Did he find Mia?"

Rys shook his head. "I don't know. She wasn't with him when he arrived."

"Where is he now?" I demanded. "Has Ezri seen him yet?"

"No. He was in the Council meeting when Zan arrived." Rys narrowed his eyes, as suspicious as ever. "Zan went to the barracks to check in while they finished. He should be back any moment."

I risked a glance over my shoulder to check that Ezri was still talking with his mother and the others. "Make sure Ezri knows, and tell Zan to meet us upstairs in the Council room when he returns."

"What's going on?" Rys asked. "Why are you sneaking off with Ezri-ruh? I heard about your betrothal."

"I'm not sneaking off with anyone." I glared at him. "I'm going up to the Council room to heal myself because I don't want to be a burden to the mages. Not that it's any of your business."

"Ayla. Wait," Rys called after me as I marched past him, but I didn't stop.

My body ached. The blood on my forehead was starting to dry into a scab that hurt whenever I scowled, which I couldn't help when I kept getting asked questions I either couldn't or didn't want to answer. I needed to be alone, and fast, before I said or did something that ruined all our careful planning.

11

THERE were no mirrors in the Council room. Nor was there a wash basin. I should have thought of that. It made attempting to heal the cuts on my face more difficult.

I was considering returning to the ground floor and turning myself over to the mages for attention when Ezri arrived, carrying a bowl of water. He'd even slung a few clean rags over his shoulder.

"Ready for some help?" he asked, setting the bowl down on the table.

As happy as I was to see him and the supplies he'd brought, I was bursting with anxious excitement about Zan's return. "He's back. Did Rys tell you?"

"Who's back?" Zan asked, appearing in the doorway.

I gaped at him for a moment before finding my words. Once I did, they began spilling out of my mouth in a nervous stream. "Uh. You. You're back. Did you find Mia?"

"No." He pointed behind him, down the stairs. "What in

the name of all the gods happened down there?"

My fists clenched. "Will. Everyone. Please. Stop. Asking. Me. That."

Zan held up his hands. "Touched a nerve, I see."

"Let me have a look at that cut on your face." Ezri dipped one of the rags in the bowl of water. "Zan, take a seat, and we'll talk while I help Ayla get cleaned up."

I took the rag from Ezri's hand. "I can do it."

Zan paced over to a window on the opposite side of the room. "I don't want to sit."

"Fine." Ezri slumped in one of the chairs. "I'll sit. You talk."

Zan pivoted, turning to face us. "She's gone."

"We knew that." Ezri folded his arms across his chest.

"No." Zan jammed a hand into his hair. "I tracked her to the docks. What possessed her to go there, I don't know."

The docks. I tried to remember what Lon had said about the traders. Had he mentioned where they were located? If they were controlled by the Shal, like he explained, then it did seem like an odd place for Mia to go.

"Maybe Forsla sent her a message." I dabbed at the cut on my forehead, using my reflection in the bowl of water to clean off most of the crusted blood. When I realized both Zan and Ezri had gone silent, I looked up. "What?"

"A message from a god? Really?" Zan stared at me. "That's what you think caused her to leave the relative safety of the forest and go down to the docks, which, I might add, are much closer to the mountains than they are to the city, and where it's nothing but traders who are just desperate enough to ransom her back to the Jahl clan who are looking for someone to punish for the old Jahl's murder."

I shrugged. "It's possible."

"I thought the gods were missing," Ezri said, not helping.

Zan gestured to Ezri. "Right. What about that?"

"Sorry." I frowned down at the rag in my hand. "Good point. Continue."

Zan glanced at Ezri, raising his eyebrows.

"I'm fine," I insisted, pulling one of the crystals out of my pocket. "Or I will be soon. Just tell us what you found."

Ezri eyed the crystal I held. "Are you sure that's a good idea?"

I glared at him, then closed my eyes and focused my thoughts. It took much less effort this time to lock onto the sensation of rose. I channeled the feeling up my arm and across my chest, letting it radiate through my other limbs and slowly rise up through my shoulders and neck to the top of my head.

"Well, that's a load more helpful than some silly illusions," Zan said.

I opened my eyes to find the pair of them staring. The skin on my forehead was still tender to the touch, but when I looked into the bowl of water, the cut was gone. Similarly, the abrasions on my arms and hands had disappeared.

I plopped down into the chair across from Ezri, exhausted. "Where were we?"

"Zan tracked Mia to the docks," Ezri said, returning his attention to Zan. "And I'm assuming she wasn't there."

"No." Zan sighed. "Worse than that. I talked with some of the traders at the alehouse. Turns out there are a few of them flush with Agrisse coin from dragging a wanted criminal back across the sea."

I sucked in a breath. "You can't mean Mia?"

Zan nodded. "It has to be her. They showed me the poster. Whoever they were after looks just like her, unfortunately."

"You think they mistook her for the real criminal?" Ezri

asked.

"Has to be." Zan shoved a hand in his hair. "How would anyone in Agrion know what Mia looks like? She washed up on our shores when she was a child."

"Now what?" I asked.

Zan paced back and forth across the Council chambers. "We have to go after her."

"Someone does." Ezri reclined in his chair. He stretched his legs out and crossed them at the ankles. "You're right about that."

"But not you," I added, trying to remain as relaxed as Ezri looked.

Now that we knew Sera's secret, we couldn't risk losing Zan as well as Mia. If anything happened to him, Ezri wouldn't just lose a close friend and his most loyal ally. And I wouldn't just lose the cousin I'd never known I'd had. Losing Zan would make it impossible for me to marry Ezri.

"You can pick a select group of your best guards and send them after her," Ezri said.

"Rys can lead them," I suggested, eager to reduce the amount of time I had to spend with him. He knew me too well, and it was too hard for me to keep secrets from him. He already suspected I was hiding something. It would be better if he went to Agrion to rescue Mia.

"I should go with them." Zan punched a fist into his opposite palm as he paced. "It will give me a chance to see what we're up against."

I frowned as my mind searched for something I could say to convince him to stay. Ezri interlaced his fingers behind his head, and I realized the answer was sitting right next to me.

"But what about Ezri?" I asked. "Now that our betrothal is off, there's nothing keeping the Jahl and Nahl clans from deciding they'd rather he not be Ruhl."

"Well, except the treaty they signed," Ezri said.

Zan scoffed. "I doubt some treaty is enough to stop them from trying something. You're right."

I blinked at him. "Did you just agree with me?"

Zan scowled. "Don't get used to it."

"I think he's finally starting to like me," I whispered to Ezri, loud enough for Zan to hear.

"What I don't like is how you keep changing the subject." Zan set his palms flat on the table and leaned forward, blocking my view of Ezri. "Some traitors who call themselves traders have captured Mia and shipped her back to Agrion. Mistaken identity or not, the Koto will be free to finish off whatever they did to the rest of her family. We don't know where they took her or how much of a head start they have. We may already be too late."

"Traitor traders," I said, repeating what Zan had said in an attempt to find the humor in the very grim picture he'd painted.

"Mages," Ezri said, drawing away the annoyed glare Zan had fixed on me. "We should send some mages with the guards you pick."

"That lot?" Zan gestured to the stairs that led down to the gathering room where we'd left the clan leaders and master mages, arguing over how to deal with the dangers of letting nearly a hundred barely trained youth on the cusp of their maturity continue to mess about with magic none of us really understood. "They'll be lucky if they leave here with all of their parts in the same place as when they arrived."

"It's not that bad," I muttered, crossing my arms.

"Do you understand what happened down there? How it works?" Zan asked.

I sighed and shook my head. "No."

"What were you trying to tell me about that center stone?" Ezri asked.

"I need to have a closer look at it, but not until we can get everyone out of there. I don't want to risk people asking too many questions about why I'm the one examining it and not you."

"All right, but why? Are you ready to tell us what happened?"

"I tripped." I exhaled, closing my eyes to recall as many of the details as I could. "The pouch of crystals spilled. I cushioned their fall with some instinctual magic. I just grabbed for white without thinking.

"Most of them scattered around my feet, but a few rolled toward the center of the room. Bez went after them. She had two or three in her hand when she reached for one that had landed on that center stone. The next thing I knew, I'd been blasted back toward the columns along with everyone else who'd been standing anywhere near her."

"So you think whatever happened has something to do with where she was standing?" Zan squinted at me. "Why would that matter?"

I studied their faces. "I know this sounds strange, but, have you ever looked at the layout of that room before? Columns set in a circle around stones laid in a circular pattern, all surrounding one center stone at the middle of the room."

Ezri shrugged. "Whoever built the tower wanted it to be pleasing to the eye? It is a gathering hall."

"Have you noticed the carvings on the columns?" I asked.

Ezri shook his head, but Zan nodded.

"You have?" Ezri asked, staring at him in disbelief.

"It's my job to notice things. Details." Zan crossed his arms.

"They're way up at the top of the column, though. I always wondered what they were."

"They look like runes," I said.

"Like the ones on the wall in the cave?" Ezri asked.

I nodded. "I'd have to get closer to look, but given the number of columns, I suspect that each one is marked for one of the gods."

"And the sixth?" Zan asked.

"Inahi," Ezri and I said at the same time.

"I think, if we look closely, we will find more markings on that center stone. Probably covered over in years of dirt." I tapped my fingers on the table. "I'm hoping it might give us a clue as to why a few crystals and a barely trained mage managed to set off an explosion like that."

"What about your little Inahi friends?" Zan asked, not letting me off the hook. "Would they know?"

"I don't know. All right?" I bit off the words through clenched teeth.

"The Midwinter Festival is in two days. Ayla might be able to return to the forest to ask them for help, but I would need to go as well if we want everyone to continue to believe I'm the Ruhl." Ezri sighed. "This lie is exhausting."

"Most are," Zan grumbled, pacing back toward the window.

"I could go alone," I said. "No one would have to know that we consulted the Inahi."

Ezri shook his head. "My guess is, when the clan leaders are done surveying the damage down there, they will insist on supervising the activation of the rest of the group. Once you're done, they will put a hold on all magic use. Then, after Midwinter, they will insist I go back to the Inahi and get them to take back the magic and return the veil instead."

"But the Inahi—" I protested.

Ezri cut me off. "I know." He set his hand on top of mine. "We have a few days. We'll think of something."

"We can't send a batch of untrained mages to Agrion," Zan said, gesturing toward the window and the glimmering sea just visible beyond it.

"He has a point. None of them have enough magic to be of any use against a true mage." I crossed my arms.

"But *you* do." Zan stalked toward me. "Don't you?"

"You can't send Ayla." Ezri sat up straight. His hands clenched the sides of his chair. "She's our only connection to the Inahi."

Zan's eyes narrowed. "If anything happens to her, they'll just choose a new Labharon, though. Won't they?"

"From the next generation." Ezri's knuckles were turning white from his grip. "We could be without a Labharon for another thirteen years if anything happens to her."

"But the clans will still believe you are the Inahi speaker," Zan said. "And nothing is going to happen to her because the guards I send with her will keep her safe."

"From mages?" Ezri didn't look convinced.

"A moment ago, you seemed convinced that my guards could successfully rescue Mia without my help. Now you think they can't manage to keep your beloved Nahla safe?" Zan raised his eyebrows.

It was an awful time for me to leave, but if the clan leaders decided to put an end to training the potential mages until after Midwinter, then there was nothing I could do in the city. I'd be better off returning to the forest to continue my own training. Or going on a rescue mission to Agrion, if it would help get Mia back.

"Zan's right," I said. "I should go."

Zan turned away from Ezri to stare at me with wide eyes. "Huh. Maybe I *am* starting to like you, Nahla."

"Ayla. No." Ezri sounded panicked.

I nudged Zan out of the way so I could move closer to Ezri. "It will be fine. No one will know who I am there. I'll have guards to protect me, and Mia, too, once we find her. We'll track her down and be back before the Midwinter Festival is over."

"Unlikely," Zan said, ruining the moment.

I turned to glare at him. "Now you're having doubts?"

"No. It's just that it takes at least a full day to cross the sea. That's what the traders told me." He hesitated as though he was holding something back. When I raised my eyebrows, signaling for him to spit it out already, he added, "That's why I didn't go immediately."

"You were going to go after her yourself?" Ezri growled at him.

"That's what you sent me out there to do."

"To the Flamehunt. I sent you to the Flamehunt. Not to Agrion. Zan—"

"Enough." I held out my arms, one palm facing Zan and the other facing Ezri. "We're wasting time."

"Ugh." Zan groaned. "Stop making me agree with you."

I stifled a grin and ignored him. It wouldn't help anything if Ezri thought we were aligning against him. "How soon can we be on our way?"

"I don't like this," Ezri grumbled.

"I need to gather my three best guards and our most skilled tracker," Zan said. "Then it's a half-day's ride from the city to the docks."

"Just three guards?" Ezri asked.

"Too large of a group will draw too much attention," Zan

replied. He waved a hand in my direction. "You'll need to go dressed as traders. None of these fancy embroidered tunics."

I looked down at the green and gold tunic Nye had selected from my wardrobe. "I don't think I have anything else."

Zan sighed. "I'll find some clothes for you to borrow."

12

INSTEAD of being rid of Rys, I ended up riding alongside him, leading a trio of guards along the coast to a protected bay near the edge of the Flamehunt. Because we'd be leaving our horses behind at the local stable, I wasn't riding Arge.

If the horse I'd been given sensed our urgency, she made it clear she didn't care. Whenever we stopped, she dipped her head into the nearest patch of grass and refused to budge. I tried using my strong blue magic to nudge her mind toward our cause, but she rebuffed my attempts to communicate.

While I struggled to get my stubborn horse moving again, Uri, Wik, and Emy shifted in their saddles. Their thoughts I could sense with the lingering effect of my blue magic. It was a tangle of annoyance, impatience, and sympathy, though I couldn't tell who was thinking what.

I grumbled about leaving Arge behind, thinking they were too far away to hear. But Rys, who had remained at my side, and in frustratingly masterful control of his borrowed horse, reminded me that traders rarely kept their own horses. I glared at him, even though I knew he had a point.

Rys made a clucking noise as he nudged his horse into a walk. The combination of sound and motion caught the attention of my mare, who finally left her mid-morning snack behind to plod along beside Rys's mount. I tried to urge her into a trot, just to put some distance between us, but she wouldn't respond until Rys's horse picked up its pace.

Traitor, I thought at her. As though it weren't bad enough to be stuck with Rys on this rescue mission, I'd ended up on a horse determined to be inseparable from the one Rys rode.

At least he seemed to sense that I was in no mood for conversation. He waited until we reached the cliffs overlooking the bay to call another halt. Ahead of us, the mouth of the Horn River cut through the plateau, tumbling down the rocks in a cascade on its rush to the sea.

Rys waited until the other guards, all dressed like us, in the plain clothes of Shal clan villagers, were stopped alongside us before pointing to the cluster of buildings and docks at the base of the bay. "We'll take that path there down to the beach. When we arrive, I'll take the lead and find the on-duty captain. Remember, if anyone asks, the trade commander has sent us to join the fleet."

Uri, Wik, and Emy voiced their agreement with a chorus of "Yes, sir." But I wasn't so quick to agree.

"I'm going with you," I said, prepared to make it clear that, though the other guards reported to him, I did not.

Rys turned his brown eyes to meet mine. "Fine."

I'd expected him to argue, so his response startled me to a momentary silence. "Fine?"

"I agree. I'm responsible for your safety. It will be easier for me to keep an eye on you if you are with me." Rys turned to the others. "Keep together while we're gone. Light chatter as though you're friends who've signed on together, but keep your ears and eyes open. Don't engage with anyone unless they address you first. We keep our heads down and our stories straight until we're on a boat to Agrion. Got it?"

His instructions prompted another chorus of "Yes, sir."

I squinted down at the boats tied to the docks jutting into the bay. There didn't seem to be much activity down there. Something about it seemed odd, but I didn't know what it might be. As my horse fell into step alongside Rys's mount, I tried to pin down the nagging sense that I was forgetting a key piece of information.

By the time we arrived on the outskirts of the little trader town, I still hadn't figured it out. We stopped at the stables first. Rys and I left our borrowed horses behind for the others to take care of. Then we made our way to the building in town that seemed to be the busiest, judging from the lights and music spilling out onto the pathways outside.

"What are they all doing in the tavern at this time of day?" I asked, reading the sign hanging above the door. "Shouldn't they be working?"

"Maybe the boats for Agrion have already left for the day," Rys suggested. "Will you let me do the talking in here?"

I frowned but nodded.

Rys shouldered open the door, then stood aside to let me enter ahead of him.

Heads turned our way, and a few groups fell silent as they stared with open curiosity. Rys guided me over to the bar where we waited for the barkeep to acknowledge us. The burly man with the thick brown beard set a pair of mugs on the counter and laughed at whatever the woman on the other side said in response.

She looked over and caught me staring, which caused the bearded barkeep to turn toward us. He wiped his hands on his apron as he made his way over to where we waited.

"Can I help you?" he asked in a deep voice that cut through the fiddler's tune.

"Greetings," Rys said, leaning on the counter. "Group of us just in from the city. Commander sent us to check in with the trading captain. I was hoping you might be able to tell us where to find them?"

Someone nearby elbowed the person sitting next to them, and they both looked over. The first spoke up, "Said you're looking for the captain?"

Rys nodded, splitting his attention between the barkeep and the pair seated nearby. "That's right."

"Captain's off duty." The woman he'd elbowed leaned back in her chair and folded her arms across her chest.

"All of them?" Rys asked.

The man who'd spoken first grinned. He lifted his mug toward a table in the back corner as though toasting them. With a nod in their direction, he said, "Off duty."

Then, he pivoted on his chair and repeated the gesture and statement to two other parties. The one near the fiddle player didn't notice, but the one in the corner and the other, at the opposite end of the bar, both paused their conversations and stared in our direction.

The skin on the back of my neck prickled, and I edged closer to Rys.

"No one is sailing today?" Rys asked.

The barkeep laughed. "It's winter, lad."

The group from the back corner was standing now, whispering with the ones at the end of the bar. That caught the attention of the table near the fiddle player. They followed both that conversation and our discussion with their eyes.

Rys straightened and took a half step back. "Right. Well, I'll just—"

The man who had spoken to him stood and clapped a hand on Rys's shoulder. "Stay. Have some ale. Until the winds die down, we won't be going anywhere."

I hadn't noticed any wind, but his words reminded me of what Lon had said about unpredictable winter weather. "We should let the others know," I said, backing toward the door.

The captain who had been sitting near the fiddle player caught my arm. I hadn't even noticed him approaching. I twisted out of his grip.

He released me, but stared down his long nose at me. "You say the commander sent you?"

"That's right." Rys angled himself into the conversation, drawing his attention away from me.

"What's the code word, then?" he asked Rys.

Rys scratched his head. "I think Wik has it. He should be right outside. I'll just go and ask."

I grabbed for Rys's arm as the trader behind him reached for the knife lashed to his waist. My movement caused the others closest to us to react, and suddenly everyone had at least one hand wrapped around a weapon.

Rys pushed me back, keeping himself between me and the traders. When my back hit solid wood, I fumbled for the latch. Together, we stumbled over the threshold and down the steps, onto the path outside.

Emy spotted us first. She nudged Wik and Uri.

"What's—" Uri didn't finish his question when he looked over and spotted the angry faces following us out of the tavern.

"They're on to us." Rys hissed the warning to the others.

"Back to the stables?" Uri asked, his voice barely above a whisper.

Rys glanced over his shoulder. A few traders loomed in the doorway. Others stared at us through the windows. But they seemed to be waiting to see what we'd do next.

"They want a code word," I whispered.

"Zan didn't give us one," Rys replied. "This isn't going to work. They don't believe us, and they're not sailing anyway because of the weather. We need to go back."

"If we leave, they'll know we were lying," I hissed at him.

Rys turned and shouted toward the traders waiting in the doorway. "We're going to check with our friend and come back in the morning."

The captain grunted, but didn't budge.

Rys motioned for us to head back toward the stables. We'd only walked a few steps before I caught a view of the empty docks out of the corner of my eye.

I tugged on Rys's sleeve. "We can't stay here, and we can't go back without Mia."

"What are you suggesting?" he asked, turning his head to look at me.

"We steal a boat." Before he could argue, I pivoted and took off toward the docks at a run, ignoring the commotion that erupted behind me.

Over the shouting, I caught the thump of boots pounding down the path behind me. A quick glance over my shoulder confirmed that Rys had followed me, as I expected he would. I nearly stumbled when I spotted Wik, Emy, and Uri behind him, still facing the crowd of traders, now pouring out of the tavern.

Rys caught my arm to steady me.

I locked eyes with him, expecting him to try and hold me

back.

"If we're doing this, we have to move." He took off at a jog down the closest dock. "Keep up."

I ran after him, past a number of what seemed to be perfectly fine boats that he only glanced at before continuing. By the time he stopped I was panting.

"Why this one?" I asked, trying to catch my breath.

He was already on board, bent over at the bow, untying the sail on the foredeck. "Just get on the boat, Ayla."

"But what about the others?" I stood frozen on the dock. "Shouldn't we wait?"

"They're stalling, and it will be completely worthless if you don't get on this boat right now." Rys reached out and offered me his hand to help me on board.

I glanced back down the dock to confirm Rys was right. The others hadn't followed. "You don't know how to sail."

"I do." The voice came from somewhere behind Rys.

He spun at the sound, pulling a knife from his belt. "Who's there?"

Whoever had spoken winced. Rys crept toward the sound. "If you know what's good for you, you'll come out of there with your hands where I can see them."

"I'd love to, really, but I'm a bit tied up."

Rys rounded the mast and dropped down, disappearing into the cockpit. Only his head was visible from where I stood, so I climbed up onto the front deck of the boat to get a better look. The position also gave me a much better view of what was going on back at the far end of the dock.

"Um. Rys?" Someone had started running toward us. I squinted at them until I could be sure it was a friendly face. "We need to go. Now."

Rys's head dipped down, into the cockpit, then reappeared

a moment later, just as Uri arrived. "There's someone on this ship."

"A trader?" Uri bent to untie the ropes attaching the boat to the dock.

"Don't think so. She's tied up. Says she's some sort of prisoner?" Rys caught the end of the rope Uri tossed at him.

"Does she look like Mia?" I asked.

"We don't have time for this." Uri glanced back down the dock. "We've got to get this boat on the water. Wik and Emy won't be able to hold them much longer."

"Should I dump her off, or...?" Rys turned at the sound of a muffled voice.

I couldn't quite make out whatever it was the prisoner was saying over the clank and slap of the boat against the dock. I grabbed for a rail on the boat foredeck and used it to steady myself as the boat rocked from Rys moving around in the cockpit.

"She said she knows how to sail," Rys shouted to us.

"Then she stays," Uri said, hurrying to untie the rope attached to the bow. "And we go."

A moment later, Uri jumped aboard, and we were free. When I turned, a stranger stared back at me from behind the wheel of the ship.

"Get down from there if you don't want to end up in the drink," she yelled. Her short red hair flew back from her face at odd angles as she squinted ahead.

Uri and I scrambled back, dropping into the cockpit on either side of the wheel.

"Grab that line." She jutted her chin in my direction.

I searched the area nearby and touched the first rope I saw. There were none just lying about, but there was one tied to the boat. Someone had wrapped it around a metal piece screwed into the railing.

"This?" I asked.

The woman glanced over. "Unwrap it from the cleat and then start hauling."

"Hauling?"

She groaned, then looked at Uri. "You. Beansprout. Come take this wheel so I can help the princess get our sail aloft."

"I'm not a princess," I grumbled.

"Well, you're no sailor." The woman took the end of the rope from me. In a flash, she had it unwound. "Now watch."

She began pulling on the rope and the sail attached to the long beam that hung just above the cockpit raised up and started flapping in the wind. I followed the line of the rope from the tip of the sail, up to the pulley at the very top of the mast, and then back down to where she was pulling, hand over hand. The pile of rope at her feet grew as a few beads of sweat dotted her upper lip.

When the tip of the sail reached the top, she wrapped the end of the rope around the metal bit again. "There," she said, flashing me a grin. "Think you can manage it next time, Princess?"

"Who are you?" I asked.

She tsked at me. "No questions until we're out of the bay. Try to stay out of the way until then."

She patted my shoulder, then returned to her position at the wheel. "Not bad, Sprout. Just keep it pointed there."

When she hopped up on the deck next to the mast, Rys lunged after her. His hand just missed grabbing hold of her booted ankle. "Where are you going?"

"Got another sail to hoist, Soldier." She scurried forward to untie whatever had been holding the lump of sail at the front of the boat down. As soon as it was free, it started flapping about. She pointed to Rys as she scurried back toward the cockpit. "Grab that line."

Rys grabbed hold of the rope flopping about next to him.

"Well, don't just stand there, pull on it." She slid down alongside the wheel and immediately began unwrapping another line from one of those metal bits.

Uri, who had been glancing behind us, turned to face forward again just in time to be scolded.

The red-haired woman yanked on the wheel. "There. Hold her on this course or we're going to end up back there with your friends."

Uri gripped the wheel so hard his knuckles turned white. He locked his arms to keep it from spinning, grimacing at the strain.

"That's it. Use those muscles, Beansprout." She flexed her own as she hauled on the rope attached to the front sail, lifting the tip of the triangle up off the deck and into the air. When it was near the top, she said, "You still got that end, Soldier? Good. Tie it off."

He glanced around for a moment before she pushed past Uri to take the rope from Rys.

"Like this," she said, deftly wrapping it around yet another metal bit.

When she finished, she glanced back at the quickly receding dock and waved. "See ya, suckers!"

I doubted they could hear her because we couldn't hear whatever they were yelling. Their voices were lost in the wind that was picking up the closer we got to the mouth of the bay. I could just make out faces and figures well enough to tell that Emy and Wik weren't among them. I sent a prayer to Lorjad that they got away.

"Don't taunt them," Rys said, grabbing her arm and yanking it down.

The burliest of the traders picked up a rock and threw it at our boat. We were too far for it to be a threat, but it still made me wince before it dropped into the water, well short of our boat.

"Do you think they'll come after us?" I asked.

The woman shrugged, then plopped down on one of the benches in the cockpit. When she started digging around in her pockets, Rys loomed over her.

"Leave your hands where I can see them," he said, reaching for the knife he'd sheathed at his waist, only to realize it wasn't there.

She grinned, then reached down to pull Rys's blade from her boot. "Looking for this?"

Rys snatched it out of her hand. "Who are you?"

"Pirate." From another pocket she pulled out what looked like a floppy stick. Before Rys could react, she put one end of it in her mouth and bit. As she chewed, she said, "You can call me Red."

A tense silence fell over the boat, broken only by the wind whipping the sails. Uri's hands remained fixed on the wheel, but he kept looking back over his shoulder to where Rys loomed over Red. He still held his knife in his hand, but she didn't seem at all threatened by the gesture.

I stepped forward and pressed my palm against Rys's forearm to guide his hand down. His eyes locked with mine for a beat before he relaxed and sheathed the blade. He kept one hand on the hilt and refused to budge when I tried nudging him aside.

Ignoring him, I turned to the pirate. "Greetings, Red. My name is A—"

My tongue froze as my brain prevented it from giving my

true name. It was unlikely that someone who had never set foot in our lands would know from my name that I was a clan leader's daughter, but I couldn't be sure.

"Ana." I gave her the name Zan had selected for me, along with the simple trousers and layers of woolen tunics he'd given me to wear. I gestured to the others. "This is Rys and Uri."

"In a hurry to escape whatever lies beyond those cliffs, I take it." She bit off another hunk of the floppy stick. "Not gonna get very far if you can't sail, though."

"We appreciate your help with that." I pushed the too-long ends of the under-layer tunic sleeves back to free my hands. "How is it that you happened to be here, on this ship?"

"Tied up and shoved in the corner? Left to rot like some unwanted garbage? Is that what you mean?" she asked, wiping her hands on the legs of her dark trousers. Her eyes fixed on the horizon just ahead of the boat. "Beansprout. Point the bow a little more starboard."

"What?" Uri turned his head back, brow furrowed.

"His name is Uri," I reminded her.

Red gave me a brief look as she stood. Then, taking one step toward the wheel, she reached an arm past Uri and pointed to the water off the right-hand side of the boat. "Starboard means right. See that point up ahead? The one with the tall trees covering it?"

Uri nodded as Red set her hands on the wheel just above his. He started to let go.

"No you don't. Put those hands back. I didn't say you were done." She waited until his fingers closed around the wheel, then turned it just a bit.

A moment later, the boat reacted, and we were pointed at the trees off in the distance.

"Now, hold her there until I say so, got it?" Red took a step back and put her hands on her hips. "Did you have a destination in mind, Princess?"

"Agrion," Rys said.

Red shivered. "Don't know what you're running from, but I can tell you that's not where I'd be running to."

"We're looking for a friend." I squinted at the pirate woman. With the sun behind her and her features in shadow, I realized that she looked a lot like Mia. Same height. Same build. "Your hair... Did you cut it recently?"

Red ran her hand through her short waves. "You like it, Princess? I could do yours if you want. Just need to borrow your boy's knife again, and we can saw that braid of yours right off."

I pulled my long braid over my shoulder, keeping my fingers on the tuft of hair at the end. "Is that what you did?"

Red ignored my question. "How about I make you a deal. I drop you lot off in Agrion, then I get the boat as payment for my trouble."

"Hey now." Rys stepped forward, but I stuck my arm out to keep him back. It didn't stop him from arguing, though. "You would still be tied up in the hold if it wasn't for me."

"And you would probably be tied up alongside me if you hadn't released me." She crossed her arms. "Those traders didn't seem real happy about you running off with one of their boats."

"If you get us to Agrion, you can have the boat," I said.

"We'll be stranded there," Rys said in a low voice.

"We'll figure something out."

"Um, excuse me?" Uri swayed on his feet. "I'm not feeling very well."

Red caught him as he slumped toward the deck. "Princess, grab the wheel. Soldier, give me a hand."

"It's Rys," he muttered as I disregarded her command and lunged forward, to help with Uri.

"Rys, take the wheel," I said.

Red looked at me with lifted eyebrows. "Looks like I was right about who's in charge here."

"Help me get him onto the bench." I repositioned my hands for a better grip and realized one was sticky and wet. I paused to have a look. "He's bleeding."

"Lift on three," Red said. "On his side, so I can get a better look at where that's coming from."

I scooped his booted feet into my arms as she counted down. On three, we hoisted him up onto the closest bench. Then Red patted him down, starting at his head and working her way down. While she examined Uri, I palmed a crystal and located the blood-soaked spot on his trousers, just below his left knee.

"I think it's his calf," I said.

Red continued to work her way down his body. Her hands explored his thighs, then stopped when she reached the spot I'd found. Reaching into his boot, she pulled up the leg of his trousers until the cuff came free of where he'd tucked it into the leather. Then, producing a knife out of nowhere, she slashed the hem, stuck the blade between her teeth, and tore the fabric up to the knee.

At first, neither of us could see where the blood was coming from. Then, as Red moved his leg, I caught sight of a smooth black mark on his skin.

"What's that?" I asked, pointing.

"Mole, probably." Red grabbed for the edges of the fabric, prepared to extend the tear a little higher up Uri's leg.

"Wait." I set one hand on his bare calf. The other I wrapped around the crystal in my pocket.

Just as it had in the tower after the accident, rose over-whelmed my senses as soon as I allowed myself a breath to focus. Every time I reached for it, that color seemed easier to grasp. My fingers skimmed Uri's lower leg, following the intuition that came with my magic.

"There's something..." I opened my eyes to find my fingers hovering over the black mark. "Whatever that is, it's not a part of him. It needs to come out."

Red stared at me. "You're a mage."

I blinked at her. Rys turned his head, his eyes meeting mine over Red's shoulder. But it was too late to try to hide it, and if I did nothing, Uri might bleed to death.

"But, if you're a mage..." Red's brow furrowed. "Agrion is the last place you should be going."

I didn't understand why she would say that when Agrion was supposedly filled with mages. But it didn't matter. I could ask more questions after we took care of Uri.

"Will you help me?" I asked, gesturing to Uri's leg. "We need to get that out."

"We need a tweezer, then. Or at the least, a small blade." The one she'd been holding was gone again, even though I hadn't seen where she'd put it. "Mine's too large. 'Less you want me to carve him open. Wouldn't recommend it, though. Probably won't end well."

I reached up and pulled one of my hairpin knives from its sheath. "Will this work?"

Red responded with an appreciative whistle. After a quick examination of both blade and subject, she got to work. "You're right. Bit of metal, this is."

As she poked and prodded with my blade, I reached for white and tried to draw the object free with the aid of my magic. But the magic kept slipping from my grasp, like the thing that had embedded itself in Uri's calf was somehow resisting. Still, with our combined efforts, we succeeded in extracting the pointed piece of metal.

Red went silent as she studied it. Without the obstruction, blood flowed freely from Uri's wound. I released my hold on the sensation of white magic and grabbed for rose, so I could use it to knit the skin closed. I'd only ever practiced healing myself, and I wasn't sure it would work, but I had to try.

At first, it seemed like nothing was happening. Red ripped off a band of fabric from the bottom of Uri's trousers and started wrapping it around his calf like a bandage.

I waved her off. "Wait. I need to see the wound to close it."

Red paused. I felt her eyes on me and closed mine to block out her intense stare so I could refocus. I took a breath, then cracked my eyelids just enough to focus on Uri's leg. With a firm hold on the sensation of rose, I tried again. Keeping the sensation flowing through me and into Uri even as my hands began to shake and sweat rolled down my spine proved to be more difficult than anything I'd yet tried.

I wobbled, very near to fainting, and Red steadied me with one hand. I held on to the magic as long as I could before collapsing onto the opposite bench. Red wrapped the bandage around Uri's leg, then turned to face me. She bent over me, slipping my hairpin knife back into the sheath in my hair. She found it easily, now that she knew the pair of pins I wore weren't just decorative ornaments.

Rys glanced over his shoulder at me before returning to steering the boat. But whatever he saw on my face made him look again. "Are you all right?"

"I'm fine." I released my grip on the crystal in my pocket and scrubbed at my face with both palms.

When I looked up again, Red was standing in front of me,

holding the bit of metal we'd pulled from Uri's leg.

I blinked, reaching for white magic without even thinking. Calling the object to me, I rotated it out of Red's hands until it hovered close enough for me to grasp it out of the air. "It looks like an arrowhead, but not one I've ever seen before."

"I have." Red frowned. "It's an Agrisse invention. Little Stinger, they call it."

"Well, it's out now." I looked over at Uri's ashen face. "He'll be fine."

Red made a low noise, almost like a growl.

"What?" I glared at her. "What aren't you telling us?"

She raised her eyebrows. "Could ask you the same thing. *Mage.*"

The way she said the word, it almost sounded like a curse. "What do you have against mages?"

"Haven't seen one in a while, that's all." She gave me a long look, then shrugged, turned, and nudged Rys out of the way so she could take the wheel.

He rushed to me the moment his hands were free. Keeping an eye on Red, he glanced over at Uri. "Is he going to be all right?"

"Doubt it," Red called over her shoulder.

Rys lunged forward, knife in hand. He held Red motionless with one hand and pointed his blade at her throat with the other. "Start talking."

In a flash, Red's body twisted free of Rys's grip. Her leg whipped around, knocking Rys to the deck. She pinned him there with one knee as she returned to steering. "No need for violence, Soldier. Just ask nicely."

My stomach sank as I stared at her. It had been amusing when she'd stolen Rys's knife without him realizing. But I'd never seen anyone best Rys in a fight. With Uri down, I didn't like the idea that we might be overpowered. This was supposed to be a rescue mission.

13

IF we passed through the veil as we sailed out of the bay, I didn't notice. The winter storms that kept the traders tucked safely in the tavern hit us almost as soon as Rys regained his footing on the deck. There wasn't much talking for a while after that. I lost the contents of my stomach and, along with it, my curiosity and any desire to pay attention to my surroundings.

Somewhere, in the back of my mind, I remembered that at the end of the spectrum of magic, just before rose, came indigo. The magic of that color provided guidance. The Inahi said it was the magic the elders had used to create the stone that guided Ruhala to our gods-protected land, generations ago.

I had practiced a little with that color during my training with the Inahi. Enough that I told Zan that I thought I could use it to help us safely cross the sea. But once we were out in the storm-tossed water, I was glad we didn't need to rely on my magic. My guts churned as our boat rode the waves, but Red never lost her nerve. She kept us pointed in the right direction, even after we lost sight of shore, singing into the wind while Rys and I moaned, too sick to be of much help.

The way she reacted when she discovered I was a mage, I doubted she was using magic to guide us. *Haven't seen one in a while*, she'd said. But she was a pirate. Perhaps she only meant that she hadn't been ashore in Agrion in a while. Who knew how long our traders had held her captive. Or why.

By the time the weather cleared enough for me to feel steady on my feet again, the sun was rising, illuminating an unfamiliar shoreline.

"Is that Agrion?" I asked.

"In all its glory." Red scowled as she pointed our boat toward a crescent-shaped bay lined with trees.

As we sailed closer, I spotted structures up and down the shore. Entire towns stretched out on the hillsides above the beaches. Near the far side of the bay, a fortress sat perched on the highest point, surrounded by buildings all tucked inside a wall. It reminded me of Shal city, except the fortress was massive and built of a stone that sparkled in the morning sunlight.

"What's that?" I asked, pointing.

"Fortress of the Green Mage," Red answered. She glanced over at me out of the corner of her eyes. "You sure about this?"

"Is that mage the ruler here?" I asked, thrilled at the idea that here, in Agrion, a mage might be in charge of the largest city.

She nodded. "I'd stay out of his way if you know what's good for you."

Down in the cabin, Uri stirred, drawing my attention away from the view. While I checked on him, Red set Rys to work, preparing for our arrival. A patch of warm sunlight streamed through the cabin window, onto Uri's face. He blinked, wincing away from the light.

"What happened?" he asked when he saw me. "Where are we?"

"Agrion. Nearly." I pressed the back of my hand to his forehead. "How are you?"

"Awful." He groaned. "Everything hurts. Except…"

His voice drifted off, and he paused for a moment. Then his eyes went wide with alarm. He scrambled to push himself up on one elbow, turning his head to stare down at his bandaged leg.

"What's wrong?" I asked.

"I can't… I don't think…" He looked up at me. "I'm not sure I can feel my toes."

With some effort, I helped him sit up. Then I pulled his boot from his foot. His toes were still pink, but he barely noticed when I pinched them.

"We'll get you to a mage as soon as we land," I promised.

Uri ran his hands through his hair. Worry lines etched his face. "What happened to my leg?"

"I don't know," I said. "I think you must have been shot with something by those traders. Red called it a Little Stinger. But she said it was an Agrisse invention."

"I don't remember being shot," Uri said.

Red called down into the cabin to let us know we were close, and they needed me up on deck. I emerged to the sight of a port three times the size of the one we'd left behind. Rys already had the front sail down and stood waiting at the bow with a rope in his hand. Red maneuvered us to the end of the least populated dock, closest to the mouth of the bay.

A few moments later, we were alongside it. Rys jumped down onto the dock while Red and I helped Uri out of the cabin. As soon as we were out of the boat, she snatched the rope back from Rys and pushed the boat away. She sailed off without a backward glance, busying herself with the ropes and sails, in a hurry to be on her way.

Rys and I stared after her for a moment, supporting Uri between us. Then, with only a shared look, we turned and made our way up to the buildings on the shore. When we reached them, we stood there for a moment, taking it all in.

Agrion's port city was much larger than the trader enclave we'd left behind. Bigger boats were tied up at the docks. More buildings lined the shore, three deep in some places, with a road that split them up the middle as it wound its way up a hillside, leading to even more structures just visible at the top of the rise.

"Where do we start?" I breathed the question out, not sure Rys could even hear me over the shouting of sailors, the clanking of tools, the cart wheels rattling over cobblestones, and the clopping hoofbeats of the shaggy short horses that pulled them.

The three of us argued, keeping our voices low and words terse as we tried not to draw unwanted attention. Eventually, we agreed to find an inn and maybe someone who could examine Uri's leg to make sure it was healing properly. We'd only made it to the door when Rys spotted a trio of papers pinned to the post outside.

Money for Mages, it said in big bold letters. The details about how much would be offered for any mages who were presented to the city guards were printed in smaller letters underneath. Alongside that hung another that said, *Wanted,* with drawings of three faces beneath the word. One of the faces could easily have been mistaken for Mia. Or Red, with longer hair.

Rys took one look at the drawings and shot me a look over Uri's slumped shoulders. I wondered if he'd already spotted the similarity of features between the guard we'd come to find and the pirate who'd sailed us here and then bolted. But I also wondered about the other posting.

"What do you suppose they want mages for?" I asked.

A few of the heads around us glanced our way. Rys must have noticed and not liked the looks we were getting, because he didn't respond as he hurried us inside.

"Wait here," he said, leaving me with Uri, just inside the door. Alone, he advanced a few steps toward the innkeeper wiping out mugs behind the empty bar.

"Greetings," the woman called, setting down her rag. "We open for dinner and ale at the quitting bell. Tavern down the way is serving now if you'd rather."

"Thank you, but we were hoping for a room," Rys said.

She eyed the three of us. "Just one?"

Rys glanced back at me. Color flooded his cheeks as he turned back to the innkeeper. "All we can afford."

"Hmm." She nodded, then shot another look in my direction just as Uri's weight went heavy on my arm.

I nudged him with my hip, and he startled. When he raised his head, his eyes were glassy and dazed. His parched lips tried to form a question as the innkeeper stared.

"What's wrong with your friend?" she asked. "Been too long at the tavern?"

"He's injured," I answered, because she was still looking our way.

"Just needs a bit of rest," Rys added.

Uri needed more than that. If we were back on the plains, I would have taken him straight to Mage-nah. But we were in Agrion where we should be surrounded by mages. Surely someone here could heal him. They couldn't all have taken the offer from the city, otherwise why would they bother posting, looking for more?

"Perhaps you could recommend a—"

"Healer," Rys spoke over me, drawing the innkeeper's attention away.

She pulled a key down from a peg behind her, then walked around the end of the bar, straight past to Rys. When she stopped in front of me, she set the back of her hand against Uri's forehead. As she held it there, her eyes scanned the skin of his face and hands, finally landing on the torn leg of his trousers and the bandage wrapped around his calf.

"Skin's warm, but I don't see any sign of the pox," she said, letting her hand drop to her side. "Probably an infection. You get attacked by pirates out there?"

Rys spoke before I could respond. "Fell on a nail," he said. "When the ship hit a wave."

"Better than pirates, but still bad luck." The innkeeper clucked her tongue as she handed Rys the key. "Up the stairs on the right. Get him settled, and I'll send for someone to come have a look."

"Thank you." Rys slung Uri's other arm over his shoulder and together we managed to get him up the narrow staircase and into the small room we'd been assigned.

Once we had Uri on the bed and shut the door, I released the question I'd been holding. "Why didn't you let me ask for a mage?"

"Ayla. You saw the posting." Rys gestured toward the entrance below.

"Yes. And?" I shrugged. "Mages are in demand here, so what? You think it would have been rude to ask for one? Red said the weapon that caused his injury was Agrisse. Don't you think that means we'll need a mage to reverse whatever magic is still lingering and making it so he's unable to heal?"

Rys shook his head. "There's something strange going on here."

"Why do you say that?"

"Did you see anyone using magic out there?" He waved a hand in the direction of the docks. "Think about it."

I tried to remember all the sailors we'd passed as we walked the long dock back toward shore. Some had been standing in small groups, talking. Others were scrubbing the decks of boats or tinkering with ropes, poking around inside hatches, hauling crates of supplies and jugs of water. If any of them had been using magic, it wasn't the kind the Inahi had taught me.

"Maybe all the mages are busy elsewhere," I said, shrugging off his concerns. "They must be in high demand if the ruler of Agrion is willing to pay a bounty for them."

"That's just it." Rys paced over to the window. He pushed aside the threadbare curtain to peek outside. "What if it's not a bounty to entice the mages but a reward to those who might encounter one?"

"But that doesn't make any sense. Red confirmed that Agrion is ruled by a mage." I scowled at him. "Why would a mage be offering a reward for capturing other mages?"

"I don't know." Rys let the curtain fall back. He turned to face me. "I don't like it, though. I think we need to be careful."

A knock on the door made us both jump. Rys crossed the room to the door, nudging me out of the way and blocking any sight of me with his body as he opened it a crack.

"Mayrn, downstairs, the innkeeper? She sent me up. Said you asked for a healer?" The low voice on the other side of the door paused.

Rys swung the door open enough to let the healer inside.

"Name's Banus," he said, spotting Uri on the bed and moving toward him without so much as a glance in my direction. "This must be your injured friend."

Rys motioned for me to step out into the hall while Banus wasn't looking.

I rolled my eyes at his behavior, but knew better than to argue with him when he got all overprotective. I slipped past him and waited just outside the door. After Rys swung the door shut, I counted to three and then opened it a crack so I could hear what was going on inside.

The healer began asking questions. Rys kept his answers and explanations brief. Then Banus suggested Rys wait in the hall while he examined Uri. Rys hesitated before retreating. I didn't bother pretending I wasn't listening.

"Spying on us?" Rys asked in a whisper as he stepped into the hall.

"Making sure you didn't need my help." I noted Rys had also left the door open a crack.

He kept one eye on the slice of view the opening provided. "He asked a lot of questions."

"Healers do that when they're trying to be helpful." I folded my arms across my chest. "At least, Mage-nah does."

Rys grunted in reply.

I sighed. My eyes fell on the bathing room at the end of the hall, and I tapped Rys on the shoulder. "I'm going to get cleaned up while we wait."

He glanced at me. His gaze traveled from my face to my feet. By the time his eyes met mine again, I could feel the heat in my cheeks. "All right," he said. "But be quick about it."

I hurried down the hall, eager to put a bit of space between us. With the door to the bathing room closed between us,

I took a deep breath. Being with Rys was easy. Too easy. I knew what every movement he made meant. I could interpret every breath without a word.

If we were going to find Mia, we'd need to work together. Falling back into old rhythms would make that easier. I took another breath.

I could do this. Rys and I could be a team again. Us against the world. Against Agrion. At least until we got Mia and were headed home. It didn't have to mean anything.

I crossed the room to pour some water into the basin. Loosening my tunic belt, I placed my knife on the table next to the basin. I unwound the fabric from around my waist and pulled my tunic over my head, then hung both from a peg on the wall.

Leaving only the under-wrap around my chest, I bent over the basin and splashed water on my face and neck. The cake of soap on the shelf behind the basin smelled like Mage-nah's herb cabinet back on the plains. I closed my eyes as I scrubbed the dirt from my face, letting the scent take me home.

After rinsing my skin clean, I blinked my eyes open and stood, catching a movement out of the corner of my eye. My fingers curled around the hilt of my knife as I turned, only to find Rys staring at me.

"Sorry," he said.

"What are you doing in here?" I released my blade and reached for my tunic.

"I tried calling to you through the door, but you didn't answer." He blushed as I pulled the garment over my head, even though he'd seen me wearing less than this whenever we went swimming in the river at home. But, I supposed, that had been before. "We need to get out of here before Banus returns."

"Is Uri healed?" I asked, wrapping my belt around my waist.

Rys frowned. "He's awake. I talked with him after Banus left."

"But?" I knotted the ends and tucked my knife into the folds, immediately comforted by its familiar presence against my side.

Rys took a step toward me and reached out a hand toward my neck. I flinched away, locking eyes with him in the process. He didn't drop his hand. Instead, he took another half-step toward me. His fingers plucked a strand of wet hair off my neck and tucked it back into my braid.

"You should cover that up before we go," he said, nodding at the clan tattoo on my neck. "Where's the scarf Zan gave you?"

"In the room. With my cloak." I rubbed my palm against the skin, covering the mark.

"Let's get it and be on our way, then." Rys peeked outside the door before opening it and stepping through. Then he waved me ahead. "Come on."

I waited until we were back in the room with Uri before I asked, "Why is the healer coming back?"

"Once he saw the wound, he knew we were lying about the nail." Rys handed me the scarf I'd left behind. "He went to find someone who can deal with magecraft. Or, at least, that's what he said."

I stared at Uri, who was lying on his uninjured side with his eyes closed. "We can't just leave him here."

"I'll be fine," Uri said without opening his eyes. "I can handle a couple of healers."

"And what if they bring the guard?" I asked.

"That's why we need to leave." Rys tossed me my cloak.

"Quickly."

"How are we going to find Mia without a tracker?" I pulled the cloak across my shoulders.

"The poster," Rys said. "We're going to find a tavern in town and start talking to folks until we find out where they take their prisoners."

"You'll be fine." Uri blinked his eyes open. "And by the time you return with Mia, I'll have secured us transportation back across the sea."

"Are you sure?" I hesitated, torn between Rys, waiting for me at the door, and Uri.

Uri nodded. "Go on. Get Mia."

I hurried over and squeezed his arm. "Be careful."

"I will." With a sly grin, he lifted the edge of the pillow under his head to give me a glimpse of the knife he held underneath it.

"Lorjad's Luck be with you." I directed my words to the Inahi, even though they were far away, across the sea, hoping my prayer would reach them, and they'd send my words to the gods.

The missing gods. I grimaced at the thought as I turned toward Rys.

His brow wrinkled when he caught the look on my face, but he didn't say anything. After a quick check that the hall was clear, he led me out and down a staircase at the back of the building. He kept us moving, and I followed, anticipating when he wanted me to hold back and wait, and when he wanted me to hook my arm in his and walk along at his side as though we were just out for a casual stroll.

The tension didn't leave his shoulders even after we started up the road toward the town above. Whatever had him worked up, we hadn't left it behind on the waterfront. By the time we were halfway up the hill, I realized he was fuming.

I read his mood in everything from the way he moved his arms to the crunch of his boots on the gravel. If I looked over at him, I knew he'd be clenching his jaw, eyes narrowed, staring at everyone we passed with a glare that would make them think he was trying to set them on fire. And not in a good way.

I sighed. "Out with it."

He continued to brood as he paced along beside me. I counted the steps, knowing that he was just gathering his thoughts. Three. Two.

"I can't believe you let her go," he said.

It took me a moment to realize who he meant. Not Mia. He was talking about Red. The pirate he'd freed. The one who'd sailed us across the sea. Of course I let her go. Didn't he know me well enough to understand why? Still, I kept my mouth shut because I knew he was just getting warmed up.

"She saw what you can do. There's nothing stopping her from going straight to the authorities to tip them off so she can claim one of those mage bounties." He turned his head to look at me. "The longer we stay here, the more people who have reason to take notice of us—of you—the greater the risk."

"You were the one who suggested going to a tavern. It's not too late. We can go back and get Uri." I stopped walking and pivoted to face him and read the worried lines on his face. "Or are you saying we should leave? Do you want to be the one to tell Zan we came this far only to return without Mia?"

Rys stared at me. "I'd rather do that than risk anything happening to you."

"Because you've sworn your loyalty to Ezri and don't want to disappoint him?" I rolled my eyes.

"I don't care about disappointing Ezri-ruh." Rys took a step closer. "And why would he care what happens to you, anyway? He broke off your betrothal."

I winced at his words, knowing I couldn't contradict him. "Why do *you* care?"

"Isn't it obvious?" His eyes softened as they stared into mine.

A flutter of feeling thrummed in my chest. I told myself it was nothing. Just an echo of what we'd once had. "No. It's not. And I can't do this right now."

"Ayla." He lifted his hand, but I stepped back before he could reach for my face. He let his arm drop back to his side. "My feelings for you haven't changed. I never stopped loving you."

"You're really going to do this *right now*?" I glanced around, expecting there to be other people, but we were alone on the path.

"Why shouldn't I?" Rys stared at me. "There doesn't seem to be any other way of getting you alone."

"And that's my fault?" I asked, crossing my arms. "You're the one who went and swore an oath of loyalty to the Ruhl."

His eyes narrowed. "Your aunt saved my mother and me from Merluks, Ayla. You would have done the same thing in my place."

"I would not have." I grimaced, suddenly unsure. The truth was, I did understand why he had done what he did. I just didn't like that he'd kept it a secret from me.

"It doesn't matter." Rys ran a hand through his hair. "All that is behind us now. There's nothing keeping us apart anymore, and I'm not about to let anything happen to you. Not before I have the chance to declare for you. And not after that, either."

I blinked at him, suddenly very aware of the approaching Midwinter Festival and the opportunity that presented for him now. "You're going to declare? For me?"

He looked at me as though surprised I would even question such a thing. "Of course."

In all my scheming and planning with Ezri, I'd never considered how Rys would react. I should have realized. If he declared at the Midwinter Festival, I would have to turn him down in front of everyone. "You can't."

"It's perfect, though. Don't you see?" Rys took my hands in his. "I'll continue as a Shal clan guard, and you'll be just down the hill from the barracks, studying to be a mage. We can see each other whenever we like, and we'll never have to hide our feelings again."

"Rys..." My heart sped in reaction to the words I'd once longed to hear him say. But it was too late. He was too late. "I can't."

"I know you'll be busy with your studies." He squeezed my hands. "We don't have to marry right away. We can wait until after you graduate from the Magery. And then, if you want to go back to the plains, I'll talk to Zan. We'll figure something out."

I pulled out of his grip. "You mean you can go back to spying on the Nahl clan for him."

"No. That's not—"

"Enough." I cut him off. "I'm not going anywhere until we find Mia. You can either help me, or wait for me down at the docks with Uri. But I'm not going to stand here, listening to you plan our future while Mia is being held captive. So what's it going to be?"

"I'm not leaving you." He frowned at me.

"Good. Then tie up my hands." I held out my arms with my

wrists pressed together. "You're going to take me to the city guard to claim the reward for bringing in a mage."

Rys took a step back. "What? No. Absolutely not."

"Remember how, in the legend about the origin of the clans, Ruhala's younger brother sacrifices himself to get closer to the raiders to figure out what's going on?" I'd made the connection when Rys started talking about mage bounties. In that story, the raiders from Valthonia had done something similar.

"Sure. And I also remember how that story is not about how he succeeded. It's about how his older sister escaped to find somewhere safe for mages because her brother was captured and probably killed." Rys crossed his arms.

"You said it yourself." I gestured to the stone fortress up on the hill. "If there's a bounty on mages, the more people who have reason to take note of us, the more I'm at risk. So, new plan. We skip the tavern and go straight to the source. All you have to do is pretend you're planning to turn me in."

"What good is that going to do?" He shook his head. "Handing you over to the city guards isn't going to help us find Mia."

"How many prisons could they possibly have?" I asked. "When you try to claim the reward, if you're right and I'm wrong about why they want mages, then they'll take me to wherever it is they're holding Mia."

"You don't know that. It might just land you in prison and leave me holding a bag of money." Rys scowled. "Besides, exactly how does having both you *and* Mia imprisoned help us?"

"I can find a way to help her, and anyone else they're holding captive, from the inside, while you find a way to help us escape." I searched the ground until I found a stone like the one I'd used while practicing with the Inahi.

"What's that for?" Rys asked.

"I'm going to infuse it with magic so it will guide you to me. Like the elders did for Ruhala." I reached into my pocket for a crystal.

Rys rushed forward, nudging me off the road and toward the shelter of the trees lining the path. "Not here where someone might see you."

It took longer than I liked for me to push the magic into the stone and link it to me. Then, Rys insisted we test it out. When he was finally satisfied that the stone would lead him to me, I held out my wrists.

"Let's go," I said. "Before they close the gates for the night."

14

TURNED out it was harder than we'd expected to locate someone who cared about taking me off Rys's hands. The first guard we approached, patrolling the outskirts of town, told Rys to continue past the cluster of market stalls and talk with the guard at the gate. Then she waved us along.

The guard at the gate sat on a stump, his hands busy sharpening a knife, and he barely glanced up when anyone passed by. When Rys approached him, he seemed annoyed that we were bothering him. Even after Rys told him I was a mage, he just directed Rys to a tall building with a peaked roof near the center of the city. He said it would be visible once we passed through the gate and rounded the bend in the road.

Rys led me past the guard, through the gate, and along the narrow side streets lined with rickety straw-roofed buildings. If I didn't know I was in Agrion, I would have thought I was back in Shal city. The streets were similarly busy, filled with people pushing carts, carrying heavy loads, or leading animals.

Mostly there were more of the small shaggy horses with packs strapped across their backs, but no riders. I wondered if the Agrisse didn't keep horses for riding. Or maybe there just weren't any in this part of the city.

Rys was right about at least one thing. Now that I was looking for it, the fact that no one seemed to be using magic seemed obvious. Agrion was turning out to be nothing like I'd imagined. Except for the stone fortress that dominated the horizon ahead, the two cities were nearly identical.

From where we walked, I couldn't tell if the fortress was located at the center of the town, or on the opposite side. It was big enough that it blocked any view of what lay beyond. Four towers marked the corners of the building. And the stone they'd used to build it glowed red in the setting sun, making the whole thing appear to be lit with god-fire.

When we spotted the building described by the guard at the gate, I realized the tiles on the roof were made from the same stone as the fortress. The building stood out from the surrounding structures both because it was taller, and because it was the only one with those tiles. A sinking feeling weighed in my gut, and I began to question the plan I'd been so sure about before we'd set foot inside the city walls.

A flash of sunlight reflecting off something shiny caught my eye in the uppermost window of the tile-roofed building. Rys saw it, too. His grip on my arm tightened.

"Guards," he said, in a low voice.

The building must be some sort of station for them. I wondered if the upper windows served as something like a tower, giving those inside a better view of what trouble might be brewing in the town below, or farther. It was possible they could see beyond the city wall from up there. As if to prove my point, a large bird swooped down and landed on the edge of the tiled roof, tucking its wings tight against its sides.

"Are you sure about this?" Rys asked, glancing at the sign for a tavern just ahead.

"It's going to work," I said, feigning the confidence I no longer felt.

His thumb caressed the skin of my wrist, the movement hidden by the way he held his grip on the rope he'd used to tie my hands together.

I let the sensation soothe my nerves. Rys was with me. He wouldn't let anything happen to me. I wasn't alone. I tried to ignore the nagging voice in my mind that reminded me that being connected by a spelled stone wasn't the same as him fighting at my side. He wouldn't be in the dungeons with me.

But with Lorjad's Luck, Mia would be.

Too soon there were no more buildings between us and the guard station. Rys whispered, "Here we go."

I inhaled deeply. After a long exhale, I began pulling against Rys's hold on me, pretending I was trying to get away from him. He dug his heels in and dragged me along behind him, playing his part.

Rys stopped in front of the door. He rapped his knuckles against the wood with three powerful, impatient beats.

Footsteps shuffled on the other side, and the door swung wide enough to allow one guard to glower at us from the opening. "What is it?"

"I've got a mage," Rys said.

"I'm not," I whined, pulling against his grip. "I'm not a mage."

"Yes you are. Liar." Rys spat the words at me before turning back to the guard. "She is. I swear it. I saw her doing magic."

"I was not." I tried willing myself to cry, but all I could manage were a few weak sniffles.

The guard eyed us a moment longer, and I was sure we were done. There was no way she believed this performance. But they must have been desperate. Even after scrutinizing my face, she pushed the door open the rest of the way and waved us inside.

"You'll have to take it to the clerk." She stomped ahead of us down a dark hallway, then turned into a small room.

She stepped aside and directed Rys toward a desk opposite the door. As my eyes adjusted to the light, I realized the person behind the desk wasn't wearing a uniform. He wore a stiff black tunic with a high collar. His head was bent over some papers on the desktop, but he looked up when we entered.

"What's this?" He tapped his pen against the wood in a staccato beat.

"I've got a mage, and I want my reward," Rys said, stepping up to the desk and pulling me up behind him.

I caught myself at his words and stopped staring at everything like a curious visitor. Slipping back into my role as prisoner, I tried to pull away from him. When I twisted my body, I spotted the row of plain wooden chairs with their backs against the wall just inside the doorway.

The guard who led us inside sat down in one of them. She grumbled at Rys. "Stop calling it a reward, you fool."

"You want mages, don't you?" He yanked on the rope he'd tied around my wrists and pushed me forward. "Well, here you go."

The clerk leaned forward with his elbows on the desk. He propped his chin on his fists and stared wide-eyed up at Rys. "And what makes you think we need mages?"

"Told you." The guard sighed. "Here we go."

Rys glanced behind him at the guard in the chair, but she

just shook her head at him. He turned to the clerk. "There are signs up. Down at the docks. I saw one."

"Did you, now?" His voice was sugary sweet. "And you're sure about that? You know what the word 'mage' looks like?"

"Are you suggesting I can't read?" Rys stumbled a half step back, but he recovered quickly. "The paper pinned up outside the inn said, 'Money for Mages.' I brought you a mage. Now I want my money."

Rys pushed me forward, and I protested.

The clerk ignored me. "I'm afraid I can't give you any money until we prove she's a mage."

Rys nudged me. "Go on. Show them."

"I can't," I whined as I pretended to make a break for the door.

Rys caught my arm as the guard stood to block the exit.

"Enough messing about, Cass. You're going to make me late for my break." The guard crossed her arms and leaned against the doorjamb. "Just call for the beast and let's get this over with."

The word beast made me tense. The look of fear that flashed across my face was real. I wanted to believe it was just a nickname for one of the other guards, but the skin on my forearms prickled with warning.

For how well he knew me, Rys must have mistaken my reaction as more of the agreed-upon act, because he turned back to the clerk and said, "I'm not leaving until I get my money."

The clerk picked up a pen and tapped it against the desktop. "Well, that is too bad, isn't it? I can't give you money until we've confirmed that this person you've brought us is in fact a mage. So you'll just have to come back tomorrow and check with whoever is on duty—"

"Oh no. You can't fool me like that." Rys's hand clasped the rope at my wrists. He tugged me toward the door. "If I don't get my money, you don't get your mage."

The guard blocked our exit. "Really, Cass?"

"Fine." The clerk sighed. He leaned back in his chair and slapped a hand against the wall behind the desk three times in rapid succession.

A moment later, the muffled sound of an alarm buzzed from somewhere behind the wall. The clerk opened one of the desk drawers and took out a familiar-looking cube. It wasn't until he held it up that I recognized the markings covering the outside.

I sucked in a breath and scrambled backwards. Rys turned to pull me closer, thinking I was still acting my part. When he saw the look on my face, he realized I wasn't pretending. It was too late, though.

The guard set her hands on my shoulders, pinning me in place as the clerk stood and opened the door on the opposite wall. A clear panel covered the opening, separating the two rooms. Beyond it, there was nothing but blackness.

The clerk hit a switch on the wall and the space behind the barrier lit up revealing a tiny chamber. He stood there, facing that empty space, waiting. His body blocked my view of what lay beyond, but from where I stood, the room didn't seem very big. I wondered what they were waiting for. There was no handle on the barrier. No way I could see to open it. Were they going to shove me inside? Or were they waiting for someone else to arrive?

I breathed in and out, trying to calm my racing heart and convince myself that this cube wasn't the same as the one we'd found among Tavo's things. The one that Mia recognized as having some connection to the Koto.

We hadn't seen any of those creatures since setting foot in Agrion, and I'd almost begun to believe that they weren't here. That we'd been wrong. That maybe they'd gone for good when Mia banished them from the caverns by killing the Jahl.

Then I spotted the horn rising up over the shoulder of the clerk. Some sort of platform was being raised on the other side of the barrier. On top of it stood a Koto. Only its horns and forehead were visible at first. When it was eye level with the clerk, the platform stopped. Then the clerk stepped aside, and Rys stumbled backward into me.

The guard behind me laughed. "Not so tough now, are you?"

She tightened her grip on my shoulders and pushed me forward, past Rys, who realized what was happening and grabbed for me a moment too late. When his hand missed my arm, he lurched after me. The guard blocked him with her body as she led me around the far side of the desk.

The clerk held the cube out to me. "Take it."

I shook my head. "No. I'm not a mage. He's lying."

"We'll see about that." He grabbed the rope around my wrists and forced the cube into my hands, cupping his own around mine to make sure I didn't let go. Then he looked to the Koto.

Mage. I heard the thought in my head and shivered.

"No. No." I realized I'd made a horrible miscalculation. If Mia had been taken to someplace like this and presented to the Koto, we were probably already too late. This scheme of mine would just land me inside an Agrisse prison with no way out. "It's a mistake."

There was a commotion behind me. The guard released her grip on my shoulders, but I barely noticed, because my mind was suddenly flooded with images. Thoughts. A language that seemed almost familiar, but that I couldn't quite understand. Then an image of a prison. That's when I caught a glimpse of a familiar face.

Mia. I called to her in my mind.

The Koto set its claws against the barrier. *Mage.* It repeated the word in my mind.

I need to help my friend. I pictured Mia's face.

The Koto growled a low warning, one I couldn't understand.

"All right, horn-head. Time's up. What's it going to be?" The clerk made an exaggerated, enthusiastic nod as he said, "Mage?" Then he gave an equally emphatic shake of his head as he said, "No mage?"

I blinked at the clerk. He didn't know. Had I been the only one who could hear the Koto's thoughts?

The Koto stared at me.

I stared back, less frightened than before, even though I could hear Rys arguing with the guard behind me.

Mage. I sent the thought to the Koto. *Tell them.*

The Koto stared at me through the barrier. Finally, it nodded.

"See. There you go. Was that so hard?" The guard slapped Rys on the back. "Looks like you were right, and you get your money after all."

I tore my gaze from the Koto to glance at Rys over my shoulder. He started toward me, but the guard blocked him.

"Hey now. Too late for regrets." She steered him toward the desk where the clerk was counting out coins. "Take your payment and go, if you know what's good for you."

Rys looked at me, and I tried to project reassurance to him. It was too bad he wasn't one of the Inahi, or one of the Koto. Even when I tried using blue magic, he still couldn't hear my thoughts. His wrinkled brow made it clear he was still worried about me.

There was nothing I could do, though. Once the clerk handed Rys his money, the guard shoved him out the door and down the hall, leaving me alone with the clerk and the Koto. The clerk tapped the wall again, and the platform holding the Koto started back down.

"You're next," the clerk said. He pressed against a notch in the doorjamb and a small door swung open, revealing a thin panel, no bigger than the clerk's finger.

The clerk inserted a key into a slot in the panel. When he twisted the lock, something clicked, and a new platform emerged from below the floor. This time without a Koto standing on top of it. The platform stopped when it was flush with the floor. Then the clerk twisted the key a second time, and the clear barrier blocking the doorway slid aside.

"In you go," he said, as though they expected me to willingly step into that box and follow the Koto down into whatever lay waiting below.

I swallowed, willing my muscles to move my body forward, but I remained rooted in place. Fear flooded my veins as my brain insisted that this was the stupidest thing I had ever done. But, I argued with myself, Mia was down there.

The clerk scowled at me, then called out, "Vix! A little help?"

"...have to do everything..." the guard muttered to herself as she huffed back into the room. She didn't bother with coaxing words when her stomping boots reached me. She just set her palm between my shoulder blades and shoved.

I stumbled forward, my balance awkward with my wrists still tied together, and tripped through the door, into the little cell that lay beyond. My shoulder slammed against the back wall, and before I could shift my momentum, the clerk was there with the key.

One twist and the barrier slid back into place. I slammed my tied hands against it, but the platform was already moving, bringing me down into the darkness below. The clerk gave me a little wave, then slammed the door shut. The lights went out a moment later, and I shrank in on myself as fear crept cold fingers down my spine.

The platform stopped with a shudder that would have thrown me to my knees if claws hadn't curled around my forearm to steady me. When my eyes adjusted to the dim light, I looked up at the creature standing next to me and shivered.

The Koto released its grip on my arm and took a step back. It seemed to be reacting to my obvious distress, giving me space to let me know I shouldn't feel threatened by it. But no matter how I tried, I couldn't regain that connection I'd had with it before.

Every time I tried to send it a thought, I felt a squeezing pressure in my head. The ache reminded me of the sensation that came from climbing up the mountain from the plains to reach the Jahl clan caverns. I winced and raised my fingers to my temple.

The Koto's claw hooked onto the rope tied around my wrists, and I opened my eyes. It shook its large horned head, then reached with its free arm to tap a claw against the stone wall. I studied the walls, trying to figure out what it was trying to tell me.

I turned to look behind me, noting that we stood in a small, carved out space, not much bigger than the clerk's office above us. There were no other doors, just one tunnel leading who knew where, and smooth stone walls surrounding us.

One lantern, similar to the ones in the Jahl clan caverns, sat on a ledge opposite the only tunnel leading out of this space.

Then, with one slice, the binding around my wrists dropped away.

"Thank you," I whispered, not sure if it could understand me, but wanting to avoid another painful squeeze in my head.

It dipped its head, and I remembered that it had followed the clerk's instructions, so it must be able to understand at least some of our language, even if it couldn't speak it. Then it motioned for me to follow before turning to plod down the tunnel.

"Will you take me to Mia?" I asked, thinking of her and automatically attempting to send the thought. My head ached from the momentary pressure caused by forgetting. Frustrated, I asked, "Why can't I speak with my mind down here?"

The Koto reached out one arm and dragged its claws along the stone wall as it walked.

I paused to stare at the walls again. This place reminded me of the Jahl clan caverns, and I'd spoken with Delna using my mind when we were in that space. What was it about this stone that was different? It looked the same.

I stepped closer to the wall and reached out to touch it. As soon as my skin scraped the rough surface, a jolt of pain surged through my fingertips, causing me to jump back.

The Koto, who I thought had continued on without me, was suddenly at my side. It wrapped its clawed hand around mine and shook its head before releasing me.

"It's the walls. They're keeping me from..." I let my voice trail off, then shut my eyes and reached for the sensation of color that had begun to come easier and easier to me, especially here, in Agrion. But there was nothing there. It was like groping into empty darkness.

I opened my eyes. "There's no magic here."

The Koto shook its head again.

"But." I slid my fingers into the hidden pocket in my tunic to retrieve the one crystal I'd tucked inside. Then I closed my eyes again. Nothing. It was just a stone, no longer wrapped in color, at least not that I could sense.

I curled my fingers around it, tightening my hand into a fist. I was alone. In a dungeon. With a Koto. Who I could not communicate with as easily as I'd thought. Cut off from Rys. And with no access to magic, I doubted the stone I'd spelled for him, the one that was supposed to lead him to me, could find me here.

The scuffle of feet on stone drew my attention, and I looked up in time to see five more Koto stomping toward us. The one with me wrapped its clawed hand around my upper arm and roared something at the approaching group.

The one in the lead of that group growled back in a series of sounds I couldn't understand, but that the one holding me responded to with more guttural noises. Whatever it said caused the approaching group to part. The one holding me led me past as the others stared at me with their orange eyes.

I tried not to cower as I corrected my assessment of the situation. Not one Koto. Many. And even if the first had turned out to be helpful, these others did not appear to be so kind.

15

LED by one Koto and followed by the rest, there was no hope of escape as we wound our way through tunnels under the city. With no view of the sky and no way to orient myself, I had lost all sense of direction and could only trod along and hope they were leading me closer to Mia.

We finally emerged into a larger room, and the sour smell of unwashed humans and their waste hit me before I spotted the cells. At least ten people huddled in the first one we passed. They clustered together toward the back, keeping their eyes and heads down and making it hard for me to tell if Mia was among them.

I stared as I was led past, swiveling my head to make sure I'd gotten a thorough look at all the occupants. My distraction made me miss what was ahead of me. The Koto who I had been communicating with was holding the door to an identical cell open. I walked right in without realizing until I stood facing another huddled group of prisoners, this time with no bars between us.

The door shut with a clang behind me, and I spun around. "No. Wait!"

The mass of Koto who had been following ignored me. They retreated as the one I had spoken with lingered a moment longer.

"Please. I need to find Mia." I tried to send the image of my friend again, only to be rewarded with another squeezing ache in my head. I grimaced through the pain. "Please?"

The Koto shook its horned head once, then turned and walked away.

I gripped the bars and stared after it, hoping it would return. When it didn't, I turned to the others I'd been shut in with. A few had raised their heads to stare at me, but none had moved out of the huddle at the back of the cell.

"Hello?" I took a tentative step toward them.

The few who had been staring at me looked away when I spoke.

"Are you mages?" I asked. When they continued to ignore me, I asked, "Can you understand me?"

One of the ones who I had caught staring at me sent a glaring look in my direction before busying himself with helping one of the others arrange themselves in a more comfortable position against the back wall of the cell.

I moved closer until I could tap him on the shoulder. "Why won't you talk to me?"

He wrenched his shoulder away as though I might infect him with my touch, but otherwise didn't respond.

"Have you somehow been silenced? Can you not speak?" No answer. None of them would even look at me. "Please? I just want to know—"

The man who had glared at me stood to face me. He pointed to the opposite corner of the cell. "Sit down and shut your mouth before you bring them back here."

"But what do they want?" I asked, retreating a few steps.

The man snarled at me. "Are you *trying* to draw the attention of the Green Mage?"

"I think she is," someone behind him whispered. "I think they sent her here to stir us up."

"I wasn't." I raised my hands. "I'm not."

The whisperer leaned over to the old woman next to her. "Proving my point, she is."

The old woman huffed in agreement and shook her head.

The man who first spoke folded his arms across his chest. He lifted his eyebrows, waiting for me to do as I'd been told.

I realized that the more questions I asked, the more I continued to argue or even try to defend myself, the guiltier I looked. So I retreated to the other side of the cell. I stopped just shy of the grimy wall, remembering the shock I'd received when I touched that stone in the tunnel, and sank down onto the dirt-covered stone floor. I kept a buffer of air between me and the wall as I sat hunched over my crossed legs. To avoid the temptation of staring at the others, I took out the crystal I'd hidden in my tunic pocket and turned it over in my palm.

There was no point in trying to stay clean in this place. Everything and everyone was covered in a layer of dirt and stink. I was stuck in a cell with no one willing to give me information. Who knew how long it would be before anyone came for us.

Mia wasn't here, and I couldn't get out to look for her. The Koto who I'd thought understood me didn't seem inclined to help me find her. And no matter how hard I focused on the crystal in my hand, I couldn't sense any colors.

As long as I remained in here, Rys wouldn't leave me. I

knew that. But it also meant that Ezri would probably never know what happened. He'd think we all died here in Agrion. Except, the Inahi wouldn't select a new Labharon until I really did die.

It seemed like being forgotten and left to rot in a crowded cell with six other humans who refused to speak with me was more likely than me being killed by either the Koto or this mysterious Green Mage anytime soon. As long as I lived and remained stuck in this colorless prison, Ezri would have no way to effectively maintain the illusion that he was the Ruhl. The united clans would suffer. All because I trusted a Koto. What in the name of all the gods had I been thinking?

I set the soles of my boots on the ground, pulled my knees toward my chest, and wrapped my arms around them. Feeling defeated but refusing to cry, I dropped my forehead to my knees and squeezed my eyes shut.

Eventually, I must have drifted off into an uneasy sleep because I jolted upright at the sound of boots scuffing against stone in the tunnel beyond the locked cell door. I pushed myself up to standing, shook some feeling into my cramped legs, and rushed toward the bars to try and catch a glimpse of what was going on.

It struck me that I had no idea how long I'd been asleep. I glanced over my shoulder to see if the others in the cell were awake, only to find them all returned to the huddled mass of bodies in the back, just as they'd been when I arrived.

They feared the Koto. That had to be why they were acting this way. I knew I should be scared of them as well, but the fear of being stranded in here forever was greater. I'd fought a Koto once. But I'd had help then. I told myself I could do it again if it meant finding Mia and getting out of here.

So, when the Koto marched past, I was ready. I jiggled

the bars and shouted at them, but they ignored me and kept walking. There were four of them. Two pairs, each supporting a prisoner between them.

The two humans pinned between hulking Koto shoulders were both dirty and slumped, shuffling along in a daze. Neither lifted their head or shifted their eyes to look at me. None of the Koto so much as flicked an ear in my direction. It was like they couldn't even hear me. Only a brief falter in the steps of the human walking between the second pair of Koto gave me any hope that they might just be ignoring me.

I slammed a palm against the cell bars as they disappeared from view. Then, as the disappointment at missing an opportunity to get out faded, I realized I was no longer holding the crystal that had been in my hand when I fell asleep.

I paced back over to the place where I'd been sitting, only to find the man who had confronted me standing there.

"Looking for this?" he asked, holding up the crystal I must have dropped.

"Yes, thank you." I held out my hand, palm up.

He held it up to examine it in the light from the lanterns in the room outside our cell. "What does it do?"

"Nothing." I didn't even have to lie. "There's no magic here."

His eyes narrowed. "You're one of them, then."

"You're not?" Taking advantage of his moment of distraction, I snatched the stone from his hand and tucked it into my tunic pocket.

The others, who had been clustered together in the back corner of the cell, began to unbunch. A few drifted closer, curious about my response to the man's accusation.

"Where were they taking those people?" I asked, waving one arm toward the cell door.

Two of the onlookers exchanged looks, then shook their

heads like I was clueless. As I opened my mouth to ask another question, their eyes went wide. They stared past me, frozen.

I turned to see what had drawn their attention in time to see a Koto unlocking the door to our cell. Behind me, feet shuffled back. I ignored them and stepped forward.

"Take me," I said, holding out my hands.

The Koto stared at me for a few tense breaths. It held a clump of chained-together metal cuffs in its massive hands. When I didn't move, it shoved me aside, reaching instead for the arms of three of the prisoners behind me, seemingly at random.

I noted this out of the corner of my eye as I recovered my balance. Then, with its attention on securing the cuffs around the wrists of the prisoners it had selected, I made an impulsive break for the still-open door.

I didn't have a plan beyond escaping the confines of the cell, but that didn't matter because I wasn't fast enough. The Koto turned on me almost as soon as I moved. It held one end of the chain connecting the cuffed prisoners in one hand and wrapped its other around my bicep, holding me back.

When I tried to twist out of its grip, it roared at me. I winced away from the sound, even as the Koto pulled me closer. It hesitated for a moment once I stilled. Then it shoved me forward and through the cell door as it held fast to my arm, claws digging into my skin through my tunic sleeve.

Once we were out, it tugged on the chain, drawing the line of shuffling, hunched prisoners out after us. Muffled sobs and a few wails came from the group left behind. As the Koto locked the cell door, my eyes found the man who had confronted me. He was staring at us already, and his eyes locked with mine.

He had one arm around a woman who was bent over, shaking with sobs, but his face was dry, his eyes clear. I couldn't interpret the look on his face. He seemed confused, possibly by my failed attempt at escape, but maybe because the Koto had taken me as well, even though there were only restraints for three prisoners.

I didn't have much time to think about it before we were moving again, this time down a different tunnel. From the strain in my thighs, I guessed the tunnel led up, but at such a slight incline it was otherwise hard to tell.

After a much longer march than I'd thought possible, one that made it clear there were nearly as many tunnels under the city as there were streets stretching between its buildings, we reached a stone staircase.

The Koto pulled the exhausted prisoners up behind us as it led the way, yanking on the chain when they dragged behind, and shoving at me to keep walking whenever my steps faltered on the uneven stairs. We paused on a landing with a wooden door set into an arched doorway. Someone had carved a line of runes into the wood, but I didn't recognize any of them.

After herding us into a corner of the landing, close to the doorway but as far from the stairs as possible, the Koto raised a massive fist and knocked in a pattern similar to the one the clerk had used back in the guard station. The action made me wonder if there would be more guards on the other side. This wasn't the way I'd come in, so they must be moving us to a different location in the city.

I searched the faces of the other prisoners, trying to determine if any of them recognized where we were. None of them would look at me. When they caught me staring, they shot nervous glances at each other before shifting their gazes down.

I wondered if any of them were mages. If that man back in the cell wasn't a mage, were any of these people? If they'd been put in that cell for some other reason, why had the Koto put me in there with them? Did this Koto know I was a mage?

The door swung open, revealing a human guard holding some sort of metal rod in their fist. It was about as long as my forearm and blunt on both ends, though one end flared out, ending in a wider disc than the other. She pointed the wide end at the Koto and she drove it forward as though she intended to stab the Koto in the chest.

The Koto didn't flinch, even though I did. Except, the blow I'd been expecting never happened. The wide end of the bar stopped abruptly about halfway between the guard and the Koto. Right in the middle of the arched doorway.

Another invisible barrier, I thought.

The guard pressed a button on the metal rod, and the barrier shimmered before flickering out. As it disappeared, the flared end of the bar started glowing with a white light. The guard continued to point the glowing rod at the Koto's chest.

"Send them through," the guard commanded.

The Koto shoved me through the opening, toward the waiting guard. I stumbled before colliding with the guard's body.

"What's this? Why isn't she chained?" The guard pushed me to one side. "Stand there and don't move."

I did as she ordered, waiting while she took control of the chained prisoners.

Once they were through the door and lined up against the wall, the guard grabbed my arm and shoved me toward the Koto. "Take this one back. He said three. We have three. We don't need her."

The Koto took a step back and shook its large head.

"What do you mean, no?" The guard's fingers tightened on my upper arm. "I give the commands here. Now take this one back to the cells until he asks for more."

The Koto roared, waving its massive hands. Those long claws sliced through the air, making me flinch back toward the relative safety of the guard.

"Ugh." The guard yanked me back as she pressed the button that slid the barrier back into place.

She slammed the door shut, then fumbled in the pockets of her leather vest until she found a cuff like the ones the Koto had secured around the wrists of the other prisoners. "Don't know what you did, but all right, looks like you're coming with me."

She snapped the cuff around my wrist and secured me to the end of the chain. Then she muttered to herself as she marched us up more stairs and down a windowless stone-walled corridor. "Useless creatures. Just asking for trouble, letting them freely roam about, even if they are confined to the tunnels."

A few people passed us, but none looked our way. They were all dressed in identical cream tunics with high collars over loose trousers. Their slippered feet made a hushed swishing sound as they scuffed against the stone floors.

I paid close attention to everything we passed, hoping something would give me a clue as to where we'd been taken. But every door we passed was closed, and the walls held no ornamentation, only lanterns hung at regular intervals. Without windows to let in daylight, I couldn't tell if it was day or night. The lanterns were the only source of illumination.

Eventually, the guard's steps slowed as we approached a door that looked identical to all the others we'd passed. She paused before reaching for the handle. With a quick glance to ensure we were all still standing alongside her, secure in our chains, she swallowed and turned the knob.

The door opened to a small, dark entryway. The guard had to hunch over to keep the top of her head from scraping against the low ceiling. We followed her into the cramped space and waited as she squeezed past us to close the door behind us.

From my position at the front of the line, I could see colorful lights dancing across the section of wall visible in the room just past the entry.

Once the door was closed, the guard led us out of the dark and into the enormous room beyond. As we emerged, my eyes were drawn upward along walls that stretched high, disappearing into the cavernous, shadowed space above us. The lights I'd seen flickering against the walls appeared to be coming from the floor at the center of the room. They zipped along invisible lines, like veins or rivers, hidden among the stones in the floor. Most raced toward the solitary chair positioned in the middle of the space.

Five columns, arrayed in a circle, equidistant from each other, surrounded the throne-like chair at the center of the room. They reminded me of the ones in the tower in Shal city, except these didn't stretch from floor to ceiling. In that way, these were more like obelisks or tall pedestals. At first, I thought they only rose to the height of a very tall human. But, as the guard led us past them, onto the floor with the illuminated lines, I realized they towered over me to at least twice my height.

The other thing I noticed was they were also covered in veins of flashing lights. Unlike the floor, where every color zipped underfoot in seemingly all directions, the lights on each column were only one color, and they flashed in vertical lines, striping down the side facing the center of the room. The one directly across from us as the guard led us toward the middle of the floor had a steady stream of white lights running up and down it, just below the surface of the stone. A golden hue lit the next one over. I glanced over my shoulder, noting the one behind us had green lights pulsing through the veins in the stone.

"What is this place?" I whispered, turning my head to note the other colors.

"Quiet." The guard yanked on the section of chain attached to my cuff before I could get a look at the ones behind us.

A moment after she spoke, a low gong rang through the chamber, echoing off the walls.

Her shoulders tensed, and she hurried us along. One of the three prisoners following me resisted, digging in their heels and refusing to budge, which pulled our entire line to a halt.

"Oh, no you don't." The guard glowered at us. She pulled on our chains, and when that didn't work, she circled around to shove at the straggler, nudging him forward, only to find another in the line had taken up the cause.

Meanwhile, footsteps beat a steady rhythm against the stones. The sound bounced around the space, making it difficult to tell exactly which direction they were coming from.

Judging from the throne-like chair at the center of the room, the gong that preceded the footsteps, and the way our guard was rushing to position us facing the empty chair, I had a strong suspicion we were about to meet the Green Mage. That would also explain the sudden wave of fear that had caused my fellow prisoners to resist.

I stared around, searching for a glimpse, only to have the guard jerk me into position and smack the back of my head, sending my gaze down until the only view I had was of lights zipping past under my boots. Curious as that was, I wanted to see the mage.

Keeping my head down, I glanced up from under my brows, waiting for a figure to step into view. My first glimpse was of sweeping black robes. They billowed around the mage's feet, sliding across the floor like a dark cloud passing a star shower. A shiver ran down my spine when he spoke.

"What's this?" he asked. "I called for three, and you bring me four?"

"My apologies, Great One. The Koto—"

Whatever she was going to say was swallowed by a choking gasp.

"I do not want excuses." His voice rasped like it strained him to speak.

My head turned toward the strangled sounds of the guard. I expected to find the mage's hand around her throat, but he stood more than an arm's length away with one hand at his side, fingers barely visible under the long sleeves of the robes he wore. The other hand was wrapped around a gold staff with a clawed tip. Nestled between the tines, a crystal with a swirling white hue at its center pulsed with a mesmerizing glow.

The mage must have felt my gaze on him because he turned his head to meet my eyes. While he stared at me, I found myself unable to look away. Some force held me pinned in place.

In that moment, I was sure it was over. I'd miscalculated. I understood the resistance the others had shown, but there was nothing I could do.

He released whatever grip he had on the guard. Out of the corner of my eye, I watched her stumble, then hunch over, as she began sucking air into her lungs in desperate gulps.

"Bring that one to me," the mage said, gesturing in my direction.

The guard swayed as she took a tentative step toward me, then another, gaining confidence in her balance as she closed the distance between us. She unclipped my cuffs from the chain and hauled me by my arm toward where the mage sat on his throne.

"What do we have here?" His fingers curled around the arms of his chair as he leaned toward me.

Up close, I noted his unlined face, sharp cheekbones, and strong jawline. His eyes were dark and flashed with reflections of the lights that ran along the floor and the columns. He didn't seem much older than Goff, though something about his voice made him sound much older. At least as old as Mage-sha.

"Take off her cuffs," he commanded, motioning to the guard.

She hesitated. "Great One, I don't think that's—"

He silenced her off with a look. "Do as I say."

I wondered if the intensity of that gaze had the same effect on her as it had on me. When she approached me, her mouth was set in a firm line, and her eyes warned me not to try anything.

As soon as the cuffs were off my wrists, the mage grinned. He spread his arms wide. "Now this. This I can work with."

In a shockingly swift motion, he grasped the golden staff he'd left resting beside his throne, and clutched it tightly in his hand. The crystal nestled in the tines swirled with green. His eyes blazed as they locked with mine. Then I felt a pull as though someone were trying to suck the air from my lungs.

But it wasn't air that the mage was pulling from me. He was drawing on my magic.

Once I realized what was happening, I forced myself to focus. We were out of the dungeon. Perhaps I could reach my magic here. The longer he retained his hold on me, the harder it became to form coherent thoughts. I forced myself to focus. As soon as I connected with the sensation of green, I wrapped it around me. Then I yanked my magic back, just as I had when I tested the young man from the Shal clan. Except this was harder.

I had a strong suspicion that this was why they called him the Green Mage. It took a moment before he noticed my resistance. As soon as he did, he released me.

He waved the hand that wasn't holding the staff at the guard. "Put her cuffs back on."

The guard grabbed my arm. When she slapped the first cuff on my wrist, my magic slipped from my grasp. With the second one secured, I could no longer sense any of the colors. But it seemed to work both ways. The mage couldn't draw on my magic while I wore the cuffs. That must have been why he insisted they be removed.

He tapped the end of his staff on the floor. "I see we'll have to try this a different way."

Two figures stepped out of the darkness and approached the mage's throne with their eyes fixed on the ground. They were both dressed like the people we'd passed in the halls. I barely glanced at them because I was more concerned about what was going to happen to me. But then, when they turned to face the throne, the lights lit the profile of the one closest to me, illuminating the scar on her cheek.

I knew that face. That was Mia.

16

W ITH her eyes downcast and her body turned toward the mage on the throne, I had no way of signaling to her. I needed her to look at me. To recognize me. And then we needed to get out of this place.

The mage was giving them instructions, telling them to fetch what sounded like a restraining device. I guessed it was for me. Something that would allow him to drain my power without me fighting back. But I didn't plan on sticking around long enough to find out.

When he'd finished his request, Mia and the other servant bowed before retreating. I followed their progress out of the corner of my eyes as I kept my gaze pinned to the floor. A plan was taking shape in my head, but I needed to act fast if it was going to succeed, and everything depended on me being right about the mage not being able to control me while I was wearing the cuffs.

The mage turned his attention to the guard who was still standing next to me. "Let's see if any of the others show as much promise."

"Yes, Great One." The guard stepped away from me.

Mia and the other servant were disappearing into the shadows, and I was about to lose sight of them, but I forced myself to wait. I knew I would only have one chance. Once I heard the clank of the prisoner chains, and I could be sure the guard's attention was occupied, I rushed forward.

The mage cried out in surprise and threw up a defensive barrier around the throne, just as I'd expected. With only one guard, I guessed he would rely on his magic to protect him. But with his magic and the guard temporarily occupied, I pivoted and took off after Mia.

Running with my hands bound wasn't easy, but fear of the mage combined with the hope of rescue drove me forward. Boots pounded behind me, followed by shouting, and I knew the guard was right behind me.

I urged my feet to go faster. As I ran, I searched the darkness ahead for any sign of the white servant uniform, but it was like they'd disappeared. The walls were black. The lights were dim. No colors striped the floor here, with their illuminating flashes. There wasn't anything to hide behind, either.

I started to panic the closer I got to the wall ahead. The guard would be on me, dragging me back, at any moment. Then I spotted the outline of what looked like a door in the wall ahead.

I ran straight for it, slamming my body into it and groping for the handle. There was none. A quick glance over my shoulder confirmed what I expected. The guard had almost caught up.

I ran my cuffed hands up and down the edges of the frame, feeling with my fingertips for some catch or latch. There had to be some way through.

When that didn't work, I banged my fists on the door in a panicked effort to see if someone might open it from the other side. The door rattled in the frame, and I realized what I had been missing. The door didn't swing open. It slid.

I set both palms on the panel and pushed, first to the right, and when that didn't work, to the left.

The door glided open, and I stepped through, sliding it shut behind me just as the guard reached for me. My movement threw her off balance, and she grasped at the air where I'd been standing.

I kicked out, shoving her backward, then slid the door shut. Lorjad's Luck was with me, as I found the iron bar that fitted into the slot on the back of the door. I slid it over and twisted the knobbed end to lock it into place.

The guard's hammering fists started pounding on the other side, accompanied by her muffled shouts. I took a step back and nearly tripped as I collided into someone.

Spinning around, I raised my cuffed hands, ready to defend myself, only to recognize the servant who had been with Mia.

"Ayla?" Mia's whispered voice came from somewhere behind the long-haired youth standing in front of me.

"Mia!" I stepped sideways until I could see her.

"What are you doing here?" she asked, unmoving.

"Rescuing you." I held my hands out to her. "Can you get these off me?"

The youth stared at me with wide eyes. "You are a prisoner. You are not allowed here."

Behind me, the guard stopped banging on the door. The youth opened his mouth as though he was going to scream, but Mia was faster.

"Sorry about this," she said, stepping between us. Then she swung her hand into the side of his neck, and he collapsed to the ground.

As she leaned him against the wall, I glanced around to see if there were any other servants or guards with us in the small room.

"Give me your hands," Mia said.

I extended my wrists in her direction as she slid a pin out of her sleeve. When she set to work on the lock, I noticed the pale band of skin around the base of her first finger.

"Your ring. What happened to it?"

Mia's hands stilled for a moment before returning to their work. "One of the traders took it."

"So Zan was right. They did capture you."

Mia's jaw tensed. "There."

One cuff clicked open, then the other.

"You should go," she said. "That guard will send for more. You don't have much time. I can give you directions—"

"No." I grabbed her hands. "I'm not leaving without you."

"You have to." She twisted out of my grip. "I'm bound here."

"By what?" I asked, searching for some sign of restraints.

"By some magic of the mage. I don't know how it works, but..." She shivered. "I've seen others who have tried to escape. It...doesn't end well."

I reached for the crystal in my pocket to help me focus my magic. Then I scanned her body again.

"Come on. We're wasting time," she said. "You need to—"

"Oh!" A tangle of colors near her right ear caught my attention. I'd had to feel my way through the colors twice before I was sure I could identify all the components. "That's clever."

A commotion from somewhere beyond the room shocked us both to silence. When Mia spoke again, it was in a whisper. "Come on. We need to get you out of here."

"Wait," I said, taking hold of her arm with my free hand. "Hold still for a moment."

With one hand wrapped around the crystal for guidance, I placed my palm near the patch of yellow and red magic that wound around her neck. When I tried to pry them apart, I lost my grasp on the magic, and the invisible noose snapped back into place. It didn't take long for me to figure out that I needed to control both sensations at the same time in order to gather up the magic and diffuse it.

Just when I thought I was nearly done, I noticed a sliver of indigo wedged into what I'd begun to think of as a red and yellow rope. This third color was like a barb that I needed to extract before I could free her completely. But once it was out, the rest dispersed quickly.

"You should be free now," I said, wiping beads of sweat from my brow with the back of my hand.

"Since when can you do magic?" Mia asked, pulling me with her, away from the sound of stomping boots coming from somewhere on the other side of the wall.

"I'll explain later." I wondered why the Inahi hadn't mentioned anything about combining colors to create different effects with magic. If I had to guess, I'd say the Green Mage had used the indigo barb as a sort of location beacon. The growth effects of the yellow magic in combination with the heat effects of red magic must cause whatever Mia had meant by escape attempts not ending well.

Mia led us toward a rack holding a row of long white garments. She shoved half of them aside to reveal a panel set in the wall behind.

"Stand back," she said.

I edged away from her as she crouched and spun, kicking out with her leg to shatter the thin panel.

"Messier this way, but faster." She ducked her head, angling her shoulder into the opening, then using her body to widen the opening as she crawled forward. "Watch yourself," she called back to me.

I bent and crawled in after her, pulling the garments back into place to hide our exit route. I'd thought they were servant uniforms, at first. But, as my hand clenched around the fabric, I realized they were full body suits with buckles and straps.

"Come on," Mia called to me. She had repositioned herself so that her feet were in front of her and was holding herself in place to keep from sliding down the sloped tunnel floor.

I gave the strange suits one last look, then hurried after Mia. "Do you know where this leads?" I asked, sliding down after her.

"In theory." Mia waited for me to catch up before continuing her controlled descent. "It's a disposal chute."

"For garbage?" I sniffed the air. There was no stench of rot. The walls and floor seemed clean, though it was hard to be sure the further we descended into the darkness. I thought of the garments on the rack. "Or soiled clothing?"

"Mages," Mia said. "After he drains them."

I shivered. "You've seen him do it?"

Mia yelped. When she spoke again it was from farther away. "Slippery patch there," she called back up to me.

I hit the slick metal before I could heed her warning. My boots slid, and the next thing I knew, my body slammed into Mia's. Then we were both sliding down, rapidly approaching an opening lit by a dim glow.

I scrambled for purchase on the smooth walls, and when that didn't slow me down, I reached for magic.

If this was a chute for disposing of bodies, who knew

how far we'd drop or what we'd land on when we emerged. I fought back the terror flooding my veins and reached for white magic to cushion our fall. Just like I'd done with the spilled crystals in the tower.

There wasn't time to consider how those had been small objects, and now I hoped to control the descent of two grown humans. And I couldn't see far enough ahead of me to get a look at the ground.

Even with my best effort, we landed with a thud on a canvas tarp stretched between four posts. The fabric swayed under our weight but held. I exhaled a relieved breath too soon.

With a clicking noise, the posts rotated, twisting the canvas so it curled over us, wrapping us inside. And then we dropped again.

I screamed and tore at the canvas.

When we landed next, it was on an uneven surface. Hard edges and unforgiving angles poked into my shoulders and legs, but my butt was cushioned by something soft. I tried not to think about it.

Mia wiggled her arm free from where it lay pinned against me. Then, reaching down, she extracted something sharp from her boot and sliced a tear in the fabric.

I dug my fingers into the hole she'd made, helping to rip it wider.

We sat up, side by side, and took in our surroundings. There was light, not from lanterns, but from the sky. The sun was hidden from view, and the light was the dim grey of dawn or dusk. I couldn't tell which. But it was enough to see that we'd landed in a gap between a high stone wall that rose above us on one side, and the outer wall of the fortress on the other. Below us lay a mound of what I could only guess were canvas-wrapped bodies that filled the space between. Mages,

I thought, with a pang of sadness.

Mia tugged on my sleeve and pointed to a cart that had been left near the edge of the mound. Wheel tracks led from it, through the gap between wall and fortress, and around the corner.

"Where there's a cart, there will be workers. We need to get out of here before they see us," Mia said, twisting onto her hands and knees.

"Which way do we go?" I asked, turning to look in the opposite direction.

The base of the mound on that side ended in a muddy pool of water that filled the gap between wall and fortress as far as I could see. The idea of wading through it when we had no idea where it led didn't seem very appealing. And who knew how deep the water ran. If we went that way, we could end up swimming through endless muck without any way to climb out. I turned back to Mia, ready to tell her I'd rather take my chances with the workers, but she was already climbing down toward the cart.

"This way," she said. "Go slow and be careful."

We climbed down in silence. Mia's boots hit the mud alongside the cart before mine. She watched and waited while I apologized to every mage I touched on the way down and whispered prayers to Estrel on their behalf.

This could have been me, I thought. This terrible plan of mine could have gone very, very wrong.

By the time I stood on solid ground, the light had dimmed enough for stars to emerge in the night sky above. I prayed they were the souls of these mages, gone to shine beside Estrel.

Mia took hold of my arm to steady me. "Follow me. We stick to the shadows and hope the workers are done for the day."

It seemed like a reasonable plan. I fell in behind Mia, matching her step for step as she cut a path toward the outer wall of the fortress.

"If we're lucky, there will be a door here, leading back inside," she whispered.

"Inside?" I caught the high note of surprise in my voice and lowered it to a whisper before continuing. "Why would we want to go back in now that we're out?"

"Inside, I can disguise us as servants. I know my way around enough that I think I could find us a way out," Mia said.

"You don't think this will lead to—"

Mia held up a hand, and I swallowed the rest of my question. She pressed her back to the fortress wall. I crept closer to her and mimicked her posture, though I couldn't hear anything beyond my own rapid breathing.

As I tried to quiet the air flowing in and out of my lungs, I heard the squelch of a boot in the mud. Neither of us had moved, so someone else had to be out there.

I sucked in the breath I'd been trying to quiet and held it instead. Something moved in the darkness ahead of us. I made out the silhouette of a person, just as Mia lunged forward.

She took them by surprise, tackling them to the ground. I couldn't make out the tangle of limbs until their grappling moved them closer to where I stood. They seemed evenly matched, and about the same size.

Mia ducked out of a hold. She scrambled back to regroup, drawing her opponent closer to where I waited in the shadows. Without a word, I understood her intent.

If there was only one of them and two of us, and one of

us took them by surprise, we could get the upper hand, even without a weapon.

I readied myself to join the fight, waiting for my opening. But the closer I watched Mia's opponent, the more familiar their movement seemed.

"Rys?" I breathed his name, barely audible to my own ears, as realization dawned.

He must have heard, because he hesitated a moment too long. Mia swiped his feet from under him with a kick that might otherwise have only caused him to stumble back within my reach. She pressed her advantage, pinning him to the ground. Her forearm found his throat, and he choked in a rasping breath.

"Wait." I stepped out of the shadows and reached out a hand to grip Mia's shoulder.

Rys grunted, eyes wide as they locked with mine. His mouth opened, but he couldn't speak. Not with Mia's arm on his windpipe.

His eyes flicked from mine to Mia at the same time she let up on her hold.

"Gods." Mia lurched back. "I nearly killed you."

Rys coughed to clear his throat. "I'm all right."

"What are you doing here?" I asked.

"Looking for you," he said, pushing himself up on his elbows.

Mia scrambled off him, then offered her hand to help him up. "How did you get in?"

"Stole a uniform. Blended into a group coming in at shift change." Once he was on his feet, he rubbed his hands down the front of his tunic.

"They just let you walk in?" I gaped at him, once again struck by how misguided my plan had been.

He raised his eyebrows at me. "I'm a spy, remember?"

"Why didn't you suggest that instead—"

"Instead of letting that creature take you—"

Mia stepped between us. "Later."

Rys dipped his head. I shut my mouth.

Mia nodded once. "Good. Now. How do we get out?"

"The guards I came in with weren't the ones assigned to the prison. But their chatter made it clear there was one under the fortress. I just needed to find my way in. When they marched out to relieve the unit at the gate, I slipped away and circled back here, hoping I could find the entrance."

Mia sighed. "Great. So the only way you know in or out is past the guards."

"Maybe we could sneak out, like Rys snuck in?" I suggested.

Mia gestured toward her servant uniform. "Not looking like this."

"There was a door back there." Rys pointed back the way he'd come. "It led to some sort of storeroom. Maybe there's something in there? At least it would get us out of the cold while we come up with a plan."

I hadn't noticed the growing chill in the air until he mentioned it. "Lead the way."

Rys waited for Mia to agree before starting back. Just as before, we kept to the shadows along the fortress wall, this time with Rys in the lead and me sandwiched between him and Mia.

We walked in silence until we arrived at the door. Rys signaled for us to stop and wait while he investigated to make sure the room was still empty.

"Do you think they're still looking for us?" I whispered to Mia.

"If the mage knows you have magic, he'll turn the fortress inside out until you're found." Mia sighed. "I, on the other hand, am easily replaceable, as far as they're concerned. They think, if I'm dumb enough to run, my head will explode, and that will be the end of that."

Rys stuck his head out of the door and waved us inside. When the door closed behind us, he lit a small handheld lantern. Mia and I turned in a slow circle, taking in our surroundings.

"I know this place," Mia said. "Or one just like it."

"Maybe all the storerooms look the same," I said.

"It's possible. But if I'm right, then we aren't far from the bathing hall." She walked over to a rack that held stacks of folded linens. "These are the towels they use. I've collected the soiled ones and brought them to the laundry."

"Is it a public bathing hall?" I asked.

Mia shook her head. "If it's the one I'm thinking of, it's for the guards to use after their rotation."

"Maybe we could steal a couple more uniforms?" I suggested.

"Maybe." Rys's brow wrinkled. His face got that look that told me I wasn't going to like whatever it was he said next. "But all that dirty water has to go somewhere, doesn't it? Most likely out of the fortress. Under the wall? Maybe a tunnel that will lead us all the way back to the docks."

"What's at the docks?" Mia asked.

"Uri. With a boat, if we're lucky," Rys responded.

"How many of you are there?" Mia asked.

"Zan sent four of us, plus Ayla," Rys replied. "But only three of us made it past the traders and onto a boat."

Mia blinked at him for a moment. I couldn't tell if she was surprised there were so many of us, or that Zan had been the one to send us, or that we'd managed to get past the traders. Perhaps all of it. I could tell she had more questions, but none worth asking until we escaped.

"Well." She shrugged. "If we need to get back to the docks anyway, a wastewater tunnel isn't a bad idea."

"You want us to crawl through a sewer?" As I expected, I did not like this plan. "When we could just walk out of here in stolen guard uniforms?"

Rys folded his arms across his chest. "How many units of guards do you think we'll make it past before someone gets curious about why we're just walking around and asks us for a passcode or something?"

I frowned at him. He didn't have to remind me of what happened with the traders.

"And they'll be looking for you, remember?" Mia added.

I groaned. "Fine. We'll take the sewer."

Rys patted my shoulder. "It's just a little dirty bath water. I think you can handle it, Nahla."

"Shut it, Rys." I glared at him.

"Enough, you two." Mia looked down at her mud-streaked uniform. With a shake of her head, she said, "It will have to do."

"What do you have in mind?" Rys asked.

"You'll pass as a guard, if we're stopped. A muddy one, in need of a bath. So that works." Mia paused to think for a moment. Her eyes narrowed, and she cocked her head to one side. "Say you're new. That you've lost your way. You found yourselves near the servant baths and asked me to lead you to the guard bathing hall."

I gestured to the clothes I was wearing. "This won't pass as a guard uniform."

"I know." Mia frowned. "That's why we're going to try not

to run into anyone. We don't have to make it all the way there. In fact, it's better if we don't have to go inside. There should be some sort of a maintenance room next to the baths. We just need to find it."

Rys nodded. "Lead the way. I'll bring up the rear."

Mia paced over to the interior door. She listened before twisting the handle and opening it a crack. Then she listened some more before waving us out into a hallway that looked identical to the one the guard had marched us down on our way to the mage's throne room.

Mia set a brisk pace. After a series of turns down branching hallways, she whispered that we were almost there. But at the next turn, her steps faltered.

I looked past her shoulder and spotted a trio of guards coming toward us from the opposite direction. They were laughing and might not have noticed us if we hadn't hesitated.

Our pause caught the eye of the smallest in the group, and he nudged the woman next to him. Their laughter died as they focused their attention on us.

Mia's body tensed. Rys moved forward to address the approaching group, but Mia put her arm out.

At first, I thought she meant to keep Rys back. Then I realized she was reaching for a nearby door.

"This way," she said, stepping aside to let me and Rys enter ahead of her. She followed us in, then closed the door behind us, locking it shut. "Find the outflow, quickly. It won't take them long to reach the other entrance and sound the alarm."

Rys hurried forward, dragging me with him. I barely had time to take in the large steam-filled room, dotted with cascading pools. A few of the occupants glanced our way as we passed, but none bothered to question us.

A commotion on the opposite side of the pools drew my attention, but Mia shoved at my back.

"Keep moving," she said in a low voice.

We reached the lowest pool just as the shouting above us began. "Stop them!" someone yelled.

Rys slid to a stop, and I slammed into him. He kept a hold on my arm as he searched the ground around the pool. Mia faced the opposite direction, searching the walls.

"What are we looking for?" I asked.

"Access hatch," Rys said.

"Got it." Mia tugged us away from the pool. "This way."

Boots pounded down the steps behind us as Mia led us through another door and down a flight of slimy stairs that ended in a barred entrance to a tunnel.

Beyond the bars, water flowed in a rushing stream alongside a stone ledge, like a walkway, built into the wall.

Mia tried the latch. "It's locked."

"Let me try." I stepped forward as Rys jogged down the stairs to join us.

"Jammed the door shut," Rys said. "How's it going down here?"

"Did you know she's a mage?" Mia asked him.

I tuned them both out as I immersed my mind in the sensation of color, gathering them together for a blast of white that clicked the lock mechanism open.

Once we were all inside, I flicked the lock closed with my magic before jogging after Mia and Rys.

17

OF course, the walkway ended. We searched for other ways out, but the hatches were all well above our heads, and all seemed to lead into the city. Rather than risk running into more guards, Mia and Rys insisted on wading through the dirty water.

At least it's just runoff from the baths, I reminded myself as I trudged behind Mia.

As long as we kept to the edges of the underground ditch, we could keep the water from sloshing into our boots. We walked for a while, unsure where exactly the tunnel would lead us, until we were forced to stop by a metal grate that stretched across the tunnel. Beyond the grate, the ditch continued in the open air, with the water flowing as though it were a natural stream. Judging from the view, it appeared we'd arrived at the city wall.

The metal bars of the grate extended into the bricks in the wall above and beside us. There was no door. No way out.

Rys suggested turning back and coming up through one of

the hatches we'd passed, but I convinced them to let me try to free us with magic, first. They didn't know what I knew about magic, and they trusted me. But what I wanted to try wasn't something the Inahi had taught me, because none of the colors, individually, held power that could help us here. I would need to combine colors, like the Green Mage had done.

I chose red, to heat the metal, and white, to move it. The only problem was, my attempts to harness white magic while trying to hold on to red individually kept failing. In the end, I used them in turns, heating and bending until there was enough of an opening that Rys, who was the largest of us, could squeeze through.

Both moons were high in the sky by the time we emerged. I didn't bother closing the gap I'd made once we were out. We just ran as fast as our legs could carry us, down the hill to the docks.

All that time in the city and then learning magic from the Inahi hadn't given me many opportunities to run. My lungs burned from lack of use, and I swore that I'd train with the guards more when I returned. If I returned.

I glanced back over my shoulder, but it was too dark to see anything much. I couldn't tell if we were being followed or not. Better to focus on what was ahead of us.

"Are we meeting Uri at the inn?" I asked, panting as I fought to keep up with them.

"He's securing us a boat. I told him to meet us on the dock where we arrived," Rys replied.

"Do any of you know how to sail?" Mia asked.

Neither of them sounded the least bit winded.

"No," I huffed, restricted to one-word answers if I hoped to keep breathing at this pace.

"We had some help on the way here," Rys said. He didn't

offer further explanation, and before Mia could ask, we were approaching the little settlement near the docks.

Rys slowed his pace to a brisk walk. Mia and I fell in beside him, and the three of us tried to look like any other group on their way to the tavern. But the eyes of the first couple we passed were drawn to us, anyway.

Once we were around the corner, I pulled Mia and Rys into the shadow of a building. "This is never going to work."

"How far do we have to go?" Mia asked.

"Too far to be drawing even that much attention." Rys ran a hand through his hair.

I stared at the pair of them. For once, it wasn't me that was the problem. Mia was dressed like a servant, and Rys like one of the fortress guards. It was too suspicious. Especially if Mia was right and servants never left the fortress. And no fortress guard would be wandering out for a drink this far out of the city while wearing their uniform.

We didn't have time to find a change of clothes for them. But it wouldn't take much to cover up what they were wearing. A cape, or even a blanket, would help. We had neither.

As I stared at them, trying to think of something, the answer became obvious. "Switch tunics."

"What?" Mia asked.

I gestured to her outfit. "All that white screams escaped servant. But if you had Rys's black tunic with those trousers, no one would look twice. Especially if it's turned inside out, so you can't see the stitching on the shoulders and cuffs."

Rys loosened the belt at his waist and pulled his tunic over his head, turning it inside out in the process. "Good thinking."

I tried not to stare at the muscles that rippled across his chest and abdomen as he traded with Mia.

"Much better," I said as Mia folded up the cuffs of her

sleeves so they didn't hang over her hands.

Rys finished tightening his belt. "All right. Let's go,"

We set out again, this time without any sideways glances from those we passed. The small success lightened our mood, and we even joked and laughed a bit as we made our way down to the very last dock.

There was a boat out at the end, waiting for us. I only hoped that Uri was the only one on board this time. Of course, that presented a different problem.

"Do *you* know how to sail?" I asked Mia.

She gave me a look out of the corner of her eye. "And if I don't? Then what?"

"I suppose we could swim." Rys laughed.

"Or row?" I suggested.

Mia shook her head. "How much planning went into this rescue, anyway?"

Uri's head popped up out of the cabin when he heard us approaching. "Anyone chasing you?"

"Not this time," Rys said, leaning over the side of the boat to bump his forearm against Uri's. "All good on your end?"

"Ready and waiting." Uri grinned. "Shall we?"

"Should we untie it?" I asked, eyeing the boat rocking against the dock in the light wind.

"It's a good thing you did find me." Mia sighed as she stepped onto the front deck of the boat. Once she was on, she turned and held her hand out to me. "Get on. Rys, you get the lines. Start with the one in the bow."

Rys hurried to do as he was told while I climbed down into the cockpit. This boat was smaller than the one we'd taken from the traders.

Uri caught the look on my face. "It's a rental and all we could afford with the bounty Rys got for turning you in. Supposed to have it back by dawn. Owner thinks we're fishing."

"If you're going to stand around and chat, do it in the cabin," Mia said.

Uri made room for me in the open hatch that led to the tiny space below the front deck. I wrinkled my nose against the stink of persistent dampness wafting out of the cramped cabin.

"How's your leg?" I asked, keeping my head out in the fresh air.

"I can walk on it." Uri shifted his weight from one leg to the other to demonstrate.

"Did the healer give you any trouble?" I asked as we watched Mia and Rys work to get us on the water.

Rys pushed us away from the dock as he stepped into the boat, looking as though he'd done it a million times.

"No trouble. Not once he confirmed I wasn't a mage," Uri said. "Though, after that was settled, he got real suspicious of you and Rys. Especially when you didn't return."

"He was fine once I told him I'd turned Ayla in to the guard." Rys plopped down on one of the bench seats in the cockpit. "Where did you stash our belongings?"

Uri ducked down into the cabin and rummaged about. He returned a few moments later with a canvas sack and passed it to Rys. "Here you go."

Rys tugged the drawstring open. The first thing he pulled out was my cloak. I shivered when I saw it, only then realizing I was cold.

Rys noticed. He handed it to me. "Put this on."

"I'm fine," I said, even though I took the garment from him and slung it over my shoulders.

"Why did they think you were a mage?" Mia asked.

I hadn't even realized she was listening to us talk. "I made

Rys tell the guard that so they would take me to the prison. I thought you'd be there."

Mia shook her head. "Not you. Uri."

"Me?" Uri frowned. "Oh. The traders shot me with something when we were escaping. What did that pirate call it?"

"Pirate?" Mia's eyes widened. "You never said anything about a pirate."

"There wasn't exactly a lot of time for catching up," I said.

"Little Stinger," Rys added, layering his own tunic over the one he'd taken from Mia.

"That's..." Mia's eyes flicked from the horizon to Uri and back. "The traders shot you with that?"

"That's not what I told the healer. I wasn't about to explain where we'd actually come from, or how we got to Agrion. But, yeah. Why?" Uri climbed out of the cabin. He sat on the bench across from Rys, who was still rummaging around in the sack.

"It's an Agrisse weapon. Not the sort of thing I'd expect them to be trading for. Unless..." Mia's voice drifted off.

Rys looked up. "You think the Shal may be stockpiling Agrisse weapons without Zan's knowledge?"

Mia scowled. "It was developed to use against mages. So, maybe. If she was anticipating an Agrion attack."

"But there aren't any mages in Agrion anymore," I said. "The Green Mage has seen to that."

"We didn't know that until we came here," Rys said. "Maybe the Shal doesn't, either."

Mia's eyes met mine for a moment. "You should be thanking the gods it wasn't you who was hit. I've seen what it does to mages..."

I squirmed under her gaze. "Right. About that—"

"Save it," she said, cutting me off. "I need to focus if I'm going to get us out of this bay before dawn. I barely remember how to sail. I definitely don't remember how to navigate. So tell me one of you knows the way home."

Rys looked at me.

I nodded. "I can do it."

"Probably best if you get started now," Rys said. "Just in case the wind picks up again when we're out of the bay."

I turned to Uri. "Switch places with me?"

"Sure." Uri slid back down into the cabin so I could take his place in the cockpit. "But what's a Green Mage?"

"You don't want to know." Mia's lips pressed into a thin line.

Rys bundled up whatever was left in the canvas sack and shoved it at Uri. "Stow this."

As Uri disappeared into the cabin, Rys reached up to hand something to Mia. "Here. This is for you."

Mia glanced down at Rys's hand then back at the horizon for a moment before staring down at whatever it was he held.

"How?" she asked, reaching for it.

"Zan took it from the traders. He said it's how he knew they had you." Rys rubbed his palms against his thighs.

It wasn't until she slid the object onto her finger that I realized it was her ring.

"Zan had it?" I asked.

Rys nodded. "He seemed pretty angry that they took it from you."

"They didn't take it," Mia said in a quiet voice. We stared at her until she explained. "I traded it to them. For passage to Agrion."

"Oh." Rys leaned back. He rubbed his palm against the stubble on his chin. "That would explain why he was so mad, then."

I squinted at Mia. "Why would you do that?"

Mia's jaw clenched. "The Koto killed my family."

"And you were going to do what? Fight them on your own?" I shook my head. "Not that it matters. They seem to be all in prison with the mages."

"Is that what that creature was?" Rys asked. "Koto?"

"Big hairy thing with horns like this and claws?" Uri asked, raising his hands to the sides of his head and sketching a large upward arc, curving out like a Koto's horns.

I nodded. "Where did *you* see one?"

"Healer brought one in on a chain. That's how he knew I wasn't a mage," Uri replied.

"Did it speak to you?" I asked.

Uri's brow wrinkled. "It spoke, but only in some language I couldn't understand. The healer could, though. He spoke a bit, himself. Sounded like a lot of grunting to me."

Uri's report meant there was at least one Koto out of the prisons, but still being treated like a prisoner if the healer kept it in chains. What was more curious was that the healer spoke its language, and that it hadn't—or maybe couldn't—speak to Uri or the healer directly with its mind.

"Nothing in Agrion is as I'd expected," I said.

Something hit our boat with a thud that sent us rocking.

"What was that?" Uri asked, turning toward the bow.

"Hit something, I think?" Mia said.

The words were barely out of her mouth when two people holding daggers jumped up onto the front deck of the boat. One grabbed Uri and yanked him up out of the cabin. Then he pushed Uri over the side.

"Uri!" I leaned over the edge, expecting to see Uri bobbing in the cold water, only to find a rowboat pulled alongside.

Two more visibly armed people grinned up at me from

inside. One of them was tying Uri's hands behind his back as he struggled. "You next?" she asked.

I glanced over my shoulder and spotted Rys fighting with one of the pair on the front deck. The other had slipped into the cockpit and was stalking toward Mia.

Mia held up her hands. "There's too many of them, Rys."

They tied our hands behind our backs and loaded us into the rowboats that transferred us to a larger boat waiting further out in the bay. One by one, they lifted us onboard, untied our hands, and replaced the ropes with cuffs. The moment the loops of metal closed around my wrists, I lost all sensation of color, just as I had in the prison. The feeling disoriented me enough that I barely noticed as they sat me down next to the others and secured my cuffs to the base of the enormous wooden pillar holding the sails aloft.

After they stowed the rowboats, we were on our way. I watched the lights of Agrion disappear over the horizon as our little rented boat trailed along behind us, attached with a line to the bigger pirate ship.

"Where do you think they're taking us?" I whispered.

"Probably not home," Uri sighed.

The pirates ignored us as they went about their duties. I tried to stay awake, but the gentle rocking of the boat, combined with the late hour and the exhaustion that had finally kicked in, caused me to drift in and out of sleep. I didn't come fully awake until the lead pirate on our boat started shouting commands to the others.

"I think we've arrived," Mia said.

"But where?" Rys asked.

"Guess we're going to find out soon enough," Uri replied. In a lower voice he asked, "Do we fight?"

Rys glanced at Mia. She scanned the ship and frowned.

"Too many."

"Maybe if we have an opportunity?" Rys asked.

"We'll see," she said, eyes narrowed.

"Look." I pointed with my nose at the bow where a small lump of land had appeared on the horizon, just visible in the breaking dawn. "I think it's an island."

It didn't take long for the pirates to glide their boat up to a long dock. Then, after tying it up, they began unloading their cargo. Us included.

Being marched off the boat, tied to the others, reminded me of being led to the Green Mage by the guard at the fortress. I tried to keep an eye on our little boat, so we could find it again if we escaped, but there were too many people moving around, and we were hurried off the dock and onto the shore.

The lead pirate on our boat shouldered past us, bumping into me as she called out to someone ahead of us. I stumbled, and Rys caught my arm to steady me. Then, a familiar voice responded to the pirate from our ship.

Rys's hand squeezed my arm as we both turned to look.

I caught a glimpse of short red hair, but no more than that before we were ushered away and into a nearby building. Inside, lanterns suspended from the beams holding up the roof lit rows and rows of crates stacked along the walls. The pirate led us around and between the stacks until we emerged on the other side. It seemed that the wooden boxes, some nearly as tall as me, filled almost half the rectangular space. The other half had been left open, with only a large, circular table surrounded by tall-backed cushioned chairs.

The pirate secured the rope chaining us together to a metal loop in the wall near the crates. Then he walked away, whistling, and left us there.

With our hands still secured behind our backs, there wasn't much we could do. Once it became clear that no one was paying any attention to us, we huddled closer together to make it easier to talk.

"Did they get all your weapons?" Mia asked Rys.

He nodded. "All of them."

She shook her head. "Uri?"

"Same." He kicked at the dirt covering the floorboards.

"Ayla? Your magic?" she asked, turning to me.

I reached for the sensation of color, even though I knew there would be nothing. I'd felt my connection to the magic shut off as soon as they secured my hands. "These cuffs are like the ones they use in the fortress."

I craned my neck and twisted my arms, trying to get a better look at my hands, and spotted the head pirate from our boat entering the building through a door on the opposite wall. She held a large mug in one hand. Her other arm rested across the shoulders of the woman who came in with her. Both were laughing until they spotted us.

The pirate from our boat slammed her mug on the table, sloshing some of the contents over the side. "You lot," she called to us. "Break it up."

I exchanged a glance with Mia. Rys and Uri sighed. We shuffled apart until we were once again standing in a line, still close enough that our shoulders brushed against each other when we breathed.

Another three pirates emerged from between the crates a few rows over from us.

The pirate from our boat waved to get their attention, then pointed at us. "Put some space between them. I don't like them all bunched up like that. Makes me nervous."

The youngest of the trio hurried over at her command. He

tugged on my arm, pulling me away from the others to spread us out. Then he forced us to sit. He found a stake, which he used to pin the section of rope stretched between me and Rys, who was next to me in line, into the ground.

Meanwhile, his companions joined the pirate from our boat at the table. With the pirate next to me using the hilt of his dagger to hammer the stake through the rope and into the ground, I couldn't hear much of the conversation. When he stopped, I caught the words "two mages," spoken by the pirate who'd captured us.

Two? I thought, glancing around to see if there were any other groups tied up like us. That's when I spotted Red. Her eyes met mine before she turned away, and I wondered if she recognized us.

I looked over at Rys. "It's her."

"I know." His head was turned as though he was focused on a different part of the table, but I could tell he was watching her as well.

"She saw me, but I don't think she recognized us." I tried to follow Rys's lead and ignore her, but my eyes kept drifting back in her direction every time she spoke.

"Let's see what she does," Rys said.

It felt like forever before the group of pirates settled into their chairs and began their dealings. Once they started, it became clear we'd been brought as prizes to some sort of conclave. They were there to trade what goods they'd claimed with each other.

When the conversation finally came around to us, it was Red who introduced the topic.

"What are your plans for the captives?" she asked. "I'm rebuilding my crew and could use a few extra hands."

The woman who captured us slapped the table with her

palm. "That's right. You're the one who found Lorhala, then stole a boat right out from under the noses of those greedy traders! How'd you do it? Are you heading back that way once you have a crew?"

Rys and I exchanged a look.

"We stole that boat," I whispered. "She just helped us sail it."

"Hush," he hissed back.

I shut my mouth and turned my glare toward the table.

"Haven't decided," Red said. She leaned back in her chair. "Depends which way the winds blow."

Everyone at the table muttered something that I couldn't quite make out beyond the words "blessed" and "mother." If they'd invoked the name of a god, it wasn't any that I recognized.

"If you need extra hands, I might agree to part with two of them. The other two I'm planning to take back to Agrion for the mage bounty. Caught them escaping." She punctuated her statement with two slaps of her palms on the table.

I resisted the urge to look at the others. The pirates must know we could hear them. They weren't trying to be subtle or quiet in their dealings. I couldn't understand why they thought any of us had magic. Had I done something to give myself away? And if I had, why did she think *two* of us were mages? Or was she only bluffing?

"I could take them back for you," Red said. "Save you the trip. You were heading to Valthonia next, weren't you?"

"Might be moons before we cross paths again," the other pirate said. "That bounty could fund a good portion of my trip."

"I understand." Red folded her arms across her chest. "How much for the other two, then?"

The pirate who captured us tapped a finger against her chin. "On the other hand, if you paid me the bounty now, you could turn them in and keep the reward for yourself."

Red shook her head. "Seems risky. Could get to Agrion and find out they've no need for mages anymore. Better to just take the other two off your hands and send you on your way."

"Or." The pirate who captured us drummed her fingertips on the table. "We could split the difference. Split the risk."

Red cocked her head to one side. "And how would we do that?"

"You pay me for three recruits, plus one full mage bounty at the last known rate. You route through Agrion with two mages. See what bounty they're offering. If it's less than the value of a recruit, you keep all four on as crew, and you're only out the mage bounty for one head." She paused to let Red consider her offer. Then she added, "I'm sure you can get at least that much value out of having a mage or two on board."

"Keeping a mage is risky. Winds don't like it," Red said. She reached into her jacket and pulled out a pouch. When she bounced the sack in her palm, it jingled. "Three head, plus a mage bounty?"

"Three head plus a mage bounty," the other pirate confirmed.

Red glanced over at us. She frowned, then shook her head like she might not agree. After a tense few moments of hesitation, she tossed the pouch across the table to the pirate who captured us. "Probably going to regret this."

The dealings continued on after that. But I found it hard to pay attention. I wanted to talk with the others, but every time I looked over at Rys, he gave a slight shake of his head. Whatever the reason for his caution, it didn't matter. He wasn't going to relay my questions to the others. I tried to find a comfortable position and wait patiently, but my legs were going numb, and my arms hurt. My wrists chafed against the metal every time I shifted positions. I didn't understand why we had to just sit there and wait.

Eventually, someone came in with two pitchers of ale, followed by another with mugs for those who hadn't been drinking. The talk of routes and trades died down as mugs were filled and emptied and filled again.

Then, finally, someone came for us. They led us out and back onto a different dock, past a boat I recognized as the one we'd stolen from the traders, to a much larger one tied at the end. She settled us on the deck of Red's ship, out of the way. Then left us.

"Why do they think two of us are mages?" I asked as soon as we were alone.

Rys ignored my question and turned to Mia. "The pirate who bought us is the one we found on board the ship we stole. She called herself Red. Sailed us to Agrion then took our boat as payment."

"Sounds like she told everyone *she* stole the boat, not us," I said.

"It's Lorjad's Luck she didn't mention us." Rys glared at me.

"Why?" I found it curious that she'd lied to the other pirates, but I didn't understand why it mattered.

"It would have cost her twice as much to buy us back if they'd known and sensed she was interested," Uri explained.

"But what does she want with us?" I asked.

Red stepped onto the boat a moment later. She didn't so much as glance our way as she paced the length of the ship, checking everything over, greeting her crew, and settling herself behind the wheel.

"Let's get her underway," she called, initiating a renewed bustle of activity around us.

We sailed until nightfall with no sign of land, and no hint where we were heading. After sunset, most of the crew disappeared below deck, including Red. Two returned with bowls of stew for us, then scurried away.

We ate in silence, watching the horizon for signs of land until the sky darkened enough for the stars to emerge.

Only then did Red appear before us. She came with the one who'd brought us to the ship and introduced her as Birdy, her second-in-command.

"Where are you taking us?" I asked.

"Didn't like Agrion, Princess?" Red pinched my chin between her fingers. "I spent a pretty purse on you. How am I supposed to get my bounty back if I don't deliver two mages?"

"You probably shouldn't have paid for two when only one of us has magic," Mia said.

Birdy stepped closer to Mia and lifted her hands into the light. "This ring says otherwise. And the captain's seen what the princess can do. So that looks like two to me."

Rys, Uri, and I turned our heads to stare at Mia, but her eyes narrowed, and her gaze fixed on Birdy.

"Sorry to disappoint, but my ring is proof my grandmother loved me and nothing more than that."

Red focused on Mia's ring for a moment. Then she tugged Mia closer to the nearest lantern. She studied Mia's face closely, then examined the ring on her finger. When she looked up again, she whispered one word. "Mia?"

"How do you know my name?" Mia flinched away, but Red didn't let go.

"You survived. We all thought you were dead."

"Who are you?" Mia asked.

"You don't recognize me?" Red grinned. "It's me. Nor. Your sister."

18

"HUH," Birdy said, in a low voice. "They do look alike, don't they?"

"That's what I thought, too," I said, keeping my voice down so I wouldn't interrupt the sisters' reunion.

"If you're alive..." Mia's voice trailed off. She swallowed. "Is Gran..."

Red—Nor—gave a brief shake of her head. "She made it through the storm. Survived long enough to get me to shore. But she'd been injured pretty badly."

"She took you back to Agrion?" Mia asked.

Nor laughed. "Gods, no. The Winds of the Sea Witch pushed us toward one of the pirate islands. They took us in. Set their healers on Gran. Raised me when they couldn't save her."

"They took you in." Mia raised her cuffed hands up to touch her sister's cheek. "I thought you'd died."

"Wait." Nor's eyes went wide. "*You* didn't end up back in Agrion, did you?"

"No." Mia dropped her hands down. "I washed up in Lorhala. The land of legends."

"You made it," Nor said, bending to unlock Mia's cuffs. "Gran died thinking she'd failed you, and all this time you've been safe. The Sea Witch answered all our prayers."

"Lorhala," I whispered the name. "That's what you call our home?"

Birdy turned to look at me. "Why? What do you call it?"

"Ramara," Rys answered.

Our exchange must not have reached the sisters' ears because Nor continued as though we hadn't spoken.

"I can't believe you still have the ring Gran gave you. After all these years." Nor removed the cuffs from her sister's wrists but held onto Mia's hand to admire the ring.

Mia tugged her hand away and rubbed the skin on her wrist. "It reminded me of what they did to our family, and the promise I'd made to myself to get revenge."

I leaned closer to Birdy. "What did you mean about that ring proving she was a mage?"

Nor turned her head at my question. She held up the cuffs she'd taken off her sister, still dangling from her finger. "It's made of the same material as these."

"Blocks her magic," Birdy added. "So the Koto can't find her."

Nor's eyes slid past me and narrowed. "Storm's coming. Birdy. Uncuff these three. Then alert the crew."

We all turned to look at the horizon ahead, where dark clouds were gathering.

"We'll talk more later. Once I get us around this." Nor handed Mia's cuffs to Birdy, hugged Mia, and then she was off.

"Hold tight to something and stay out of the way," Birdy instructed as she removed my cuffs. "If it gets real bad, we'll send you below."

Birdy released Rys and Uri, then carried our cuffs over to a locker to stow them. With one last look at us, she ducked through the cabin door.

Within moments, the weather shifted. Winds whipped against the sails. Waves broke against the sides of the boat and sprayed water across the deck. Our knuckles went white from gripping hard to our holds as our feet slipped out from under us and we stumbled with every surge.

The boat rose and fell on the waves. Nor shouted instructions to her crew over the wind. People slid and skidded on the deck as they hurried to haul on ropes, adjust sails, and secure loose gear. My grip slipped as water sloshed past us, and I flailed for something to hold on to so I wouldn't go over the side along with it.

Rys threw an arm around my waist, pulling me close. "I've got you."

I regained my hold on the rail but didn't move away from him. A shiver of fear ran down my spine. We'd survived Agrion. Rescued Mia. Even escaped from pirates. After all that, I didn't want to drown in a cold sea.

There was nothing my untrained magic could do to help Nor or her crew. So I prayed to Jusala for a positive outcome and asked Forsla to grant us the strength and the endurance to survive. I begged Solnat to see us through with no injuries. From Estrel, I requested the gift of calm seas and a clear path home. Then, I pleaded with Lorjad to lend us his luck just a little bit longer.

When I finished, I looked up in time to see a wall of water loom over us, blocking out the stars. I sucked in a breath just before it crashed, and the world went dark.

I woke wet and cold, sprawled on a beach under the night

sky. Everything hurt. Salt stung my eyes. Sand chafed my skin. And every muscle in my body ached like I'd been beaten in a fight.

When I turned my head to the right, I spotted another person-sized lump washed up beside me. When she moved, the long braid that hung from the back of her head told me I was looking at Mia's silhouette. She groaned and cradled her arm to her chest.

I tried to call out to her over the sound of the crashing waves, only to find my lungs still waterlogged. My words got swallowed in a wave of coughing.

When it passed, and I'd expelled most of whatever seawater remained in my lungs, I turned to look for Rys, only to find him kneeling in the sand beside me. He'd paused in the process of reaching for me, his eyes trained on the sand behind me.

I turned my head to look and found a scattering of flowers arranged in the sideways S pattern that mimicked the rune for Estrel's Mouth. In an instant, I knew this was a sign from the Inahi. They'd heard my prayers and brought us home.

Only where was Uri? When I turned to look for him, I found Rys staring at me. His eyes were dark, and for once I couldn't tell what he was thinking.

Unlike Ezri, Rys knew the runes. The important ones, anyway. Had he guessed what this meant?

"Where's Uri?" I asked, hoping to distract him.

"Are you all right?" His hands jolted toward me, breaking free of the frozen moment to help me sit up. He wiped the dripping water from my cheeks and pulled the seaweed from my hair.

"I'm fine." I rubbed at a sore spot on my hip. "Mostly. Have you seen Uri?"

Rys glanced up as Mia approached from my other side. "No."

I tried to stand but fell back on my bruised hip and winced. "He has to be here. We have to find him."

"We'll find him," Rys said, helping me to my feet. "But where are we?"

Mia's eyes scanned up and down the thin stretch of beach we'd washed up on. "Considering this is the second time in my life I've found myself washed up here..." Her voice drifted off as she gazed up the cliff face rising like a wall behind us. She pointed up to the top of the tower, just visible over the edge of the cliff.

Even though I'd already figured it out, I breathed a sigh of relief at the evidence. "Home."

The scuffle of rocks crunching under boots drew our attention to the stairs that led up the face of the cliff. A cluster of guards were hurrying down, weapons at the ready.

"They don't know it's us," Rys said, starting toward them.

Mia held out her hand to stop him. "I outrank you. I'll go."

"But what if they arrest you?" I grabbed for her arm, trying to hold her back.

She brushed my hand away. "It's all right. I've had plenty of time to think about this. Trust me. I need to face what I did."

Mia walked briskly away before either of us could say another word. We stared after her for a moment before Rys jolted in reaction to something and began patting at his clothing.

"What's wrong?" I asked.

"My knives." His hands stilled. "I never got them back, and now they're gone."

I lifted a hand to check my hair, only to realize that the hairpin knives Rys had given me on my naming were also missing. Not only that, but my braid had come undone, and the long strands of my hair hung in cold wet clumps that stuck to my shoulders and back.

My thoughts flashed to the pirate ship.

Nor. I stared out at the dark, churning sea.

"Do you think they survived?" Rys asked, following my gaze.

An image appeared in my mind. Their ship, sailing away from the storm. Confusion among the crew about cargo they'd lost to the waves. But no memory of the four of us. The storm we'd passed through had been a part of the magic of the veil. It had kept the pirate crew out, but let us in.

The look of relief on my face must have given Rys a clue as to what I was thinking.

"You know, don't you?" He took a step closer to me. "Because it's you. Isn't it?"

"Rys..." I didn't know what to say. Lying to him should have been easy. He'd lied to me. But for some reason I couldn't do it.

He pointed to the flowers on the sand. "That's why we washed up here. The Inahi. They're protecting you, aren't they?"

"I'm sorry. I couldn't tell you."

"Who else knows?" He paused. "Besides Ezri-ruh, obviously."

"Zan and Mage-sha. There wasn't any way to keep it from them. Delna and Sera, too." I glanced over to where Mia was talking with the guards, who had stopped at the bottom of the stairs. They were too far away to overhear us.

Rys raised his eyebrows. "Not much of a secret anymore, is it?"

I glared at him. "You can't tell anyone."

"I won't if you don't want me to." Rys frowned. "But, Ayla... How long do you plan to keep this up?"

"Forever, if I have to." I shivered in the cold wind blowing off the water. "It doesn't matter."

"What do you mean, it doesn't matter? Are you joking? You're the Ruhlini."

I shook my head. "Not the Ruhlini. That's just a title the clans gave to the Ruhl's family because there had been so many chosen from that line that it began to look like the power was inherited. But it's not. The Inahi choose the Labharon."

"Labharon." Rys tested the word on his tongue. "All right. That's exactly my point, though. You were chosen. Not Ezri-ruh."

"So?" I rubbed my arms, trying to get some warmth into them.

"So, why are you giving him all the power?" He kept his voice low as a pair of the guards Mia had been talking with jogged past us down the beach.

I watched them go, guessing they'd run off to try and find Uri, then squinted at Rys. "We are talking about the same person you swore an oath to protect, right?"

"I swore that oath because your aunt saved my life, and she wouldn't take anything in return. I didn't do it because I thought he could speak with the Inahi." Rys wrapped his arms around himself.

"Fine. Well, it doesn't matter. So long as the clans believe that he's the Ruhl, they'll follow him." I started walking toward where Mia was waiting.

Rys fell into step beside me. "They'll follow you if you give them a chance."

"They will not." No one thought I had what it took to be a leader. I'd heard my brothers and the Jahlos talking about me at Cala's wedding. They'd doubted I'd succeed at being the partner of the Ruhl. "They'd laugh if they knew."

"Ayla, no. They wouldn't." He pulled me to a stop, turning me to face him. His fingers curled around my shoulders. "They'd see, just like I do, how it makes perfect sense. Of course the Inahi chose you. I doubt that even the master mages know more about the Inahi and our folklore than you do. And, even if they do, they aren't half as respectful to the gods as you are."

Mia called to us from the bottom of the stairs that led up the cliff side.

I glanced over at her. "Come on. We're both sopping wet and freezing. We can argue about this later when we're warm and dry."

"I'm not going to forget you said that." Rys released his grip on my shoulders.

"I know." I shivered again. My teeth started chattering. "I'm so cold I can't think straight."

Rys put his arm around my shoulder and pulled me close against his side, matching his steps to mine. I wanted to push him away, but he was warm under his wet clothes. So I let him hold me until we reached Mia. Then I slipped out from under his arm and immediately regretted the missing heat from his body.

"The Festival has already started," Mia said. Her eyes watched me and Rys, but if she had any feelings about what she'd observed, she kept them to herself. "I sent one of the guards back to report to Zan and the others are searching for Uri."

"Let's go." I glanced up at the stairs carved into the cliff face. "At least the climb will warm us."

"Be careful on the steps," Mia said, taking the lead. "I don't know about you, but I can barely feel my toes."

I wiggled mine in my boots as I started up the stairs. As soon as Mia drew my attention to my feet, I realized they felt as though I'd frozen them into blocks of ice. I put one foot down and then the other, deliberately, and tried to use the repetition to help me focus. I reached for red magic to warm me, but it kept slipping from my grasp.

We were nearly halfway up before I finally managed to hold onto the sensation long enough to send a little warmth into my bones. But it didn't last long. The wind continued to whip at us as we climbed. Between the shivering and the frozen heaviness in my legs, I wasn't sure I'd make it. By the time we were within sight of the top, it was hard to take a deep breath.

I missed a step. The toe of my boot slammed into the front of the stone step instead of clearing it to land on top. I flung my arms out to break my fall as strong hands grabbed my waist.

"I've got you." Rys held me steady until I regained my footing.

My heart wouldn't stop pounding. I could feel its frantic beat pulsing in my ears over the waves crashing against the beach below. As I resumed climbing, Rys kept a steadying hand on my hip.

Mia took off for the barracks as soon as she reached the top. She called back over her shoulder to let us know she'd meet us in the tower after she changed into warm, dry clothes.

I started toward Ruhl house, but Rys grabbed my hand before I could go. "I'm glad it's you they chose."

"Thanks." I shivered.

"Go. Get warm." He grinned at me. "We can talk about it later. Tonight we celebrate your maturity."

19

Y arrival surprised everyone at Ruhl house, even though they admitted Ezri had told them to expect me. He'd instructed them to be ready to help me dress, if I returned in time for the Festival. Nye had a selection of dresses prepared for me to choose from, but she took one look at me and rushed me into a warm bath.

I stayed there until the frozen feeling melted away, then longer as I tried to put my thoughts in order so I could share them with Ezri. That's when I remembered that I no longer had any reason to approach him. I'd have to wait for him to find me.

No longer willing to waste any more time, I called for Nye to help me get ready. I picked a dress with a cream bodice and golden skirts, not wanting to draw too much attention to myself. It would be easier to sneak away with Ezri after the Festival if all eyes were not on me.

Sitting while Nye arranged my hair, I realized I was still cold and asked for a shawl. Nye found one in green with golden highlights woven into the warm knit. It added a touch of festive color to my dress, in honor of Jusala, who ruled with Forsla over Midwinter.

"Shall I add the comb, Nahla?" Nye asked.

I nodded. "Yes, please."

She inserted the gold crescent moon into my upswept hair so the arc of the curve framed my clan tattoo. Then she stepped back to await my approval.

After thanking Nye and admiring her work, I made my way across the courtyard to the tower. Kilm spotted me shortly after I stepped inside. I'd barely had time to admire the greenery strung in swooping arcs along the walls before he started toward me. Torches made to look like black horns lit the room, their flames flickering above the heads of the dancers twirling amidst the green-wreathed columns.

I remembered the very first time I'd set foot in the tower. I had wondered what it would look like decorated for a Midwinter Festival. Now I knew. And Jace had outdone the splendor of my imagination.

Then I blinked, and for a moment, I was back in the Green Mage's throne room. The similarities struck me once again. My eyes drifted up, past the torchlight, to the runes at the top of each column. I was squinting at them, struggling to grasp something important that seemed just out of reach, when Kilm arrived at my side.

"Where have you been?" he asked, taking my arm. "The Council has forbidden us from practicing what you've taught us."

"They didn't allow anyone else to activate their magic?" A bolt of panic ran through me. Ezri had promised he'd oversee it. I'd left all but one of my crystals with him for that reason.

"They did. But then they refused to let us practice," Kilm

said, easing my fear. "A few of us have been meeting in se-cret—"

"You mean you and Jace?" I asked, searching for any sign of Ezri in the crowd.

"More than just us." Kilm blushed. "Bez and Ivn. Katz and Tavo and some of their friends from the Jahl clan."

I finally spotted Ezri on the far side of the room. He was surrounded by a trio of women. Based on their sun-streaked blond hair and golden-olive skin, I guessed they were from the Shal clan. Filna-sha stood nearby with her pair of assis-tants, and I caught the way her eyes strayed to Ezri's group. When, with every look, the corners of her mouth quirked up into a satisfied grin, I became sure of it. These were Shal clan women, celebrating their maturity, eager to marry the newly available Ruhl.

And who wouldn't be? Ezri practically glowed with charm. His smile lit that corner of the room, drawing in everyone around him. Even though I was too far to see the sparkle in his eyes as he waved a hand to emphasize whatever it was he'd been saying, I knew it would be there.

Kilm elbowed me. "You're not paying attention to a word I've been saying."

I blinked at him. "Sorry."

"What has you so..." Kilm looked where I'd been looking. "It can't be Ezri-ruh. Not after... Do I need to kick his ribs in for hurting you?"

I laughed. I wondered if I should tell him what Ezri and I had planned for later. But Ezri spotted me before I could say a word. His eyes met mine across the room. The briefest hint of relief flashed across his face. It was gone so quickly, I thought I'd imagined it.

Zan, who'd also been watching, cast a pointed glance

toward the closed balcony doors where two figures lurked in the shadows. I recognized Mia and Rys, both dressed in the black tunics and trousers of their guard uniforms, even though I doubted either was on duty. From their tense posture, I guessed they'd only arrived moments before me and hadn't had a chance to speak with Zan alone.

"Oh." Kilm stood close to me, following my gaze. "Not Ezri after all, then."

Rys had stepped into the light when he spotted me. His dark hair was still wet, slicked back from his face at the brow and falling in short clumps that curled over his ears and at the nape of his neck. He didn't glow the way Ezri did with sunny charm, but the look he gave me still burned into my core. His dark eyes locked on mine and held on, causing everyone else to slip away.

When he looked at me like that, I knew what he'd said was true. He'd find me anywhere. And a traitorous part of me still couldn't resist that connection. We'd always been like magnets, drawn to each other despite everything holding us apart.

"He's going to declare for you, isn't he?" Kilm's question in my ear momentarily broke the spell.

Every muscle in my body tensed as I remembered my conversation with Rys in Agrion. The plans he had made for us now that I was free. But I wasn't free.

I didn't dare look at Ezri and give myself away. Instead, I tore my eyes away from Rys and turned to my brother. Wrestling my churning emotions into control, I said, "I hope not."

"What?" Kilm gaped at me. "Are you joking? That's all you've ever wanted."

"You knew?" I glared at him.

Kilm rolled his eyes. "Ayla. Please. Everyone knew."

"But—"

My ready protest and denial were drowned out by Jace, calling for everyone's attention. He'd created a platform in the center of the room, directly over the stone that I believed had in some way interfered with our magic. The way he stood there, with his hands raised, he reminded me of the Green Mage.

The thought caught hold of me and wouldn't let go. If I squinted, I could almost imagine the layout of the Green Mage's throne room overlaid onto this room. The pillars with the rune carvings stood in nearly the same place as the obelisks with the flashing lights. There had to be a reason for the similarities. It seemed so obvious, yet just out of reach. If I could just concentrate for a moment.

A hush had fallen over the room, and Jace began his speech. "May the blessings of Midwinter be with you all! And to those of you here to celebrate the blessing of maturity with me, I wish you the insight of Forsla's Navel, grown from the wisdom of Jusala's Scales."

The rumble of "May it be so," cascaded through the room.

When the response faded, Jace continued. "On behalf of the Shal, I thank you for coming to this celebration. Especially our Master Mages from the Magery, who have joined us to lead the maturity ceremony." He gestured to where Mage-sha stood with five others, all wearing rose-colored mage robes, embroidered around the collar and down the front with a pattern stitched in the colors of the rainbow. The colors of magic.

It was the first time I'd seen the Master Mages dressed in their ceremonial clothing, and the sight filled me with awe. Mage-sha's worn rose robe was nothing like these.

"If our mages are ready?" Jace paused, waiting for Mage-sha's nod. "Then, let those celebrating their maturity step forward, and we will begin!"

A cheer erupted from the crowd as Jace stepped down from the platform to formally greet Mage-sha as she approached, followed by the other Master Mages. Jace bowed his head as they passed, then slipped into the crowd gathering around the platform.

The mages circled the base of the platform, each carrying a small offering table. They stopped walking when they were equidistant from each other, positioned in a ring facing the crowd. When they were all in their places, they set their trays before them and raised their hands to the sky.

Kilm nudged me. "Aren't you going to join them?"

I'd been so absorbed in the spectacle that I'd almost forgotten I was also celebrating my maturity. I squeezed past a few of the older Shal clan members who had moved to the outer edges of the gathering to observe the ceremony at a distance and joined the group of my peers clustered around the mages.

I paced the outskirts of the group, searching for the others from my clan. I found them not too far away, standing in a tight group, sandwiched between the black-and-red-clad Jahl clan and the much larger representation from the Shal clan, who were all dressed in a bold array of colors and fabrics, embellished with some combination of beading and lace and shimmering silk.

The six from our clan all wore wide brown belts woven with patterns in golden thread over high-collared cream tunics that belled out at the wrists. The embroidery on their tunics matched the golden threads woven into their belts. It made me glad that I'd chosen the dress with the golden skirts to wear. The fabric may have looked as though it belonged among the Shal clan, but the color was pure Nahl clan. As was the comb I wore in my hair.

My parents spotted me as I approached. A small smile formed on my mother's lips, and my father dipped his head. I lowered mine in response before taking my place between Bez and Abi. My sister's friend reached out and took my hand, curling her warm fingers around mine and squeezing. She flashed me an excited grin before returning her attention to the mages.

I glanced over at Bez, searching her profile for any sign of lasting damage from the explosion. She turned her head, caught me staring, and gave me a wink before shifting closer to me.

"Are you excited?" she whispered.

"Are you all right?" I asked.

She scoffed. "I'm fine. Not going to let a little danger hold me back. Wait until you see what I can—"

Ivn hissed at us to be quiet and Bez closed her mouth but held onto her manic grin. I reached for her hand the same way Abi had reached for mine and gave it a squeeze. Together we listened as Mage-sha completed the ceremonial blessing.

"Forsla, god of courage and strength, we call you forth through your messengers, the Inahi, so we may humbly ask you to bestow the insights of maturity on those gathered this Midwinter in your name." Mage-sha lowered her arms, extending them toward us. "May those who wish to receive your blessings come forth with their offering."

When she finished, she bowed her head, opening her arms wide to invite us forward to present our offering and receive our blessing. Groups formed around each of the master mages. I hesitated, dropping Abi and Bez's hands, as I realized I had forgotten to bring a stone, representative of Forsla's Rock from the legends, to mark with my maturity prayer rune.

Someone tapped me on the shoulder, and I turned to find Kilm at my elbow.

"Here." He handed me a stone, still gritty with sand, but otherwise smoothed by the waves. "I don't know how you forgot, or what you're going to use to mark it, but Rys said to give you this."

There wasn't time to wonder how Rys had guessed I'd forget my offering, or where he'd found a suitable stone on short notice. The others in front of me were already taking turns stepping forward to bow before the mages and place their offering on the low tables. As they straightened, the mage whispered Forsla's blessing and marked their forehead with the rune representing Forsla's Navel.

I glanced behind me. My eyes followed Kilm's retreat and found Rys standing beside Zan, Mia, and Ezri. Both Ezri and Rys grinned at me when they saw me looking. I twisted away, casting my eyes down on the stone in my palm.

How do I mark it? And with what rune? I let my eyes flutter closed and turned my thoughts inward to consider what insight I wished for my maturity.

I wanted to strengthen my connection with my magic. I wanted to be a good Labharon. I wanted the knowledge and guidance that would help me find the gods and restore their connection, through the Inahi, to our clans.

Marking the stone with Estrel's Mouth, the symbol of the Labharon, didn't feel right, though. I considered Jusala. She offered wisdom. Her Scales, as Jace had said, were invoked to bless us on our naming and bring us balance, harmony, and wisdom. Except it wasn't just wisdom that I sought. That's when the answer came to me.

I called on orange magic, finding the sensation with ease. Then I drew, using conjured indigo ink, the rune I'd etched over and over in my search for the Inahi. The one that still expressed what I was seeking. Divine gifts and guidance. Using my gift from the gods, I marked the stone with Estrel's Hands.

I was one of the last to step forward. By the time it was my turn, there was already a steady buzz of happy chatter behind me. The clatter of plates and clink of goblets meant the food had been laid out and people were already helping themselves to the feast.

I didn't mind. Even though I was hungry, I was more eager to get through with the ceremony so I could sneak off and speak freely with Ezri and Zan. I wouldn't be able to relax or celebrate until I'd shared with them everything we'd learned.

When I stepped in front of the Master Mage at last, he smiled at me. I caught the glint of recognition in his eyes as I bent to set my stone on the overflowing offering table at his feet.

"May Forsla's Rock give you strength and her Navel grant you the insight you desire, Nahla," he said, dipping his finger into the inkpot before reaching out to brush the rune of Forsla's Navel onto my forehead.

"Thank you, Master." I wondered if he knew who I was because I was scheduled to start my studies at the Magery soon, or because he'd spotted my clan tattoo when I bowed my head.

As I backed away with the last of the celebrants, the Master Mages lifted their offering tables and proceeded in a line out of the reception room, through the entry, and out into the courtyard. I guessed they were taking the offerings someplace where they could leave them for the Inahi. Perhaps to a waiting cart that would transport them to a shrine located outside the city walls.

I wanted to follow and find out, but my desire to find Ezri was stronger than my curiosity. Only this time, when I looked for him, he was nowhere to be found. I began to doubt that I'd be able to get him alone before the secret meeting we'd planned with Sera for after the Festival.

Mage-sha approached and linked her arm with mine. "Shall we get some food?" she asked.

I agreed, hoping I might find Ezri among the crowd gathered near the refreshments. Matching my steps to Mage-sha's, I said, "I was thinking I should move my belongings to the Magery tomorrow, so I am ready to begin my classes with the other novices."

"Yes," she agreed. "I suppose that makes sense now that you will not be staying at Ruhl house with Ezri-ruh."

I winced at the reminder of the act we needed to maintain. "Do you have my class assignments?"

"Of course. I will give them to you tomorrow." She lowered her voice before adding, "I was worried when I heard where you'd gone."

"Ezri told you?" I asked, surprised.

"Mmm." She slowed, keeping us at a slight distance from the people piling food from the banquet tables onto their plates. "He came to me for a reading the morning you left."

"What did the cards say?"

"He was worried when the first card he selected was Lorjad's Nose. Danger. Of course, he had to know there would be some, given where you were going. Then he pulled Estrel's Light, and I think that gave him some measure of relief. Especially when it was followed by Jusala's Crown." Mage-sha squeezed my arm, drawing my attention to where Mia stood near the foot of the stairs leading up to the Council chamber above. "I see that the cards were right, and you brought her home."

I caught Mia's eye, and she gave me a slight nod of acknowledgment. "That wasn't the only thing Estrel's Light illuminated. Agrion is nothing like we thought. For one thing, the Koto, they're prisoners there. As are all the mages."

"You are brave for facing them again." She patted my hand.

"They're not what I thought." I paused to make sure no one was close enough to overhear. "I spoke with them. The way I can speak with the Inahi."

"Perhaps it is just the magic you've been gifted," she suggested.

"I suppose that could be true." I wished there had been time to find out more, but I was also glad we escaped when we did. I was no match for the Green Mage. At least, not yet. "If you'll excuse me, I'd like to check with Mia and see how she's doing."

"Of course, dear." Mage-sha beamed at me. She brushed her fingertips against the mark on my forehead. "Enjoy your celebration."

I thanked her and slipped away, avoiding groups of people I knew as I circled around to where Mia waited by the stairs.

"They're up there," she said. "Waiting for us."

"That's why I couldn't find him." I sighed.

She gestured for me to go ahead of her up the stairs. I glanced around the room once, hoping no one would notice me sneaking off. Then I crept up the steps, trying to keep to the shadows. Mia followed in silence.

When I reached the top, the door was open. I stepped inside and found Ezri pacing. He stopped as soon as he spotted me and rushed over to wrap me in his arms.

"You're back. Thank the gods." He kissed my cheeks before brushing his lips against mine.

Zan cleared his throat, as though we needed to be reminded that we had an audience.

Ezri grinned against my mouth, then led me to one of the chairs. "Sit. Tell me everything."

He perched on the arm and held my hand between his as I told the story of how we'd made a mess of things with the traders, and how we suspected, because of what happened to Uri, that Filna-sha might be stockpiling weapons.

"Did the guards find Uri?" I asked, looking back and forth between Zan and Mia.

Zan scowled. "They did and brought him straight to the Magery."

"But all the mages are here," I said.

"There are apprentices tending to him," Mia replied. "He'll be fine. He wasn't fully healed from the Stinger. They think that's why the cold hit him harder than the rest of us."

"The storm," I said, remembering that she didn't know. My eyes locked with Mia's. "It was an effect of the veil. What's left of it, anyway. That's why we got through and the others didn't. But they're fine. The Inahi showed me."

"Thank you," she said.

"Others? What others?" Zan asked. "The other guards I sent you with have been back for days."

"There were pirates," I explained, leaving out Nor's relationship to Mia. She could tell them later, if she wished. "The first one we encountered was on the boat we stole from the traders. She must have made it through the veil, which doesn't surprise me, since we know it's fading. But we never found out if the traders brought her here or if she arrived on her own and they captured her."

"Pirates." Ezri sighed. "You really did have an adventure, didn't you?"

As he lifted my hand to his lips to kiss my knuckles, the door slammed open. We turned to find Rys panting in the doorway. His eyes focused on Ezri's hand holding mine, just a breath away from his mouth. A cloud of emotion crossed his face, then disappeared.

He gave his report in an even tone. "The Shal is arguing with Sera in the courtyard."

"Arguing?" Ezri slid off his perch, pulling me up with him. "What happened?"

Ezri didn't wait for a reply before rushing out the door. The rest of us followed him, speeding down the stairs and through the guests in the tower until we emerged in the courtyard. As soon as we stepped out the door, we spotted the two figures standing about halfway between the tower and Ruhl house.

Their voices carried, and we heard their argument long before we reached them. Rys and Mia hesitated when Ezri and I rushed forward. Zan fell in on the other side of Ezri and motioned for Rys and Mia to stay back.

"I know you lied," Filna-sha snapped at Sera. "I know that baby didn't die."

I sucked in a breath, risking a glance past Ezri to Zan. He was focused on the scene ahead, but Ezri had turned his head to look at me. Our eyes met, and we exchanged a knowing look.

"Why would I tell you anything?" Sera kept her voice low, but it still carried. She leaned toward Filna-sha, pressing hard on her cane. "It was you, wasn't it? Trying to poison Delna. You'd figured it out, hadn't you?"

"I did no such thing." Filna-sha flinched back.

"You did." Sera shoved a finger at Filna-sha's chest. "And you would have done the same to Belyn and Harn's child. And that's why I'll never tell you anything."

"What's all this yelling?" My father emerged from the tower behind us. He strode forward, reaching my aunt and positioning himself between her and Filna-sha.

The pair fell silent once they realized they'd drawn a crowd. Filna-sha looked at her son, standing next to me, and her eyes narrowed. Then she returned her attention to my father and aunt.

"Teron." Filna-sha spoke in the taunting tone of someone with a juicy secret they might be tempted to share. "Do you know that your sister has been lying to us all these years?"

Sera's lips pressed together as she glared at Filna-sha.

My father, to his credit, didn't take the bait. "I'm not sure what you mean. How could Sera be lying to me when I haven't spoken to her in years?"

The shift in his position was subtle, but I noticed how he leaned his weight ever so slightly on the leg he'd planted closest to my aunt. I knew that stance. Whatever their differences, he would side with his kin in the face of the Shal.

"Ezri isn't the true Ruhl, is he, Sera?" Filna-sha locked eyes with my aunt.

"If your son isn't the Ruhl, then who is?" my father asked. He was playing into her hand, but not changing his position.

Sera turned to look at Ezri. Her eyes fell on me briefly before shifting to Zan. When she spoke, she directed her words to her brother. "Harn and Belyn's baby didn't die, Teron."

"I knew it." Filna-sha spat the words.

"Your father and Ber-ruh would have killed him." Sera stabbed her cane at the dirt in front of Filna-sha's feet. "I heard them talking when I came to tell them Belyn died. You can't deny it."

"My father was a fool," Filna-sha scoffed. "He thought helping Ber-ruh destroy the truth about our connection to the Inahi would be enough."

"By killing an innocent baby?" My father shifted closer to my aunt.

"Of course not." Filna-sha waved a hand at him. "That's not how the speaker is chosen. Is it, Ayla-nah?"

I flinched as she said my name. Her eyes locked with mine. I opened my mouth, only to hear Ezri's voice cut the silence.

"Enough, Mother." He set a hand on her arm, trying to guide her back toward the tower. "The Inahi chose me, even though I'm not the true Ruhl. The title is meaningless. We can vote to have it abolished if you like. Tomorrow. After the celebration."

Filna-sha twisted out of Ezri's grip. Zan took a half step forward, ready to defend Ezri from his own mother, if needed.

Filna-sha's eyes moved past Ezri to Zan. "You two. Always following her around. She corrupted you with her tales of the gods. That's why this—"

She swallowed whatever else she had been about to say and spun on Sera. "It's him. Isn't it? You wanted to be sure, so you kept them both close."

"Mother—" Ezri tried again to steer her away from the confrontation.

"You know." Filna-sha stared open-mouthed at her son. "How long have you known?"

"For the love of the gods!" My father's voice boomed as though he spoke with their power. "Will someone please tell me what's going on?"

"Belyn gave birth to a son." Sera spoke barely above a whisper. "She named him Edarn."

Filna-sha stared at Zan and cackled. "Edarn."

Zan took a half step back. He looked at Ezri. Whatever he saw on Ezri's face must have confirmed that Filna-sha hadn't lost it completely. "I'm not..."

"I'm sorry," Sera whispered.

20

THERE was no secret wedding after the Festival. Ezri caught my eye and gave me an apologetic look. Then, before Filna-sha could make things worse, he hauled Zan with him back to Ruhl house. Mia trailed in their wake, most likely to guard Ezri's door and make sure they wouldn't be disturbed while Ezri explained things to our cousin. Meanwhile, I took charge of Sera, leading her down to the Magery.

I paused when we reached the stables to give Sera a chance to rest. That's when I spotted Rys following us. At first, I thought he was just returning to the guard barracks. When he remained standing just up the path from us, I shouted back to him, "What are you doing?"

"Keeping you and Sera safe," he answered, closing the distance between us.

"We're fine. You can go." I pointed to the barracks across from the stables. "Get some rest."

Sera squeezed my arm. "Ayla, he has a point."

"What point is that?" I snapped at her, even though it was

Filna-sha I was mad at. She'd ruined my reunion with Ezri and the plans we'd had for after the Festival.

"Your aunt has been kidnapped once already because of what she knows," Rys said. "And the Shal is not someone you want as an enemy."

As much as I didn't want to admit it, he had a point about the first part. And I knew from experience what it was like to be on Filna-sha's bad side. I didn't want to imagine the ends she might go to against someone she actually considered an enemy. Especially if Sera was right about her poisoning Delna.

"She'll be safe at the Magery," I said, hoping it was true. "Filna-sha can't touch her there."

"It is safer there than anywhere else in the city, I agree," Sera said. "But having the additional protection of a guard, especially one Zan and Ezri trust, does bring me some measure of relief."

Her comment about how much Zan and Ezri trusted Rys reminded me of the oath Rys had sworn to them. The oath he'd said was meant to repay Sera for helping defend his family from Merluks, and then saving his mother's life after she'd been injured. Sera had more than enough reason to trust that Rys would do everything in his power to protect her. It wasn't fair of me to deny her that.

So the three of us made our way down to the Magery together. And I spent the long Midwinter night discussing Agrion and the Green Mage with my aunt, rather than enjoying a wedding night with Ezri.

The longer we talked, the more difficult it was to stay mad about it, though. Especially after I told her about the similarities I'd noted between the Green Mage's throne room and the tower room.

While I was gone, Sera had gone with Ezri and Zan to note the rune markings on the columns in the tower. She pulled out her notebook and showed me the sketches she'd made. Zan had been the one to climb up the ladders to make the etchings of the marks, but Sera had transferred all the information he'd gathered onto a drawing she'd made of the room's layout.

I'd been right that the columns were marked for each of the five gods, with the sixth marked for the Inahi. But there was another mark on the Inahi's column. One that I remembered seeing in the cave Ezri had taken me to on the beach. It was the mark that Mia said represented the Koto.

"Why would that be there?" I wondered. "There's nothing about the Koto in our folklore."

Sera shrugged. "We know our written legends have been tampered with at least once. What's to say they haven't been altered more times than that?"

"To what end?" I asked.

"For the same reason Ber-ruh did it." Sera scowled at the drawing. "To control the clans."

I had to admit she had a point. "I'd love to compare how this arrangement of columns compares to the drawing on the cave wall. I can't remember exactly the positions of the gods in relation to each other. Perhaps I can go back tomorrow and copy the drawings there."

Sera found a piece of paper and a charcoal stick. "In the meantime, why don't you sketch the Green Mage's throne room. Maybe I can help you figure out the piece you're missing."

I sketched what I remembered of the Green Mage's throne room while Sera made us more tea. Next to each column, I noted the color I'd seen glowing in cracks in the stone. I also noted the colors I'd seen flashing across the floor, just in case any of that was useful.

Sera took hold of my drawing when I finished. She held it alongside the one in her notebook, and we compared the two. After a few moments, she rotated the paper with my drawing, comparing the colors I'd seen on the columns to the rune markings on the columns in the tower room.

"There were only five of the obelisks," I explained. "So, it's not a perfect match."

Sera rotated the paper again. Then she set it down. "Hand me the charcoal."

In her notebook, she jotted down a letter on each of the columns.

"What's that?" I asked.

"How familiar are you with the rune deck?" she asked.

"I've seen Mage-nah and Mage-sha give readings with them. Why?" I asked.

Sera nodded. "I keep forgetting that you weren't educated at the Magery like me."

"What does that have to do with it?" I bristled, ready to defend Mage-nah and all I'd learned from him. "I bet I know more about our legends than anyone in this building."

"And I agree." Sera set her hand on mine. "But the Masters have a particular way of teaching their disciplines. You'll see once you begin your classes."

I frowned. "What does this have to do with rune decks?"

Sera smiled. "I made one when I was a novice. I still have it somewhere. I'll find it and show you. But you'll make your own. And by the time you're done, you'll have the colors of the gods ingrained in your mind the way I do."

"The colors of the gods." I gasped. "That's it, isn't it? In Agrion, the obelisks aren't marked with runes, they're marked with colors. Because colors are magic."

I jumped up, grabbing hold of my drawing in one hand and pulling her notebook toward me with the other. I hadn't seen the color on every column, but I was hoping Mia could fill in the ones I'd missed. She'd been there longer and had more time to notice little things like that. But there was enough there to get a sense of it.

"They match," I said, showing the drawings to Sera. I pointed at the column I'd marked as having white lights, then at the tower column marked with Lorjad's rune and the letter W written in Sera's hand. It was next to the one with golden lights, just as the corresponding column in Sera's drawing was marked with Solnat's rune and the letter Y.

"I think you're right," Sera said. "But why? Were these places used for worship? Like the temples in the city? Or the ones in the Jahl clan caverns?"

"Maybe." I stared into the fire as I rearranged pieces of the puzzle in my mind, waiting for them to click into place.

Sera's soft voice interrupted my thoughts. "Why are you keeping it a secret?"

It took a moment for me to realize what she was asking. I looked at her. "I'm not a leader. Father trained Goff and Cala and Dern to lead clans. This is what I'm good at. Where I belong."

The corners of Sera's mouth pulled down as a crease formed between her brows. It was several quiet moments before she responded. "I've been in Cala's place, yet I chose this. You are not what you were born to be. You are what you make of it."

She paused. "Ezri is no better a leader than you just because he was born here, in Shal city, eldest of his line."

I frowned and turned my eyes back to the fire. "It's better this way."

She didn't argue with me. She only refilled our cups with the last of the tea and sat beside me a while longer, until Mage-sha knocked softly on the door.

Mage-sha poked her head inside at Sera's call to enter. "You're still awake."

We filled her in on what we'd been discussing. She offered a few thoughts of her own, then insisted that I get some rest.

It wasn't until she asked how long it had been since I'd slept that I realized I couldn't remember. She led me upstairs to the nearly empty novice dormitory, explaining that almost all the students had gone home for the holiday. After locating a spare tunic and leggings for me to change into, she led me to an unclaimed bunk in the large, shared sleeping room.

"I'll send your dress back to Ruhl house for cleaning," she said. "And I'll ask the staff there to send a change of clothes down so you'll have them when you wake."

"Ask for Nye," I said, crawling into the bed, already half asleep.

"Rest well, Ayla-nah." Mage-sha's whispered words could have been part of a dream given how quickly sleep took me.

A small stack of fresh clothing lay at the foot of my bed when I woke. I changed quickly and followed my nose down to the dining hall. It was empty, but one of the staff waved me inside.

"Ayla-nah?" he asked. When I nodded, he motioned for me to sit. "Mage-sha asked us to have a plate warming for you. I'll bring it out and let her know you're awake."

"Thank you." Before I could sit, someone called my name from the other end of the room, near the door.

I turned toward the sound and found Jak, the novice I'd met, standing in the doorway.

"Thought I heard voices in here," he said. "Saved me a trip

up to the dorm."

"Were you looking for me?" I asked.

He nodded. "The Ruhl is here, and he's asking for you."

"Oh." I glanced toward the kitchen, feeling bad about having to abandon my breakfast. "Is there somewhere private I can meet with him?"

"There are private meeting rooms in the central hall. I'll show him to one of those and tell him you'll meet him there?" Jak's voice rose, seeking confirmation that his suggestion met with my approval.

"Whatever you think is best." I couldn't tell if it was the presence of the Ruhl or the fact that he knew I was a Nahla that had him deferring to me. Either way, I didn't like it.

"Do you know the way?" he asked.

"I'll find it," I said. "Just as soon as I tell them I won't be needing that plate they saved me after all."

"Take it with you. They won't mind." Jak grinned, then hurried off.

The man from the kitchen returned soon after Jak left. I took my warm plate from him as well as some directions, then set off to find Ezri with my mouth watering from the tantalizing smells wafting up from the platter. Warm bread, berry jam, and ripe cheese were piled atop a mix of colorful diced vegetables combined with some sort of grain I didn't recognize. I resisted the urge to take a bite as I wandered down the central hall, poking my head into any room with an open door. My stomach rumbled in protest, and I nearly gave up and turned back to find Jak for help.

Then, in the last room, at the very end of the hall, I found Ezri sitting at a small table, his leg bouncing with his barely contained energy. He bolted up from his chair when he saw me. After an awkward embrace, he shut the door and gave me a brief kiss.

"I'm sorry about last night," he said.

"It's all right." I set my plate down on the table so I could stretch both arms around his neck and claim a more satisfying kiss.

He sighed, resting his forehead against mine when it ended. "I shouldn't have waited so long. I could have been doing this with you all morning."

"How late is it?" I asked. There were no windows in the novice dormitory, or in the central hall with the meeting rooms. It had been light outside when I glanced out the windows in the dining hall, but it hadn't occurred to me that it might not be morning.

"Just after midday," Ezri replied.

I sucked in a shocked gasp. "I've only just woke up!"

Ezri cupped my cheek in his palm. "Good. You deserve to rest after all you've been through."

I frowned. "How's Zan?"

"Hard to tell." Ezri stepped back, pulling me over to one of the chairs. He waited until I sat before continuing. "The Council met this morning. After I told them what we'd learned about Ber-ruh, they agreed unanimously to abolish the title of Ruhl, so that's good news."

"For us, and for Zan," I agreed, taking a bite of bread slathered in cheese and jam.

"He can reclaim his birth name and his affiliation with the Nahl clan, if he wants." Ezri cocked his head to one side. "But I doubt he will. At least not yet."

"I imagine it will take him a while to get used to the idea of having Belyn and Harn as parents," I said. "I should ask Sera if she'll let me share her journal with him."

"I already took care of that." Ezri grinned. He reached for

my free hand as I took another bite. His fingers curled around mine. "There's a bit of bad news as well, though."

"What's that?" I asked, still basking in the thought that we'd succeeded. With the title of Ruhl abolished, there was nothing stopping us from being together.

"The Council decided to put an end to the training of mages." Ezri paused, grimacing in sympathy at the shock that must have shown on my face. "They want me to make a new deal with the Inahi. Tell them we don't want magic and ask them to take it back and restore the veil instead."

I gaped at him. "But the Inahi already said they can't do that."

Ezri released my hand as he sat back in his chair. He folded his hands behind his head and sighed. "I know. But, maybe it's worth asking again. We know more now. Maybe there's a way... I don't know. If they can't restore it, maybe they can make a new one. Or you and the other mages can use your magic to make one."

I pushed my plate away, leaving the rest of my food unfinished as the uneasiness with what Ezri was asking me to do sank in. "But what about Agrion?"

"What about it?" he asked.

I reminded myself that he hadn't been there. He hadn't seen what I'd seen, and I'd barely had a moment to tell him about it. "There is no army of mages to fear. Just one. He calls himself the Green Mage."

Ezri nodded. "Mia told us last night."

"Then you must know." I pressed my palms flat against the table and leaned toward him. "He's killing them. All the mages. Draining their power with his powerful green magic and taking it for himself. We need to help them. It's just like the legend of the origin of the clans. Ruhala led us here to escape something similar. And now we have the power to fight back."

Ezri leaned forward and took my hands in his. "That's just it, though. Ruhala led us somewhere safe, where we would be protected. Those mages gave up their magic, and we can too. Don't you see? We'll be safe. And our lives can go on. We can get married. There's nothing stopping us now. You can study here at the Magery, and I'll use my position on the Council to ensure the clans remain united."

"But the Green Mage is terrorizing anyone with magic, including the Koto. He's keeping them imprisoned under the city. And we can stop him."

Ezri tensed. "You really think you and a bunch of barely trained mages can stop someone like him?"

"If the Council lets us train, we could." I slid my hands from his. "Besides, the traders have weapons designed for use against mages. Did you tell the Council about those?"

Ezri frowned. "Not yet."

"We need to save those mages, Ezri."

"I told the Council I'd ask the Inahi."

"Fine." I pushed my chair back from the table. "I'll go to the forest and ask them. But when they say no, will you at least try to convince the Council to help the mages in Agrion?"

I didn't mention the Koto again, because I knew it was too much to ask for him to have compassion for the creatures who poisoned him. Even if their alliance with Vehlm-jah had been part of a desperate attempt to free themselves from the shackles of the Green Mage, as I suspected after what I'd seen.

"You don't have to go right now." He scrambled to his feet when I stood.

"The sooner I get an answer, the faster we can move on." I picked up my half-finished meal.

"But I need to go with you, and your father said he and the others from your clan are departing this afternoon. I thought you'd like to see them off. Once they're gone, I can let the others on the Council know I'm leaving to meet with the Inahi."

"It will be dark before you're ready to leave," I said.

"Then let's go in the morning."

I sighed. I didn't want to wait. Then I remembered his mother's comment to me amidst the accusations she made against Sera. "Your mother already suspects it's me who is the Labharon. If you want the Council to continue to believe it's you, then it's better if we're not seen leaving together."

"I suppose that's true."

"I'll ride out with my clan and see them through the gates. Then I'll make my way to the forest rather than returning directly to the city."

"That's a good idea." Ezri placed his palms on my shoulders. "If everyone sees you leaving with the Nahl, they'll think you're going home."

"At least until classes start again at the Magery. Assuming they know I'm planning to attend."

"I don't like the idea of you camping in the forest alone." Ezri scowled. "Perhaps I should send a guard with you."

"No," I responded instantly, not wanting to risk the chance he'd ask Rys to join me. Then, in a calmer voice, I added, "I'll go straight to the Inahi. When you ride out tomorrow, camp in the Heartgrove, and I'll find you after I leave them."

"Do you think it will take you more than the day?" he asked.

I shrugged. "I don't know. I have other questions for them related to the magic I saw the Green Mage using. It might help with this idea you have about combining our powers to create a new veil."

"All right." Ezri leaned down to kiss me. "I'll wait for you in the Heartgrove."

I nodded. "I'll go to the stables and see if I can catch up with the others from my clan."

Ezri kissed me again before leaving. I watched him go with sadness in my heart. Maintaining this lie was going to be exhausting, but I didn't like the alternative. Even if the clans would accept me as Labharon, it would mean giving up my dream of being a mage and filling my days with politics and negotiations like this instead.

I shook my head. There would be time for considering all this later, when I was alone, riding out to the forest. I needed to hurry if I wanted to say goodbye to my family and ride with them out of the city.

By the time I got to the stables, the Nahl clan horses were already saddled, and my parents were saying their goodbyes to Filna-sha and Jace.

I waved to Kilm, then snuck in through a side door so I could get Arge ready to ride.

Kilm found me a few moments later. "What's this? I thought you were staying in the city?"

"I am." I grunted as I secured Arge's saddle. "But I wanted to ride out with you, so I have time to catch up before we have to say goodbye."

Hearing that, Kilm pitched in, helping me get Arge ready in record time. As I led her from the stall, Zan found us.

"Ezri asked me to bring you this," he said, handing me the leather pouch filled with crystals that I'd left with Ezri when I went to Agrion.

"Thank you."

Zan's eyes flicked between me and Kilm. "I would have

liked to see you prove me wrong."

I grinned at him when I realized he was referring to our conversation before I left for Agrion when he'd insisted that the magic that had been returned to us was useless. "I would have liked that, too."

"Maybe if one or two go missing?" he suggested.

I laughed. "If they do, I'll be sure you don't find out."

"Good." Zan dipped his head, then turned on his heel and left.

"Is he really our cousin?" Kilm whispered to me.

"I suppose Jace told you that?" I led Arge out into the hazy winter daylight.

"Katz, actually." Kilm blushed when I looked at him with wide eyes.

"Really?" Before I could find out more, Bez, Ivn, Abi, Paj, and Oly spotted me. They hurried over to greet me. Only Lon was missing.

"He's already on his way to join the traders," Bez explained when I asked.

I hoped he'd been given the passcode.

Father and Mother signaled that they were ready to depart, and everyone fell in behind them as they rode through the courtyard, past the tower, and down the switchback trail that led into the city below. Abi and Paj rode behind my parents, then Oly and Ivn, leaving me, Bez and Kilm to bring up the rear of the procession.

There wasn't room to ride three abreast on the trail, so Bez went first with Kilm behind her and I rode alongside them, about halfway between so that the three of us could catch up. By the time they'd finished filling me in on all the declarations, petty jealous arguments, and inter-clan liaisons that I'd missed, we'd ridden halfway through the city.

"There was a Council meeting this morning," Kilm said after a brief lull in the conversation.

I guessed he wanted to know if I'd heard what was discussed. "Did you hear that from Katz as well?"

"Jace told me that bit," Kilm replied with a smug grin.

"Which one is it, then?" I asked. "Jace or Katz?"

"Both." Bez chuckled. "I was wondering if he'd told you about that."

"He hasn't," I said. "Sounds like quite the story."

"Just doing my part to unite the clans," Kilm grinned.

"Ugh." I groaned. "I didn't need to hear that."

"Did either of them tell you if they're going to allow us to practice magic again?" Bez asked. "I was just starting to grasp the sensation of red and orange magic when they collected all the crystals and made us stop."

The little pouch Zan had returned to me weighed heavily in the pocket of my cloak. "That reminds me. I'd like to talk with Father a bit before I have to turn back. If you don't mind, I think I'll ride ahead and catch up to him."

Bez and Kilm waved me off, and I nudged Arge into a trot. I slid back into line behind my parents and just ahead of Abi and Paj, who slowed to make room for me. Father glanced back and gave me a nod when Mother turned to greet me.

"You looked stunning last night," she said. "I tried to find you after the ceremony to tell you, but then I couldn't find you."

"I'm sorry," I said. "There was a problem—"

"I know." My mother cut me off. "Your father told me what happened. I'm glad you were there. How is she?"

"Good." I didn't say more because we were approaching the Shal clan guards at the gate.

Once we were past them and across the bridge, I urged

Arge into a faster walk. The road leading into the city was wide enough for me to ride alongside my parents. As I closed the short distance between us, my heart raced at the impulsive plan that was taking shape in my head.

Guiding Arge alongside Father's horse, I swallowed my fear and said, "I need to talk with you."

Father looked over at me. He nodded once, then slowed his horse, waving my mother and the others in our group ahead. He waited until Bez and Kilm had passed us and there was a good buffer between us and the rest of the group before he spoke.

"Is this about your aunt?" he asked.

"No." I took a deep breath. "Would you believe me if I told you that Ezri isn't the Labharon?"

He squinted at me. "Based on what I know of that family, I would believe almost anything. Why?"

My heart pounded as the truth found its way to my lips. "It's me. The Inahi chose me as their Labharon."

21

I RODE toward the Heartgrove Forest secure in the knowledge that my father would see to the training of the mages in our clan. When I finished telling him everything, leaving out only the part about how I'd been planning to marry Ezri in secret, he turned to me and asked what I'd like him to do to help.

"I'm not ready to step forward as Labharon," I said. "But I'm confident the Inahi are not going to change their minds about the veil. Whatever is happening, they cannot stop it. We need to train all those with potential to their fullest abilities so we can end the tyranny of the Green Mage."

Going against the Council's agreement didn't bother him. He agreed without hesitation. I gave him the bag of crystals and asked him to put Kilm in charge of training the others in our clan. He asked if it would be all right to tell Tavo what I'd learned and pass a few on to the Jahl clan when they stopped at our compound on their way back to the caverns.

Together, we came up with a story that he believed would

support why he changed his mind about the Council's decision, but that didn't involve sharing my secret with the Jahl clan. I warned him that Delna knew, and she'd likely suspect the real reason for his change of heart. He promised to have a private word with her if she chose to return with the others in her clan.

"You think she'll stay in the city?" I asked.

He shrugged. "Delna wasn't born in the caverns. Her children are there, but they are her only happy ties to that place."

We talked more about our plans and when I would return to the compound. When it was time for me to turn back, he reached into a pocket in his cloak and retrieved a folded and sealed paper.

"When you return, will you give this to Sera for me?" he asked. "I was hoping I'd see her before we left."

"Of course." I slid the letter into my pocket.

"And Ayla..."

"Yes, Father?"

"I'm proud of you."

Tears welled in my eyes. I swallowed them down and whispered, "Thank you."

Then, I turned Arge away and rode hard for the Heartgrove.

As I neared the forest, I spotted a lone figure on horseback, waiting near the trail that led into the forest.

Recognizing Rys, I called out as I approached, "I told Ezri I didn't need a guard."

"Ezri didn't send me," he called back.

I reined Arge in alongside Rys's mount. "Then who did? Why are you here?"

"Sera." Rys reached into his vest and pulled out a notebook. "She told me to tell you she spoke with Mia this morning and then asked me to give you this."

I took the notebook from him, recognizing it, and the folded drawing stuck inside, marking the page with Sera's drawing. When I unfolded the paper, I realized there were new notes. Sera had filled in the missing information from the Green Mage's throne room with Mia's help.

I gasped as the pieces finally clicked into place. "I think I know where the gods are."

Sign up for my newsletter to be the first to know when new books release and get some Mage Lore bonus scenes! http://www.emenozzi.com/newsletter.html.

ACKNOWLEDGEMENTS

Thank you to my Struggle Bus Crew for your support, to my Wednesday night writing group for all the writing sprints, and to my WRX Indie friends for helping me stay accountable to my goals along the way.

Thank you to my excellent cover designer, Elizabeth Mackey, and to my stellar copy editor, Shannon Page.

I know I always say this, but especially this time, I might never have finished this novel without my mom cheering me on and my husband patiently listening to my angst and encouraging me to keep going. Big hugs and thanks to both of you!

Special thank you to my favorite first reader, Kaitlin who won't settle for anything but the best where this series is concerned. A huge thank you to my friends Tony and Zoe for distracting me with F1 and board games when I needed it (and especially when I didn't know I did).

And finally, thank YOU, dear reader! I hope you enjoyed exploring this world with me and are excited to read more!

About the Author

Elizabeth Menozzi is an award-winning writer of science fiction and fantasy with romance. A former Midwestern girl, she currently resides on Orcas Island with her husband. In her spare time she is a trail runner, planner geek, and devourer of books.

You can find out more on her website at http://www.emenozzi.com/.

ALSO BY E. MENOZZI

The Mage Lore Series

Heir of Gods

Poison of Power

The Modern Fae Series

Eve of the Fae

Dawn of the Fae

Will of the Fae

Hunter of the Fae

Ash of the Fae

Tales of the Fae